W9-API-674

VISITORS

Anita Brookner

Visitors

A Novel

Doubleday Canada Limited

Copyright © 1997 by Anita Brookner

All rights reserved under International and Pan-American
Copyright Conventions. Published in the United States by
Random House, Inc., New York.

Published in Great Britain by Jonathan Cape, a division
of Random House UK, London.

Canadian Cataloguing-in-Publication Data

Brookner, Anita.
Visitors

ISBN 0-385-25692-2

I. Title.

PR 6052.R5816V57   1998   823'.914   C97-931891-2

Printed in the United States of America on acid-free paper

24689753

Book design by Carole Lowenstein

Published in Canada by
Doubleday Canada Limited
105 Bond Street
Toronto, Ontario
M5B 1Y3

VISITORS

1

Towards evening the oppressive heat was tempered by a slight breeze, although this merely served to power drifts and eddies of a warmth almost tropical in its intensity. But this was England: somewhere in the atmosphere was a memory of damp. Truth to tell, the day had been almost uncomfortable: one was not used to such temperatures. The light, however, compensated for everything. Not quite crystal clear, but blinding in the absence of cloud, and gaining authority from the becalmed stillness of the garden, it put Mrs May in mind of novels and stories celebrating gardens other than her own, gardens which were part of estates, demesnes, where richly endowed families conversed in idleness, sat on terraces, or awaited visitors. 'What meads, what *kvasses* were brewed, what pies were baked at Oblomovka!' The great sun, clearer then, must have shone down on that Russia as it did now in London, at six o'clock on a Sunday evening in early September. It was the hour at which she was accustomed to experience a slight failure of nerve. At seventy she understood how closely she was being subsumed into the natural process, feared the dark, welcomed the light. On this particular day the sun had provided a respite from bodily ills; she identified with its power, put her faith in its continuation. The sun was constant, encouraging one to regard it as a familiar. Winter, even autumn, seemed far away, almost unimaginable. She shut her mind against both.

There was Turner's sun, of course, a real English sun, dilute in the watery atmosphere, mirrored in the inevitable sea beneath. There was the great sun of antiquity, of which perhaps just an echo reached one at torrid midday. And there was the sadness with which one saw it depart, even though the resulting slight drop in temperature was refreshing. This, for Mrs May, signalled the end of the day, even though some hours remained before she could decently go to bed. And she must not anticipate those darker hours which were to her so precious: solemn hours, hours of infinite recall, of the mind on automatic pilot, throwing up fragments of conversations decades old, or memories of a school-friend not seen for even longer, until that other ancient god, sleep, conducted her into what she privately thought of as her true dimension, in which she became a vivid actor, weightless and sometimes joyful, embroiled in obscure adventures which puzzled her only when she woke. More troubling dreams she was able to discount: the effect of old age, she imagined, since nothing so very terrible had befallen her, although it almost certainly would do in that very near future about which she preferred not to think. The body would betray her; the body was therefore taboo, glanced at without amenity in the bath, and ignored once it was covered. It still functioned, more or less, although there were now pills to hand in both bedroom and bathroom. It was almost a comfort to her to know that there was no-one intimate enough to share the stoicism and distaste with which she endured herself. Strangers, introduced to her for the first time, assumed that she had never married, thinking her self-sufficiency no more than the sum of others' indifference. That was their business; hers was to give no sign of anything out of order. This she succeeded in doing. Unbeknown to herself, she was considered slightly forbidding. She had few friends now, but that, she thought, spared her the pain of losing them.

When she closed the French doors to the garden she was surprised how dark it seemed in the flat. On this ground floor of an Edwardian mansion block darkness was to be expected. She did not particularly mind this; in winter it intensified the pleasures of reading. The advantage was direct access to the extensive communal garden. She was told, even by relative strangers, that she put herself at risk by leaving her doors and windows open, but she was not nervous, although everyone she knew seemed to be, on guard against imaginary dangers. She was a Londoner born and bred, but she liked to imagine country emanations in the stillness of the early morning. She rose at half past five, donned her late husband's dressing gown, made tea, and took a tray out to the small table she was entitled to place on that portion of the terrace that was judged to be hers. This too was a blessed hour. At six-thirty, when she thought there might be neighbours about, she went in and had her bath. Dressed, the imperfections of her body superficially disguised, she would sigh briefly and prepare to confront the day. This was sometimes difficult.

Mondays were substantially different from Sundays, even for those who no longer worked. On Monday morning there was a tension in the air, which she could sense even as she drank her early morning tea, in solitude, without a newspaper, without the radio, with nothing to alert her to the day's events. Monday mornings made her feel vaguely ashamed of her idleness, of her unpartnered state, though neither was blameworthy. Rather she had been cast up on the barren shore of old age by a process of natural wastage, and she in her turn would disappear, unlamented. Given the inevitable disappointments of Monday, Sunday had to be prolonged, particularly such a resplendent Sunday as this had been. She stood at the window gazing out, until the outline of the trees turned a more sombre green. It would soon be dim enough to light her lamps, although left on her own, as she invariably was these days, she preferred not to bother.

It was at this point on a Sunday evening that her thoughts turned to Henry, her husband, and their past Sundays, unvarying, obligatory, occasionally enriching. For there was no time to enjoy the garden on those distant Sundays, but rather an afternoon trip to Hampstead, to visit Henry's twin sister, Rose, whom they could not disappoint. Henry had felt guilty at abandoning his sister; he had married not once but twice, leaving Rose forlorn. It had taken Mrs May, the second wife, a whole afternoon to understand that Rose was of rather feeble intelligence, not quite backward or retarded, but responding best to a sheltered life, looked after by her parents' former housekeeper. She had somehow imbibed a little knowledge, mainly from the Swiss establishment to which they had sent her; she had certainly acquired exquisite manners, though these might simply have been the natural outcome of her quiet nature. Her welcome was rapturous; she ran to her brother like the girl she had once been, though she was now a stout woman in her late fifties. Dressed, scented, she awaited their arrival with a girl's ardour.

After Henry had disengaged himself from her embrace it was the turn of Mrs May to be exclaimed over, patted, and led to a chair. Coming from a naturally austere background, she had found this alarming, until, timidly at first, she allowed herself to relax, for there was nothing of which to be afraid. There was little conversation, but a wealth of largely mimed gratification. She sat in a chair next to Rose and allowed her hand to be stroked; she admired Rose's clumsy embroidery until Henry returned from the kitchen and his settling of the household's accounts. The tea was served, with the cakes of which Rose was so fond. Henry teased and indulged her like the child she still was, and although she did not quite understand that he had become a man and she therefore a woman, she laughed delightedly at his remarks, hearing the sound of his voice rather than the sense of his words.

Mrs May said little but was attentive, removing a slopped saucer, unobtrusively substituting a dry one, marvelling quietly at Rose's dexterity with a cake fork when her remarks were so random and repetitive. But there was always the delighted laughter, until Henry looked at his watch and announced that it was time that they were on their way. Then there were tears, and the housekeeper had to intervene, to put an end to Rose's prayerful embraces, and lead her to the window for the last goodbye. 'Until next week, Rose,' Henry would say, but she did not quite believe him. They waved exhaustively, until they saw her form retreat into the room behind her. Then Henry would shake off the burden of the visit, and they would walk back into town, glad of the activity. A different Sunday then impinged on their consciousness: tourists in T-shirts, tired children, decorous Asian shopkeepers and their families strolling in the park. All this, which could have been entertaining, became alien, as they silently compared it with the life, or half life, they had just left. Henry would sigh intermittently throughout the evening, though Mrs May was naturally equable. She was more than willing to share Henry with his sister; for both of them Henry was of equal importance. Tired, therefore, but uncomplaining, she would set about preparing the evening meal, with scarcely a glance through the window at the garden.

And they were both dead, both Henry and Rose, within weeks of each other. Rose, supported by various cousins, had fainted at Henry's funeral, although that had been as sparse and unemotional as Mrs May could contrive it. In that other garden, at Golders Green, Rose had finally understood the facts of death. An ambulance was called; in the ambulance she had a stroke, and in the hospital soon surrendered what consciousness she had left. Her bedside was thronged with those same relatives. Mrs May came and went silently. And then it was over. The relatives dispersed, and she was alone.

Alone except for the telephone calls, routinely made on a Sunday evening to ascertain that she was still alive. Henry's married cousins, Kitty Levinson, Molly Goodman, his doctor and distant connection, Monty Goldmark, all paid her faithful though absent-minded attention. She felt herself to be a stranger in their midst, a truth on which agreement was more or less unanimous. Hospitality was invariably offered, but at the same time there was a tacit acceptance that she would continue her alien life at a distance. Both parties felt some relief at this convention; the cousins, guilty at even feeling relief, redoubled their expressions of goodwill. Again there was little conversation. Mrs May was in no doubt that the calls were motivated by love for the absent Henry rather than for herself. She did not take exception to this; she knew that Henry had been a superior character, that she was little more than his shadow, his relict. It was because they felt so sorry for any woman whom Henry had left alone that their ready emotions overflowed on Sunday evenings, as if even they acknowledged the sadness of those hours, sadness that was perhaps little more than a pause for unwanted reflection, and the knowledge that time was slipping away.

The conversations seemed to follow an unseen rota, as if Kitty had previously agreed with Molly which one of them was to undertake the task. Mrs May took a small wager with herself as to who was shouldering the obligation on any particular week. If anything she dreaded the interruption of the silence in which she now lived, yet once the routine enquiries had been exchanged she surrendered almost pleasurably to Kitty's or Molly's invariable recital: their health, the health of their husbands, the dinner party of the week, the menu served at the dinner party, the projected visit to Kitty or to Molly, whoever was speaking or not speaking, reminiscences of Rose, whom these good women had been assiduous in visiting on days other than those sacrosanct Sundays, the fears they had entertained on Rose's behalf after the death of her parents, the subsequent splendid behaviour of Henry, and ultimately of herself. This was what really spurred them to keep in touch, not her own health (monotonously good, they supposed, since she never complained), not the reminiscences, but their own unquestioning acceptance of Henry's priorities. Even though she remained so puzzling a stranger, she was still Henry's wife.

It seemed to surprise them that one not of their immediate kin could identify so closely with Henry's life, and Mrs May could not tell them that Henry had been her subject, as if she had been studying him for a degree and was intent on knowing as much of him as it would be discreet of her to know, without impinging on his own sorely tested privacy. She was a novel reader, which helped, and the cousins were not. So she could not explain her deep appreciation of the differences that existed between them. Henry was festive, emotional, easily moved, extravagant; when he brought her flowers his own cheeks would flush with pleasure. Her own response, though outwardly moderate, was deep. How to explain this to Molly or to Kitty, whose own husbands were usually described in terms of physical ailments? So that the telephone calls were usually a disappointment, at least on their side. After her meagre stock of news was exhausted, after she had made the usual response to accounts of the rheumatism or the recipe for lemon chicken, aware that she was letting them down, and sincerely sorry for the fact, she would ask after every extended family member—fortunately her memory was excellent—and thus repair her reputation.

'I hope you're looking after yourself, Thea,' was usually the concluding remark. 'What are you eating tonight?'

'Gazpacho and baked cod,' she would say, or, 'Cold tongue with Madeira sauce.'

In fact she would eat a banana, as she usually did, and settle down with a book. Kitty or Molly would then think more kindly of her, guiltily reassured once again, although after the call they would telephone each other to deplore her coldness. This too she knew and did not resent.

For if they pitied her she did not pity herself. She had had Henry, so puzzlingly absent. His presence was somehow denied her, owing perhaps to that same rationality or coldness that the cousins deplored. For she could not tell of the loyalty, and gratitude, that had united her with Henry, and was therefore judged unfeeling. Because nothing had prepared her for this unlikely marriage she was profoundly surprised to be acknowledged as a wife. Not to be found a novice, to be made a companion, was her endowment from Henry. Yet there were no photographs of him in the flat, and she was not afraid of the dark, nor did she commune sentimentally with his shade. Simply, he was gone, leaving her as alone now as when he had found her, neither more nor less. As a widow she cut a poor figure, she knew. If she wished for anything now it was to be left alone, to furnish her own silence. She knew that she was approaching the end of her life, and that silence was appropriate. She was unaware that she gave no sign of this, and was thus not understood. But to express her acceptance of these facts, of this situation, would be to invite the charge of morbidity, which she rejected with something of the same distaste as would be felt by Kitty or Molly if she so much as voiced her thoughts. Therefore her conversation consisted largely of enquiries as to the health and welfare of her interlocutor. These protected her and at the same time gave pleasure, easing her into another week with a consciousness of duties fulfilled and obligations discharged. Without this consciousness she would have felt undressed.

Since that remote day when she had tripped on an uneven paving stone and fallen, and had been rescued by a passer-by, who was Henry, her life had hardly been her own, and on occasion she had difficulty in recognising it. Therefore she felt a certain familiarity with these latter days; this was the solitude she had always known before and until her marriage. She had been rescued in more senses than one, though, strangely enough, on hot still evenings such as this, she could remember the involuntary surrender of the fall, before the strong hands had restored her balance. Now that they would never hold her again she sought no substitutes, was chary of affectionate gestures, a fact which estranged her even further from the cousins, as did her apparently unsupported status. She had no family, which to Kitty and Molly made her pitiable, even shameful. Yet she was still too loyal to her origins to describe her relief at her escape from home, from the tall narrow house at the far end of the New Kings Road, in which she and her mother and father had passed their harmonious but largely silent days. Conversation was somehow a luxury, confined to Sundays. Thus she had learned nothing except to visit the Public Library: fiction taught her all she knew of life, taught her to interpret the lives of others. And she had not been found wanting: that was also Henry's gift to her. Even the cousins, once introduced, could not fault her, little knowing that their immaculate carpets and voluptuous sofas provided such a contrast with the serviceable upright furniture and plain curtains of home. She had bought her present flat with the proceeds of the family house after the deaths of her father and her mother. They too had died within weeks of each other, as if their largely coded conversation could only be pursued beyond the grave.

Her first efforts at furnishing had been awkward; it had taken some time for her to settle on the blue-grey carpet and curtains that had so soothed Henry. And of course there was the outlook onto the garden, to which she paid so much attention these days. She had never really known whether Henry had loved the flat as much as she did. On those visits to the cousins, which could not be avoided, he seemed to reveal an affinity with the amiable husbands who put aside their newspapers to wave a cheerful greeting, leaving the formalities to their wives. Something wistful and pleasure-loving then emanated from him. The coffee, the cake, which appeared as though by magic, were just as magically consumed, as though they were a birthright, as natural as mother's milk.

Their life alone together was courteous, deeply considerate. This enabled Mrs May to endure her sparse attractions, which the cousins, so abundant, so fecund, openly deplored. Had she been guilty of weaning Henry away from his family? Perhaps she had; perhaps he had it in him to be just such an amiable husband, comfortably ensconced in just such a soft armchair, served coffee and cake by the sort of mother figure that Mrs May could never be. Yet alone with her he became more of a man; not merely the provider, through a family trust, of an extended network of cousins and nephews, but thoughtful, dignified, mature. He had been the director of a small charity for refugees, from which he took no salary, being satisfactorily financed through investments. There had been factories in Germany when the name was Meyer: as Henry May a native charm, together with his own resources, made him a respected figure in his own world and in hers. She had thought herself his debtor; only now, in old age, and in solitude, did she ever think of herself without reference to Henry.

This puzzled her. Although lonely she was not unhappy. A day like today, spent watching her neighbours' children playing in the garden, hardly moving for the duration of the long Sunday afternoon, had not been unduly burdensome. If she saw herself, even in her memory, she did not see the brightness that had been hers as a wife; she saw the lined and ageing woman she had become, as if these lineaments had been waiting to emerge since her features had first been formed. For Henry's sake she kept up appearances, had her hair done, applied discreet colours to her face, yet when she looked in the mirror, lipstick in hand, she saw a drained countenance, its expression wary, as if at any minute it might undergo disintegration, as if there were no longer any cells to separate the skin from the bone. This was a bad moment every morning. Once she was packaged for the day, in one of her navy-and-white print dresses, she thought no more of this sly transformation. Housework occupied a bare half hour; she was not untidy.

Once a fortnight a cleaning firm turned out the flat, during which time she sat politely in the garden. She had got rid of her daily, Olive Gage, who was so devoted to Henry, because she could no longer endure her tearful reminiscences. The cleaners sent by the firm were Vietnamese and silent. This suited her much better. She was aware of herself as a selfish old woman, but she knew that her character, like her appearance, was unlikely to improve, might even deteriorate to the extent of asking other people to be quiet, in a voice now almost rusty from misuse. The only voices she really welcomed were those she heard on the radio, since no response was called for. Yet these days she listened only to the news, and a little music in the evening. She had grown used to her own company, paid it little attention. At the same time she was aware that the world made demands even on one as undemanding as herself.

In these days of her solitude her own history reclaimed her, her life before Henry and her life since. She saw an intimate connection between the two, as if Henry had been an improbable interlude for which nothing had prepared her. On the contrary: his company, his presence had been a source of surprise as well as pleasure. It was in fact when she saw him buttressed by Rose, by Rose's housekeeper, who always greeted her kindly, by Kitty and Molly and their husbands, that the breathtaking realisation struck her: these people are my relations. For her youth had been a long apprenticeship, her parents too busy, too abstracted, too conscious of each other, to satisfy any longings she might have had for gossip, for fantasy, such as she was to encounter in Kitty's and Molly's drawing rooms. Her youth had been an affair of studious long walks, trying to appreciate the wonders of nature in the dusty shrubs of her dull suburb; as soon as she was old enough she took the bus to Kensington Gardens and walked round Hyde Park. This excursion usually occurred on a Sunday afternoon, when her parents settled down for their customary nap; her absence was tolerated unquestioningly, and on her return there would be a proper tea, with cake, as if the day had some significance after all. Now, her days once more unaccompanied, she remembered those timid celebrations (for that was what they were) with a sense of recognition that surprised her. Between the Public Library and her long walks she had preserved her youth in innocence, unaware of either happiness or unhappiness, unmarked by anguish or rebellion.

She had been thirty-nine when she married Henry, still shaken by the death of her mother and hardly prepared for change. Yet she had acceded calmly to Henry's surprising fervour, though it rather embarrassed her now to think of it. She was a born spinster, as the cousins shrewdly perceived; at roughly the same age as herself, or a little older, they were looking forward to further festivities, were in the throes of planning them, so that no time would be lost. She had sat with her cup of tea and listened to their news; it was as if they were showing her what she could never be. She intuited that they were severely put out by this union. Henry, having returned to the bosom of his family after his unhappy first marriage, was once again to leave them, and to leave them for this thin plain woman who compared so unfavourably with the petulant Joy. She had endured their baffled annoyance, until their better natures reasserted themselves. They made amends by giving her the names of their dressmakers, suggesting lunch in town. Yet they were kind women, if easily put out, and because they judged her to have passed some test of conformity, or obedience, because Henry appeared contented, because Rose was not neglected, they admitted her to their company, while privately expressing astonishment at the fact that she lived in Fulham. They saw immense difficulties in the way of visiting—Hampstead and Highgate were so distant!—and had to be brought over by car by complaisant husbands whom they contradicted, uneasy away from their familiar surroundings.

She had made them welcome. The fact that Henry had married her gave her confidence, and her fledgling dinner parties were surprisingly convivial. In addition to the cousins and their husbands they had invited Monty Goldmark and his wife, Hélène, so that the conversation was animated and she could slip out of the room into the kitchen without being noticed. Reabsorbed once more into his family, Henry expanded: old anecdotes were repeated, ancient relatives recalled. She could hear them laughing as she prepared the coffee. The dinners having proved a success—almost an initiation—efforts at hospitality were somewhat relaxed. They kept in touch, even after Henry's death, and if their plaintive voices arrived at her from a distance both geographical and metaphorical, she was still moderately pleased to hear from them. She did not know that they thought her eccentric, that they had to overcome a mild uneasiness before they spoke to her. They thought that she could never understand them, in which they were mistaken; they thought that she could never, now even less than formerly, become one of them, in which they were correct. At the funeral, after Henry's death, Molly had tearfully clasped Mrs May's light frame to her capacious bosom. She was as shocked by Mrs May's unyielding thinness as Mrs May had been by Molly's abundant flesh. Now that it was accepted that they should remain apart, contact was easier. They were no longer critical of each other, having jettisoned many of their prejudices along with their combative middle age. In their seventies—Mrs May the youngest of the three—they understood each other much better. If the cousins telephoned one another to marvel at Mrs May's oddness, it was in order to revive an old pleasurable subject, as others might read, or indeed write, a novel. Mrs May was calmly pleased to provide them with such a diversion.

But those timid walks round Hyde Park, those bus rides, how they came back to her! It was as if no time had passed between the ages of sixteen and seventy, except that she no longer had the energy or the stamina for such walks. The newsagent in the early morning, the Italian café at lunchtime were as much as she could encompass these days, though she regretted her passivity. In her mind she strode out, even on these hot days, remembering the healthy tiredness of times gone by. That was all over now, yet the memory of her training in solitude had stood her in good stead. It may even have been a rehearsal for the ultimate solitude, which would be revealed to her in due course. For the moment she was unencumbered, almost ready to depart. Only the memory of her first meeting with Henry was allowed to intrude into her present becalmed state.

'These paving stones are a disgrace,' he had said, helping her to her feet. 'I shall write to the Council.'

He had insisted on walking her back to the office and delivering her into the kind hands of Susie Fuller, her fellow secretary.

'May,' he had said, holding her by the elbow. 'Henry May.'

'Jackson,' she had said. 'Dorothea Jackson.'

'Really, Thea,' Susie Fuller had remarked, after he had left. 'I sometimes wonder whether you should be out alone.'

That was the day when everyone was good to her. He had come back at five-thirty to see whether she had recovered from her fall, and had invited Susie and herself out for coffee. He was so beautifully considerate that they had had no thought of refusing.

'Lovely manners,' Susie had whispered, as they had gone to collect their coats. And he had demonstrated those lovely manners by making no distinction between them, although interested only in Dorothea—but this she had learned later. And the rest had followed quite naturally, as if they had both willed the same outcome. Fifteen years of harmony had followed, and if she was puzzled that they had not changed her, had in fact left her as they found her, so that Henry was a memory only, she bore the absence uncomplainingly, and was more at home with those phantom Sundays before the advent of Henry, seeing quite clearly the leaves falling in the park, and turning her steps quite contentedly towards home.

It was still very hot. The light had almost faded, signalling the last hours of liberty before the working week began again. She would make coffee, she decided, take a cool bath. Then the night could begin, and if she were lucky unexpected images would surface. She could be young again, the only reasonable wish at her age. Once she had distinctly recaptured the appearance of a dress she had worn when she was fourteen. She might see her parents, no longer ailing, as they had been so often in their lives, but smiling their placid smiles as they offered her tea and cake. She was not disconcerted by this process, did not confound it with the onset of senility. Rather it was her pastime since Henry had left her. His memory was evanescent now, as evanescent as she was herself, yet somehow she must pursue her course to the end, whatever that would be.

When the telephone rang, a little later than usual, she noticed that it was almost dark.

'Good evening, Kitty,' she said. 'And how are you this week? And Austin? Oh, dear, I'm so sorry. Perhaps the hot weather doesn't agree with him. Yes, very hot today.'

There followed the ritual medical bulletins, the news of married friends and familiars, and a reminder, yet again, that they would be going away for three weeks in ten days' time. This took just over seven minutes. At the end, like an orchestral conductor embarking confidently on the final bars, she said, 'Yes, I'm perfectly fine, dear. My love to you both. Until next week. Goodbye.'

2

Absence makes the heart grow fonder; prolonged absence makes the heart grow cold. In these latter days Mrs May was at ease only with strangers, to whom she appeared affable, released from the anxiety that something—anything—might be required of her. When she ate her lunch at the Italian café she was always gratified to see the owner's old father sitting by himself at a far table, with a carafe of wine in front of him. They understood each other perfectly. To the owner, Giorgio, certain questions had to be put: his health, the health of his wife, Paola, the health of his two daughters, and of course of the little grandson. She was then allowed to eat her pasta salad in silence. To the owner's father she waved a hand on entering; he briefly semaphored back. She knew that it had broken his heart to give up the restaurant when he was no longer as quick on his feet as he once had been. He was the first to notice that he had reached the age when retirement was not simply a matter of discretion but of necessity.

Yet he could not keep away. Every day he sat at his table, with his carafe of wine, simply in order to watch the customers, to note if a regular were absent. No-one paid much attention to him; in his careful suit he might have been a normal diner. But Mrs May felt for him. She knew, because he had once told her, that when he went home, at about half-past three, he would see no-one until the following lunchtime. After he had taken note of the fact that she had finished her meal he would come over to her and shake her hand. 'Everything all right?' he would enquire. The larger question remained unanswered. She would invite him to sit down but he preferred to stand, his body curved in a waiter's deferential stoop. 'And you?' she would ask. He would shrug, as if the evidence were there to see, in his sparse grey hair, his carefully trimmed grey moustache. He had grown stout, stiff, yet he still had the suave manners of the professional restaurateur. 'Changes,' he would sigh, indicating a young man talking on a mobile phone. 'Changes all round.' It was at this point that she laid her money on top of her bill, as if to forestall a confession that would have pained them both. 'Until tomorrow, Mario,' she would say, and, shaking his hand once again, would get up to leave.

This exchange satisfied them both, each aware without need of explanation of the other's frailty. Mrs May was not a robust woman but she thought of herself as durable and on a good day still was. She was simply and on the whole uncomplainingly conscious that at her age something unpleasant was to be expected. That was how she thought of her inevitable decline: as something unpleasant that could no longer be avoided. With her odd attacks of breathlessness she was almost at home. They had been with her for some little while, and she had even gone so far as to consult Monty Goldmark, Henry's doctor, and, she supposed, her doctor now, although she never visited him. To visit him would be to acknowledge that something was wrong, that something stood in the way

of that easy friendship that had served him so well in Henry's
case. There had been a single consultation. As if conscious of
his status as a sometime friend, he had made light of her stud-
iedly careless explanation, had merely taken her pulse and felt
her throat, and had then filled out a prescription for some
kind of sedative, which she took only rarely. 'You are a sensitive plant, Dorothea,' he had said. 'Anxiety is all that is wrong
with you. No wonder, after losing Henry. Such a dear boy.
Appetite all right?'

She was grateful to him for dismissing her complaint (although it was hardly a complaint at all), grateful to him for
maintaining an approach more social than medical, although
it did occur to her that it might be sensible to consult a car-
diologist. This matter occasionally preoccupied her, more so
when she felt out of sorts, but the prospect of a visit to Harley
Street was enough to frighten her into precisely the attack of
breathlessness she so feared. In time she no longer dreaded the
attacks; rather she congratulated herself on having nothing
further to do with doctors. The attacks were infrequent, and
if she were at home when they occurred could be controlled,
if she sat quietly in her bedroom, without recourse to the
pills. The pills were on her bedside table; they kept vigil there.
That was their function. She preferred to rely on her own
inner resources, which must be considerable, although she had
never noticed them. Henry had told her that he had married
her precisely because he admired her inner resources. At the
time she had not thought this much of a compliment. She was
enough of a woman to wish to be thought attractive, but
enough of a realist to know that her modest looks would pass
unnoticed in even the most indulgent company. It was a curious fact that she was no worse-looking now than she had
been in middle age. It was only when she raised a liver-spotted

hand to quell her fluttering heart that she noticed that she had grown old, and was then obliged to summon up what inner strengths she possessed. Yet, knowing how much these strengths would have to exert themselves, she still sometimes wished that she could do without them, could throw herself on the bounty of others, could simply charge a doctor with the task of making her better, could sit back irresponsibly and wait for the miraculous cure, the miraculous gratification. She was obliged to exert her will in most of the circumstances that others took for granted. Only the most placid routines stood between herself and exhaustion.

Part of her sympathy with Mario was for his sorrowful anticipation of his empty afternoon. She knew how hard this must be for a man in retirement. In some ways it was fortunate that Henry had not had to endure this, had been in touch with his fellow directors even when confined to his room. Of those last weeks she preferred not to think. Sitting dry-eyed by his bed, she was at least grateful that she was up to the task. She had kept him company throughout the afternoons as he dozed; her wordless presence comforted him as no words could have done. In the course of those afternoons, the summer then as hot as this one was proving to be, her mind would wander, almost free of associations, as if with Henry she was embarking on the same uncharted territory. Even after his death this habit had proved impossible to lose. So that when she thought of Mario in his silent house in Parsons Green she would also be preparing to spend an afternoon not dissimilar to his. Not for Mario, as she imagined him, the torpor of an afternoon nap; not for her either. She would sit in her drawing room, the doors open onto the terrace, the sun flooding in, and reflect that she was in many ways a fortunate woman. This, however, was somehow only possible in the summer. In the winter, darkness seemed to gather almost as soon as she was home after lunch, and then indeed she did have to summon her strengths, exert her will to endure the dead time ahead of her. It puzzled her that she had so few duties, that all duties seemed to have come to an end with Henry's death, leaving her idle, unoccupied, so unoccupied that others had no inkling of how she spent her days, imagining that she shopped and cooked as enthusiastically as they themselves did, or met friends in town, or went to galleries and concerts, spent evenings at dinner or cocktail parties where such matters were discussed. She no longer did these things, although with Henry she had travelled, had visited the museums of which he was so fond. It was in Munich, in the Haus der Kunst, that he had received the first warning of his malady. Prescient, although he had made light of it, she had got them back to London, and there, only six months later, he died. Goldmark had attended then, treating the matter as gracefully as Henry had; somehow they had carried it off. But she had been left unoccupied, with this habit of sitting idle in the afternoons, for all the world as if it were disloyal to spend the afternoons in any other way.

At first people had made an effort with her. They had telephoned assiduously, inviting her to their entertainments, but eventually her polite refusals had antagonised them. 'She's aged dreadfully,' they assured each other, as if they themselves were eternally young. Maybe they thought they were; activity is beneficial in this respect. The cousins were the most insistent, and the most disapproving, and though it cost her something to disappoint them, it did so only for a little while. By this time she was immured in her own silence, as old Mario was in his. He was the same age as herself, exhibiting the same symptoms, outrunners of a possible greater age, yet they never overstepped the mark of their acquaintanceship, their brief daily contact. To do so would have offended them both. It was ordained that she would greet him as she entered, would eat her solitary meal, and would offer a few formal words before she left. Each knew that the other would go home to an empty house. Each knew that dignity was the best, indeed the only defence, not only against the weariness and disappointment of age, but against pity, which strangers— and almost everyone was a stranger now—of their munificence offered so unstinting a portion.

It pleased Mrs May to think of the dignified old man as she removed her jacket, smoothed her hair, and took up her position in her armchair, facing the open French windows, for her afternoon reverie. On this Monday the weather was still breathtakingly hot. She pitied those at work in the city, although at other times she almost envied them, remembering her own days as a highly efficient secretary, so anxious to be a model employee that she was unaware of how out of date she must appear. Susie Fuller's insouciance was simply not within her competence. It never had been, she reflected, letting her head rest on the back of her chair, either in or out of work, either as a secretary or as a wife. It was only as a widow that she had managed to relax a little, yet even now she felt herself to be bound by certain rules, of observance, of behaviour, of formality. That was no doubt why she welcomed her quiet afternoons, as intervals in the great continuing task of keeping up appearances. She hoped that she never gave any sign that the task was wearisome. People of her age complained freely; their children sighed, not suspecting that they would do the same. The old man in the restaurant knew this, as she did,

childless as she was. One should spare young people the spectacle of old age. But she had discovered that the middle-aged
dreaded it even more, rejecting the comparison.

When the telephone rang she felt a brief spurt of alarm, as
though she were only safe if she remained undiscovered.
When she heard Kitty Levinson's voice she immediately concluded that something dreadful had happened. For Kitty to
break with tradition to the extent of telephoning on two suc-
cessive days was without precedent. Her own heart trembled
in anticipation of bad news. That was another thing she had
discovered about old age: anyone's bad news, anyone's illness,
had the same effect as one's own.

'Kitty? Is anything wrong?'

'No, Thea, nothing at all.'

But there was an alteration in her normal tones that alerted
Mrs May that Kitty had something difficult to say.

'Is Austin well?'

'Perfectly well. In fact we're about to have visitors.' She
paused. 'So we shall both have to be well, shan't we?'

'Visitors?'

'Ann is coming over from America. You remember Ann,
my granddaughter, don't you?'

'I remember her as a little girl, certainly.'

'Well, she's a big girl now, twenty-four. And she's getting
married! And she wants to get married here, in London, with
us. Between ourselves, Thea, her mother isn't up to it, and I
understand that they don't get on too well. There are younger
children, apparently, not that she's ever bothered to marry the
man she's living with. Partners, they call them nowadays, don't
they?' She gave a little laugh, revealing tension. 'As you know,
we have no contact with Clare, nor do we want to see her
again. After the way she treated Gerald . . .'

Here a great sigh threatened to disrupt the conversation, as it always did when Gerald, the absent son, was mentioned. Mrs May knew that, in this most delicate of matters, she was hardly to be reckoned part of the family circle, must never introduce Gerald's name into the conversation, but only accede sympathetically to Kitty's references. For Gerald was mysteriously taboo. All she knew, and this merely from Henry, was that Gerald had failed his parents, had most noticeably failed his mother; that after a perfectly satisfactory childhood, and a reasonable university career, Gerald had lost his head, married Clare, fathered a child, and to all intents and purposes disappeared.

'He can't have disappeared,' she had reasoned with Henry.

'He had a few medical problems' was the vague reply. 'He's living quietly in the country somewhere.'

For the offence to Kitty was so grave as to preclude further enquiries. Clare had divorced Gerald and had left the child with Kitty and Austin, before taking both the child and herself off to live in America. This offence was added to the offence of Gerald's virtual disappearance, for Mrs May had never encountered him, though Henry had.

'He's different from us,' he had explained, again vaguely. 'Likes the simple life. Living on a farm somewhere.'

'Doesn't he want to see his daughter?' she had asked.

'Not at the moment' was the cautious reply. 'Anyway, she's in America.' The whole subject was under a cloud.

If she thought of Gerald at all—and there was no reason for her to do so—it was as some sort of country gentleman, living in exile from all that Hampstead and his mother had to offer. She saw nothing blameworthy in this, although Molly had assured her that Gerald had broken Kitty's heart. It was even more grave than this: Gerald was responsible not only for

Kitty's heart but for her nerves, which were famous. Austin's task in life, somehow handed on to Mrs May, was to prevent anything from upsetting Kitty. It was possible that she did not wish to see this granddaughter, certainly did not wish to re-establish contact with her erstwhile daughter-in-law. At the same time, Mrs May knew, Kitty liked to keep lines of communication open, always in the hope that a message from Gerald might miraculously come through.

'So she's getting married from here,' Kitty's voice went on, now and then broken by the deprecating little laugh, indicative of keen annoyance. 'Grandma's faced with the task of arranging the wedding. The silly girl doesn't realise how long it takes to plan these things. They're arriving at the weekend, Ann and David—that's her young man. It's not what I'm used to, Thea. Not the way we do things in this family.'

'I can see that. It must all be quite a strain on you.' For tribute must be paid to Kitty's nerves whenever an occasion presented itself.

'This is where you come in, Thea. I have a favour to ask.'

'Yes, of course.'

'Ann and David will stay here, unless I can persuade Molly to put David up. I don't think he'll be any trouble.' David was dismissed, a mere accessory. 'The thing is that David's bringing his best man with him. At least I assume it's his best man. Ann merely said, "David's friend." I'll be frank with you, Thea; we know nothing about him. We were wondering if you'd help out.'

'I? How?'

'Well, we've no room for him here, and I can't ask Molly to take both of them, and you've got all that space . . .'

'Wait a minute, Kitty. Are you asking me to give house room to a complete stranger?'

'Best, his name is. Steve Best.'

'His name is neither here nor there. I simply don't want anyone in my flat, let alone an unknown young man.'

'It would only be for a day or two. Until the wedding.'

'And when is that?'

'Next week, some time.'

'That is more than a day or two, Kitty. And anyway it's out of the question.'

'I thought you'd be glad to help us out,' said Kitty, her voice stiff. 'After all, what are families for?'

'What indeed?'

The question hung in the air between them. Mrs May knew what families were for: they were for offering endless possibilities for coercion. She had become aware of this as soon as she had entered Kitty's drawing room for the first time, a nervous bride on Henry's arm. At that time she had not understood why Kitty was so aggrieved, why Henry had to cajole and placate. It had all settled down, of course, but Kitty had never been averse to letting her hurt feelings show. They had won her many a concession, but from men. Mrs May was not of that number.

'I thought you might be glad of the company,' Kitty's voice went on, now as mild as milk. 'All alone in that big flat. Molly and I often wonder why you haven't thought of taking a lodger.' This was the insult direct, and was noted as such on both sides.

'I have all the company I want,' she said. 'I'm afraid I can't do anything for your friend. I don't want a stranger in my flat.'

'Oh. Austin will be very disappointed. "Thea will help us out," he said. I really didn't want to ask you; it was Austin who insisted. "It's too much for you," he said. "You've got the wedding to cope with. I don't want you overdoing it. If it's only a

question of a few days Thea won't mind. After all, she's part
of the family . . ." '

'When exactly do they arrive?' she interrupted tiredly. 'And
how long is a few days?'

'Sunday or Monday,' Ann said. Of course I'll have to have
everything planned by then. The caterers . . .'

'No more than a week, Kitty.'

'Of course not, dear. I knew you'd help out. He just wants
a room to sleep in. I expect he'll be with David most of the
time.'

'Steve Best.'

'Yes. I know no more than you do. Of course it's all mas-
sively inconvenient, I'd be the first to admit. But she is my
granddaughter, and she wants to get married in London . . .'

'That's the bit I don't understand.'

'The poor girl wants a proper wedding, I suppose. Her
mother takes no interest, probably can't afford to. I know what
this is about, Thea. I'm not stupid. Austin and I can provide
for her in a way that her mother can't. That's why we're being
honoured with her presence.'

'Yes, I see.'

'Still, I couldn't refuse. How could I? And of course she'll
need something to wear . . .'

'I hope Steve won't need something to wear.'

'What?' Tinkling laugh, flirtatious now. 'Oh, I see. Your little joke. We've always appreciated that dry sense of humour of
yours.'

'No more than a week, Kitty.'

'No, of course not, dear. And thank you so much; we appreciate it. We'll see you at the wedding, of course. Austin was
saying it's been too long since we got together. Must go now.
So much to do.' Again the little laugh, the different timbre sig-

nalling that she had got her own way. 'Goodbye, Thea. And thank you again.'

Mrs May replaced the receiver slowly, as soon as it was clear that Kitty had no more to ask of her. She was aghast at herself for the abrupt tone she had heard in her own voice, aghast at Kitty for manipulating her so shamelessly, aghast at herself for allowing herself to be so manipulated. Kitty was a monster, of course; this opinion was strictly private, not revealed even to Henry, but for once Kitty's monstrousness was not the point, or not the whole point. Mrs May did not like what she had heard of herself, either when voicing her objections or when waiving them. She had heard a whole lifetime of polite re- fusals in that voice that strove to be so calm, so reasonable. A real woman would have laughed and said, 'Really, Kitty, it's out of the question. Why can't he go to a hotel?' Or produced a full agenda of visitors to prove that her spare room was oc- cupied. But since Henry's death, fifteen years ago, she had had no visitors, was known as a solitary, made no bones about the fact. Yet for all her solitariness, or her self-sufficiency, she lacked an overriding philosophy to help her deal with en- croachments, incursions, and thus fell at the first fence. And it was not as if she even knew this person, knew anything about him. Her life did not bring her into contact with young peo- ple, and it was so long since she had been young herself. And were young people nowadays anything like the young person she had been, young only in age, hardly in requirements? One heard about drugs, raves. Even if he were as innocent as she had been, and that was unlikely, he would be an unwelcome presence. She would have to make rules, see that he obeyed them. And supposing he took no notice, saw her for the harmless old girl that she was, and took advantage? At the back of her mind was an archaic fear, a fear that went so deep that it suddenly seemed to her that her whole life had been designed to outwit it. Until now she had been successful. It took only one telephone call to bring her defences down.

Her values, she would be the first to admit, were entirely suburban. One ate plain food, was careful not to give offence, and stayed at home until one married. But these were the suburban values of her youth, when suburbs still knew their place. One did not accommodate random strangers without at least an introduction, or some sort of previous acquaintance. One rarely encountered wealthy matriarchs like Kitty; matriarchs belonged to a higher order of things, or were read about enjoyably in books. Mrs May knew that even now Kitty had forgotten her all too timid protests; they would have been brushed aside by the far more agreeable prospect of planning a lavish wedding. For it would be lavish, as all her entertainments were lavish, and she would have the wholehearted encouragement of Molly, who also knew a matriarch when she saw one, and behaved accordingly. The young people, Ann and David—but did Molly know what had been decided for her? And if she did would she object?—would be dealt with superbly, as if they had nothing to say for themselves. Gratitude would be expected of them at all times. The expenditure of the wedding would ensure this. The preparations would be so dazzling that the merest hint of an objection would be silenced. Mrs May felt almost sorry for the girl, getting married in such circumstances. But having no resources of her own, or being presumed to have no resources, she would think the price worth paying. For what other reason would she decide to marry so far from home?

Everything these days seemed to be a matter of resources. Perhaps Ann was cunning, seeing her grandmother simply as one more-than-adequately resourced. In that case she would have to play her part. And whom was she marrying? Did this David have anything to say in the matter? Mrs May remembered Ann only as a recalcitrant child, with a will that might yet be adequate to Kitty's. They were, after all, of the same stock. And Austin! Brought in to clinch the argument, as if no-one could oppose a man! Mrs May doubted that Austin had anything to do with it, although she could not be sure. Austin was entirely amiable; she had always liked him best of all the family. But Austin had for so long been subjected to Kitty's will that he underwrote everything she said and did. For Austin loved Kitty, as Kitty no doubt loved Austin, but in a different manner. Austin loved Kitty for her faults, as well as for her undoubted virtues. That was the strength of their union, which had withstood even the defective son, who had, she seemed to remember, joined a commune at some point in his rake's progress. This, in itself harmless, was a defiant gesture. And he never came home. This was the reason for Kitty's broken heart, to which mysterious allusions were made. 'Of course Gerald was a disappointment,' her friends wisely opined, without knowing exactly the nature of that disappointment. Kitty was expert at deflecting questions which were too probing and might not be entirely well-meaning. Mrs May could see her, head lowered, fingers joined at the bridge of her nose. Nobody would be bold enough to demand a further explanation. Nobody was.

And in the meantime she was landed with Steve Best. This is the last thing I do for them, she thought incoherently, until she realised that it was also the first. Good sense, momentarily recaptured, told her that this was a routine favour, extended quite naturally by people of a more robust disposition. But she was not of a robust disposition, had never had anything more to cope with than a husband who had already been through one marriage, and who asked nothing more from her than a peaceful and secure setting for his future existence. Neither of them had had any contact with the young, whom she saw—common sense momentarily deserting her once again—as dangerously dynamic, like Puck, or Pan, with movements that would shatter the calm of her silent home. Why could Kitty not have had Steve, and sent Ann off to her? That would have been the considerate thing to do. Yet immediately she saw the futility of this reflection. Ann was the granddaughter who must be spoiled. Bullied too; certainly made privy to Kitty's moods. Mrs May, remembering Kitty's way with Ann as a child—ardent, but also dissatisfied, reproachful—did not think that these wedding preparations would proceed harmoniously. But that was Kitty's problem, Kitty's and the faithless Austin's. If he had so much as volunteered a suggestion, which she was now inclined to doubt.

And now she was to be invaded by this unknown Steve, with whom she hoped she would manage to be on polite terms, not showing him how deeply she resented his presence. Would he respect the atmosphere she had cultivated, even now with Henry in mind? She thought not. In the street young men on Rollerblades rushed past her like demons, or dropped nervelessly from the high cabs of articulated lorries, taking for granted an equilibrium which they had as yet no reason to distrust. She could hardly tell this Steve to go out all day, although a moment's reflection told her that this was what he would choose to do. In herself she held no attractions for a young person. That was part of the humiliation of being overruled . . . She would be nervous, apologetic, regretting her lack of experience. She could at least make him comfortable, she decided. And then she would keep out of his way. She would convey, somehow, that she was not to be disturbed, regretting that she had no great work to occupy her. He was not to know this. 'You'll forgive me if I leave you to your own devices,' she would say, pleasantly. 'There is something I have to get on with. I suggest you make arrangements to see your friends, Ann, and, yes, David. I'm sure you have plenty to talk about. I'll give you a key. But really, Steve, I expect we shall see very little of each other, don't you?'

3

There were three bedrooms in the flat, her own, the room in which Henry had died, and a small spare room in which he occasionally took a nap. The narrow divan bed seemed to retain the impress of his body, as if his ghost slept there. She stood in the doorway, reluctant to enter. It was a pleasant room, sunny and quiet, although it overlooked the street. In the daytime the street was silent, empty except for old people like herself. It was an elderly neighbourhood of quiet middle-class residents, most of whom she knew by sight, and with whom she exchanged greetings when she went out to do her morning shopping. This restraint occasionally made her sigh, although it was natural, if not entirely reassuring. She would have preferred evidence of a robust male presence, of someone who would take control in an emergency, but through the spare room window she could see only mute closed doors and undisturbed curtains. Many people were away, of course; it was still summer, although the first week in September, and exceptionally hot. Yet the houses looked closed against the street, which was itself deserted, without even the sound of a passing car to disturb this prolonged holiday trance.

The room seemed abandoned, as all rarely entered rooms do, given over to the memory of Henry lying there on winter afternoons. He had always slept voluptuously, had had easy access to sleep, could sleep at any time. It was when he felt sleep gaining on him that he repaired to the spare room for an hour, to reappear, fully restored, when she prepared tea. Christmas day was his favourite time for sleep, so that she spent the lightless hours of that long silent afternoon on her own, reading, and reflecting that in essence nothing much had changed since her girlhood, when she had spent most of her leisure time reading on her bed. She did not mind the temporary solitude, to which she was after all accustomed; what she did mind was the winter, with its stealthy darkness, and the mortal quiet of the garden. For this reason, when it was time to make the tea, she clattered the cups a little more than was necessary, until Henry, his face still blank from the onslaught of his sleep, came to join her.

Of that other unentered room she preferred not to think. It was empty now, empty of Henry and also of all evidence of his illness. When the last oxygen cylinder had been removed she had closed the door behind her as if the room had been condemned, as if it had been decreed that death had marked it forever. There was no question of anyone ever using the room again, and yet it was agreeable and overlooked the garden, as did her own. It was a sign of Henry's elegance, of his desire to spare her, that made him move to what became his room when certain of his symptoms became noticeable. He had known what was in store for him. When the evidence could no longer be concealed they had entered into a conspiracy, the three of them, she and Henry and Monty Goldmark, to carry the whole thing off as best they could. It had been done, although it had left gaps in their conversation. At times a monstrous cheerfulness prevailed. She had been there throughout, had been there on the day he died, holding his hand, and yet it was with a savage relief that she had thrown away all his pills, stripped the bed, opened the windows, and, ten days later, after the funeral, had made up the bed again with clean linen, had closed the windows, and shut the door behind her forever.

Nothing of Henry remained in that room except the knowledge of his disappearance from her life. Yet in the spare room, the room that was to be invaded, plundered, she could still see him as she had so often seen him when he woke from an afternoon nap, his hair wild, his gaze turned inward. She had not felt easy until he put himself to rights and drank his tea. When he was once more cheerfully back to normal, and as likely as not on the telephone, she would go in and straighten the coverlet on which he had lain, glancing out at the street in the hope of seeing lighted windows, signs of life. There had been none, only the pall of darkness and a fear that all might not be well, that the night would bring no comfort because sleep had become inimical, and because Henry's sleep had held a warning that she had not fully understood. Later, sitting by his bed, in the course of one of those lengthy dozes which had become habitual in his last illness, she had understood her fearfulness. Consequently she had rather taken against the spare room in which he had slept so many times. She strove to be reasonable, and on the whole succeeded. She regretted anything nebulous, mysterious, immanent. She abhorred atmospheres, portents. Nevertheless she preferred to keep the door of the spare room permanently closed.

Now, however, it was necessary to open it once again. In the sunlight, as opposed to the darkness of those distant winters, it looked reassuringly ordinary, if a little bare. Mrs May contemplated the Indian bedspread on which Henry had lain and decided to get rid of it. The room deserved something light, something new, without associations. She would go to one of the stores, John Lewis, she thought, and see what she could find. It was a point of honour that this Steve should find nothing amiss with her hospitality, even though the thought of him made her quail. It would be the same with any stranger, she told herself, even a woman. Revising her earlier estimate of the situation, she reflected that a woman would be worse. At least a man, and a young man at that, would want to keep out of her way, no doubt repelled by the very idea of sharing living space with a pensioner. Another woman would want to chat, wash her clothes, wash her hair, whereas a young man could be confined to his room, like a prisoner. She did not quite see how this was to be managed, but hoped that he would take his cue from her. She would prepare his breakfast and then make it clear that she did not expect to see him for the rest of the day.

In the midst of these calculations, standing in the middle of the room, the Indian bedspread in her hands, the irony of her position struck her anew. She was about to become a prisoner herself, at the behest of Kitty and her ruthless arrangements. And yet she could not blame Kitty for her own unprepared-ness. What did she know of young men? There had been few in her own young years, which had been all duty, uncom-plaining duty. She had thought that duty ruled everyone's life, and in her heart of hearts still did. That was why she had ac-ceded to Kitty's request, seeing her own idleness as a refuge from the world and therefore of no value. She viewed herself as this young man might view her, as something worthless. He would be in favour of social justice, as all the young were, would think her an example of undeserving privilege. Therefore she must be prudent, less authoritative than she would like to be. She might, however distasteful the prospect, be required to win him over. Therefore a certain welcome must be prepared. She would meet him as she would wish to be met, smiling, composed. She opened the wardrobe, saw that there were plenty of hangers, then bundled up the Indian bedspread and took it through to the dustbin.

Glancing once more at the impassive street, she decided that movement, activity, were what she needed. She was hungry for faces, crowds; she had been immured at home for far too long. She left the flat, locking the door impatiently behind her. But the street, which she knew so well, seemed unfamiliar, alien. She felt the first creeping inroads of anxiety and put a warning hand to her fluttering heart, slowing her pace. In her head she felt an impatience that her steps could not match. At some level it was clear to her that this excursion was unnecessary, that she could turn back at any moment, and probably should. Yet it was with something like eagerness that she took her place at the bus stop, gazing at passing cars as if any one of them might carry her off to a better life. She knew that for her there was no better life, was even on the whole contented, yet had she been able to see herself she would have been astonished at her ardent gaze and her unseeing stare. It was only after climbing onto the bus that she remembered her stiffness, her unhandiness. She composed her expression, embarrassed that she had entertained thoughts of flight.

It was hot, very hot. In Oxford Street the crowds seemed to saunter luxuriously, as if they were on a promenade, an esplanade. They wore garish holiday clothes, walked three or four abreast, seemed, to her unaccustomed eye, overweight. She was carried along like a dry stick on a stream, wincing as she was struck by a gesticulating arm, apologising as she made her way through the loitering crowd. She began to think more kindly of home, understood what it was that kept her there. The shop was reached with some difficulty, and once inside the doors she felt that the crowds had followed her, were stepping on her heels. The same or similar fat women, absorbed in conversation with their companions, blocked the aisles, turned suddenly when least expected, and as far as she could see made no purchases. As she found her way to the bedding department her heart gave a premonitory lurch; she felt in her bag for her pills. They were not there. She could see them quite distinctly on her bedside table, where they were wont to remain. The small bottle in her bag was empty. She had meant to fill it, but now she remembered with alarm that she had put off this task for another day. The sight of so many duvets and pillows, wantonly plump and pale, made her feel faint, as if they had absorbed whatever air was still circulating. The potential urgency of the situation directed her to pick up a cream cotton bedspread and make her way, as if swimming through a heavy current, to the till. 'Nice, aren't they?' said the assistant. 'Portuguese.' Haggard now, she paid with her credit card and was handed a large and pneumatic plastic bag, as inimical to her breathing as the pillows had been. There is no need to panic, she told herself. I shall walk out of here, find a taxi, and soon be home. It was foolish not to have eaten; she could not now remember why she had been in such a hurry to get out. It had been something to do with the sun, with the play of light on the windows across the street, with the sudden hatefulness of the untenanted room. With the grateful assumption of a duty, even one as negligible as this.

Now, the plastic bag sticky against her leg, she was obliged once more to push her way through the implacable crowds, and as she did so she felt the familiar dread that signalled the beginning of an attack. She stood on the edge of the pavement, her head bent, willing a taxi to notice her plight and pull over. By the time that one did so she was already so breathless that she had difficulty in telling the driver her address. Breathing as best she could she extracted a ten pound note from her bag and held it in front of her like a talisman. The cotton bedspread tipped out of the plastic bag as the taxi swung round Hyde Park Corner, and it was only the prospect of familiar surroundings that gave her the strength to retrieve it.

When the taxi stopped outside her building she climbed out gracelessly, her bag dangling open. She dropped her keys, bent to pick them up, intent only on reaching her pills. As she straightened, with some difficulty, she became aware of a young man coming forward to help her. 'Hi,' he said, as she turned her desperate eyes up to his face. 'I'm Steve.' No doctor, no attendant, no guardian angel could have been more welcome. Indeed he was rather better than any of these, being utterly unimpressed by her plight, or perhaps simply not aware of it. The gaze with which he favoured her was neutral, yet he helped her indoors, sat her down in her own drawing room, vanished, and came back with a glass of water. 'My pills,' she managed to say. 'Room on the right, bedside table.' He vanished and reappeared once more, then stood, watching her calmly. Within minutes, it seemed, she was looking at him with amazed gratitude, cautiously restored to something like health. It was only the heat, she told herself, and nerves: Monty was right. There is nothing to be alarmed about. Nevertheless she retained from the experience the sensation of falling that was becoming habitual. If this young man had not been there she might indeed have fallen, might have had to clamber to her feet in full view of any passer-by. 'Your room is next door,' she said. 'I'll show you.' She got to her feet and preceded him down the corridor. 'In a minute,' she announced, 'I shall make tea. There is a fruit cake. I'm sure you must be hungry.'

Why she was sure of this was not explained. He did not look hungry. He looked careful, expressionless. But he had been kind, and there was no-one else, no friend, no neighbour at hand to succour her. He was neatly made, of middle height, with a patient abstracted air, as if he too would rather be elsewhere. 'No hurry,' he said. 'I'll get my bag.' It was a pity that the pills had such a sedative effect; she was ready for a nap, in her own room, in silence, the curtains drawn. She knew that she should be asking him questions, making it clear that she expected him to be out all day, showing him the kitchen and the bathroom, feeling a tug of despair at the complications still to come. And the coverlet was not yet in place, was still in the plastic bag, which she was carrying like a visitor, a stranger in her own home. Yet he seemed unoffended, took off his linen jacket and hung it in the wardrobe, as of right. In his position she would have offered thanks and a mild compliment on the aspect of the room, with its view of the silent sunny street, but he continued to say nothing. Fortunately, or unfortunately, she was too becalmed by the pill to care about this. Tea, she thought; I must have tea. 'I'll put the kettle on,' she said to the room generally; his back was towards her, and he was extracting clothes from a large nylon holdall. Turning to face him at the door, she saw his bright incurious eyes on her, his closed lips wearing a half smile.

'The tea,' she repeated. 'Do join me when you're ready.'

'Right you are,' he said. 'Take your time.'

'If you want to wash,' she suggested.

'I bathe in the morning,' he told her. 'If that's okay with you.'

Mrs May also bathed in the morning. Fortunately there were two bathrooms.

'Or I can get a shower at the swimming pool, if there is one.'

'I'm sure there is,' she said. 'But of course you must feel perfectly free.'

'If I could just put a few things in your washing machine— you know what it's like, travelling.'

'Of course,' she said. 'But have your tea first.' She felt extraordinarily tired. As long as she could endure him until she could decently go to bed, she did not much mind what he did.

Tea restored her somewhat, permitted her to take stock. He seemed civilised, she thought, was quiet and contained, but with a patent lack of interest, of engagement, in his expression. One silent circular glance had apparently told him all he wanted to know about his surroundings.

'I wasn't expecting you until the weekend,' she said. 'I don't know what you'll have for supper—an omelette, perhaps. I myself don't eat in the evenings.'

'We came on an earlier flight,' he explained. 'There was no point in hanging about. Ann said her grandmother would put me up. Then when I got to her place I was told to come on here.' He looked annoyed, as well he might. 'Anyway, I'm going there for dinner tonight. That way I can bring the rest of my stuff back here.' Mrs May felt anxiety return, but forced herself to remember his kindness.

'How did you all meet?' she asked. 'Of course you must know Ann better than I do. I haven't seen her since she was a little girl.'

She remembered a stolid child, encountered one afternoon at Kitty's when she and Henry had gone there to tea. The child's thick body had been encased in a smocked Liberty print, a white ribbon in her flat dark hair. She had opposed a considerable will to Kitty's rage and love, which had not prevented Kitty from endowing her with a wardrobe of unsuitable clothes. At least they would have been suitable for a baby. Mrs May had a vision of Kitty in shops that sold clothes for toddlers, although on that occasion Ann would have been about six. There was dissension in the air even then, an embryo battle of wills. And Kitty had not entirely managed to subdue the little girl; the grown woman would offer even greater resistance.

'Have you known her long?' she asked, coming back with a start to the present.

'David's my friend,' he said. 'We hang out together. When he said he was coming to London I said I'd tag along. He said Ann's grandma could put me up.' Annoyance once more flitted across his generally impassive face.

'Ann's grandfather is not in good health,' she explained. 'That's why you're here. He needs quiet. And anyway it's only for a few days.'

'I may stay on for a bit,' he said. 'Check out the music scene. I won't be any trouble. You won't know I'm here.'

'I'm afraid you won't be here at all,' she rallied. 'I shall be needing the room. A relative may be coming to stay.'

Mrs May had no relatives, as this young man would un-doubtedly discover. I shall invite Susie Fuller, she decided. Susie might be glad of a break in London, although she would be astonished at the invitation.

'I think it best to make things clear at the beginning, don't you? You'll be able to look for something else; I should do that as soon as you can. To tell you the truth, Steve, it is not convenient for me to have you here. You're welcome to stay until you find something else, which I'm sure you will. Per-haps your friend David—whom I haven't yet met—could help you.'

'Sure,' he said equably. 'Mind if I have a quick bath? And you'd better let me have a key. I might be back late tonight.'

'The Levinsons keep early hours, as I do—I doubt if you'll be late. I'm sure you won't make a noise. I've noticed that you move very quietly. Your key is in your room. Don't lose it, will you? I shall undoubtedly be in bed, when you come in. Or perhaps not, knowing Kitty and Austin. They will be tired too, as I'm sure you will.'

His flat level gaze did not leave her face. 'I might take David out for a few beers,' he said pleasantly.

She gazed steadily back at him, confident that Kitty would forbid such an excursion. Oh, how the young must hate us, she thought. We try to stop them doing what they want to do; we forget their unrelenting energy, since we no longer have much energy left to us. And Kitty would have one of her headaches, and would be obliged to rely on Molly, even on herself, would complain—justifiably—at the inconvenience, whereas she would really be complaining about the unfair competition between youth and age. Mrs May could see Kitty, red-faced, furiously attending to her oven, while Ann leaned on the jamb of the kitchen door, supplying monosyllabic answers to questions Kitty directed over her shoulder. And all the while, between them, stood the missing link, the absent Gerald.

'By the way,' she said. 'Has Ann been in touch with her father?'

'No idea,' replied Steve, uninterested. 'Lives in a commune, doesn't he?'

So that rumour was true, not that Kitty had ever confirmed it. Kitty gave it out that Gerald was working as an ecologist. Fortunately few people knew what that meant, apart from prolonged absence. 'Doing very well,' she would say, if anyone were imprudent enough to ask. 'He moves around a lot. We see him when we see him.' But they had not seen him for an unconfirmed length of time. Austin had gone in search of him at one point, when Henry was still alive. The meeting had been either unsatisfactory or fruitless, was in any event overshadowed by the bad attack of angina that Austin had suffered as a result. Mrs May had a distinct impression of Austin, in his polished shoes, among the bracken and dead leaves, as he made his unsteady way back to his car. This had been so frightening that the visit was never repeated. That Gerald might have caused his father's death became a possibility; the matter was shrouded in silence. Shortly afterwards Austin had lost heart, had sold his business, and now sat at home, devoting his life to Kitty. Gerald was a closed book, and would remain so until, if ever, he came home. So far he had given no sign that he intended to do so.

'And when is the wedding?' she asked, pretending an interest she did not feel.

'I reckon some time next week.'

'You'll be the best man, I suppose.'

His face darkened, as though she had uttered a threat. 'David doesn't want any fuss.'

'In that case I'm afraid he's in for a disappointment. Ann's grandmother will certainly want to do things properly. She has very high standards. It will be a register office, I dare say, unless David is religious.'

'He is.'

'Oh? I didn't think young people had much time for religion.'

'David's a religious teacher.'

'Is he? Where?'

'He teaches sport and religion in a school.'

'What a curious mixture. Well, perhaps not really. Where is this school?'

'Northampton. That's in Massachusetts.'

'And that's where you met?'

'I'd been travelling,' he replied evasively. 'I was passing through, got to know him, stuck around. You know how it is.'

She had no response to this. 'And will Ann be happy with him?' she asked. She felt that someone, anyone, should put this particular question.

'Should do. He's a really nice guy. A bit heavy sometimes, you know?' There was no response to this either.

'And what about you? What do you do?'

'I'm looking around, getting it together. Like I said, I've been travelling for about a year. I'm into music.'

'That's nice. Music must be a very uplifting profession. What sort of music?'

'I play guitar.'

The guitar had always seemed to her the most specious of instruments, a parasitic offspring of the harp and the harpsichord. Suddenly she longed to be listening to a full orchestra playing something majestic, Schumann or Brahms. She longed to be seated alone in the drawing room, listening to the radio. This she was only able to do when her upstairs neighbour was away, as he was now. The neighbour, a small peppery man who avoided her eyes whenever they met at the entrance, had once sent down a note, complaining. She had felt rebuked, had blushed, the note in her hand. But she had seen him going off in a taxi, his fishing rods propped up by the driver, and in his absence had enjoyed whatever Radio 3 had to offer. She would know when he came back; he always banged his doors. She had not mentioned this, an unruly exchange between neighbours being unthinkable in her quiet respectable building. It was simply now that she was missing her chance, and would continue to do so for as long as this young man was on the premises. She felt a great weariness. Henry would never have let things get this far, she thought. It was true that Henry did not enjoy loud music either. She had only been able to indulge her tastes since his death. And until she met him she had only had reasonable tastes to indulge.

'All right if I have my bath now?' he enquired patiently.

'Good heavens, is that the time? I had no idea. Yes, you have your bath. I don't expect we shall see each other again this evening. I get up very early,' she told him. 'So I'll be able to get your breakfast. Then I'm afraid you'll have to look after yourself. I go out to lunch; I expect you'll do the same.' Fleetingly she remembered that she had had no lunch, had had nothing to eat since breakfast. That was no doubt why she had felt so poorly. She rose. Obligingly he got to his feet: a good sign. At the door she said, 'I'll see you in the morning then. Give my love to the Levinsons. Tell Mrs Levinson I'll be in touch.'

She was aware of backing out of the room, of retreating, the flat no longer her own. Her own room was a haven in which she humbly took refuge. In vain she admonished herself for what she saw as unfriendliness. It is because I never had children, she thought. That is why I appear so unnatural. That is what Kitty knows, and Molly too, though Molly has no children either. But Molly still yearned foolishly over young people, exclaimed over babies, tried to capture their little hands. Useless to tell them that she and Henry had come to terms with this apparent inability, that each had become the other's child. In his last illness she had washed and changed him but had not otherwise treated him as a baby. The most she had done was hold his hand when she saw that he had a moment of fear. Together they had watched the light change, until the room was in shadow. In that way Henry was spared disappointment, for her attention remained undivided. Maybe he had had regrets. Who did not have regrets at the end of a life, knowing that life was receding daily? Maybe he had longed secretly for children, making it a point of honour not to let her know of this. Disillusion had not soured him, though she could date her own increasing coldness from her own disillusion, which she in turn had kept to herself. Without children one was always lonely, yet she was thought to be merely independent, as if independence were not simply an alibi, and a concealment for one's losses.

After a desultory restless evening—the flat surprisingly quiet once he had left—she prepared for bed. Tomorrow she must telephone Kitty and ask to speak to Ann, or the unknown David, to suggest that he and Steve go to an hotel. She would offer to pay, her contribution to the wedding expenses. This seemed to her utterly reasonable. On this suggestion, which she thought she could put quite forcefully, she dozed off. She slept fitfully, kept awake by the need to hear Steve return and lock the front door. And it seemed to her that he never did come back, so that in the morning she crept to the door of the spare room and listened for a sound. There was no sound, only a smell of heated flesh, as if he had been lying in his bedclothes for at least a week.

4

'You're a sensible woman, Thea,' said Austin, lying concave in
his armchair. 'What do you make of all this? Ann rings up a
week ago, tells Kitty she's getting married, says she wants to
get married in London—putting Kitty to a lot of trouble, in-
cidentally—announces her arrival for next Sunday, and then
the three of them turn up like nomads nearly a week early. No
consideration. Kitty's all ready to organise a champagne buffet when Ann says she doesn't want any fuss. If she didn't want
any fuss she should have seen to it that her young man stayed
somewhere else, and that that friend of his . . .'

'I've had an idea about that, Austin.'

'They only wanted to share a room, you know, Ann and
David. Kitty put a stop to that. "But Grandma, this is a mature
relationship," she said. "Not in this house," I told her. Poor
Kitty. She wants to feel happy, but she can't. She wants it so
much, Thea. She's shed tears at night, when she thinks I'm
asleep. She thinks of Gerald all the time. Whereas I know I've
lost him, that's the difference. After I had that little attack you
might have thought he'd make some enquiries, wouldn't you?
Not a bit of it.'

'Will he be coming to the wedding?'

'Of course not. For one thing we can't get in touch with him. For another he might have moved on. His lot occasionally take to the road. No, I've lost him, that's the beginning and the end of it. And he was such a beautiful boy, Thea, so brilliant, so loving. I don't know what went wrong. I torture myself, sitting here. Of course, I should never have retired— that was Kitty's doing. But to tell you the truth I lost heart after that little attack, particularly when Gerald failed to enquire . . .'

'How are you now?' she managed to interpose, mainly to get him off the painful subject of Gerald. She could see how he was. He presented a caved-in appearance, with a collapsed-looking chest and an expansive stomach, and she remembered him as a handsome upright man, an excellent dancer and a surprisingly strong swimmer. She and Henry had spent a holiday at the Levinsons' house at Freshwater, and had been so happy that she had never wanted to go back. To walk those cliff paths again with no-one holding her arm or her waist was not to be borne.

'Not too bad' was the cautious reply. 'Of course I keep my pills to hand.' He indicated a small onyx box on the table beside him. 'This wedding I could have done without, mind you. Not that it affects me emotionally. I'm just paying for it. But to tell you the truth, Thea, I don't like these young people very much. Ann is a complete stranger to us. Kitty can't understand her, and I could tell she had hopes. But she doesn't look like us, doesn't even speak the same language.'

'What does she do?' asked Mrs May.

'I'll give you three guesses. No? Homeopathy,' he brought out triumphantly.

'I understand it's what they call a sunrise industry.'

'There are a million therapists out there, Thea, and not one of them can cure our broken hearts, Kitty's and mine.'

'And David? What does he do?'

'He's a teacher of some sort, in what I suspect is some kind of religious establishment. "I think of myself as bearer of the Christian message," he told me. I told him not to expect much of a response in Hampstead, in that case. A moron. And she's completely taken him in hand, orders him about, tells him off. Kitty is bewildered.'

'Maybe he's turning the other cheek,' Mrs May said, and was happy to see that she had brought a smile to his lips. Seizing the moment as propitious, she introduced the subject of Steve.

'I really can't have him in the flat, Austin.'

'No reason why he should be there, as I pointed out to him over dinner last night. He's got a perfectly good family in Cheltenham, as I managed to ascertain. Father's some kind of civil servant. But this Steve dropped out, joined what he called a rock band. I doubt if he's got an ounce of talent. What's more he doesn't appear to have any means of support. David paid for him to come over. He was wandering all over America, had been for the last year. It was his lucky day when he met David, who is quite well off, apparently. David, for some reason, saw him as a kindred spirit. Of course the person we need now is Henry. He'd sort them out. Dear boy, we all miss him. It must be so sad for you.' He looked at her affectionately. 'You look well, though. Too thin, of course. You were always too thin.'

She smiled back at him, grateful for the kindness. 'I want this Steve to go away,' she said. 'In fact I'll pay for both the boys to stay in an hotel. But for a limited period only.'

'Excellent idea. I'll put it to them this evening. No doubt

Steve will want to dine here—again. Kitty was cooking all the afternoon. In this heat! And she's not a young woman, Thea. We're none of us young. The young shouldn't expect us to put up with them.'

'The world has moved on since our day. We no longer set the standards.'

'Too right,' he said gloomily. 'Where's Kitty? I know she's been longing to see you.'

Not knowing how to respond to this *politesse,* Mrs May put her faith in the arrival of Kitty, which could surely not be long delayed. She was well aware that gargantuan preparations were in train. 'What meads, what *kvasses* were brewed, what pies were baked at Oblomovka!' To her surprise she was almost enjoying herself. Kitty's tense telephone call, as if she were under duress, had been welcome, since she had no intention of staying in the flat waiting for Steve either to go out or to come in again. He had been with her for two days and it felt like a lifetime. The taxi ride to Hampstead had been in the nature of a novelty, and through the windows she had renewed acquaintance with the parks. She almost wished the journey had gone on for longer, but in these dog days of late summer, with so many people still away, the roads had been quite clear. And then the Levinsons' flat was very soothing, with its silk shades pulled half way down against the strong sun, and the faint smells of beeswax and carnations from the many small tables. And Austin had always been courtly: Henry had been fond of him, and he had seemed so genuinely glad to see her. She was sure that she could trust him to get rid of Steve, and indeed of Ann and David, whom he clearly disliked.

'If you could just mention my suggestion of an hotel this evening . . .'

'Aha! At last! Where have you been, darling? Thea's had to

put up with me for the last half-hour. Not that I haven't enjoyed our chat.'

'Good afternoon, Thea, dear,' said Kitty, exhausted but immaculate in a tightly fitting silk print.

'Kitty, what a marvellous dress.'

'Hardy Amies. It is good, isn't it? This is Ann. Where is she? Ann? This is Thea, Henry's wife. I don't expect you remember her.'

'But I remember you,' said Mrs May, seeing in the large dark-haired young woman the clumsy recalcitrant child she had once been. 'How are you, Ann? And I see that congratulations are in order.' She referred to the sizeable emerald ring on the equally sizeable hand.

'This?' Ann laughed, revealing two slightly crooked incisors. 'Grandma gave me this. She thinks I'm not doing things properly.'

'Tea,' said Kitty, avoiding Austin's severe look. 'I've laid it in the dining room. I thought it would be easier. That way if the boys come in they can have it on their own. We won't wait.'

Mrs May followed Ann's broad back and legs across the room, feeling overdressed in her linen suit, which she had thought rather smart. She noted the slightly creased minidress, the skirt too tight. Not what Kitty would have wanted, she reflected.

'Sit down, everyone,' ordered Kitty, somewhat reassured by the evidence of what she thought suitable as an accompaniment to a cup of afternoon tea. Tea cakes were piled in a silver chafing dish, a banana loaf and two Victoria sponges, silver knives beside them, waited to be destroyed, and a pyramid of coconut tarts was placed to the right of the silver tea and coffee pots. 'I didn't make any sandwiches,' said Kitty apologetically. 'I'm afraid you'll just have to put up with us today, Thea.'

'Magnificent as always, Kitty. But how are you? And when is the wedding?'

Kitty flashed an exasperated look at her granddaughter. 'Next Wednesday, if I can get the caterers in time. I've been on the phone all morning.'

'Relax, Grandma. It's no big deal.'

'We have certain standards in this family, Ann, even if you seem unaware of them.'

'Kitty, Kitty,' murmured Austin, crumbling a slice of banana cake with his fork.

'I'm sorry,' said Kitty. 'But Ann, if you eat so much you won't be able to get into your wedding dress.'

Ann released a peal of laughter. 'What wedding dress? Grandma, get real! I'm not going to get dressed up just to get hitched. It's archaic, anyway.'

'Then why are you doing it?' demanded Austin.

'We think it's kinder to the baby,' said Ann, reaching out to replenish her plate.

Kitty, Austin, even Mrs May, were for a split second united in carefully dissimulated speculation. Of course this in itself was not unexpected, or was not to be received as such. She felt them all struggling with disapproval, even with disappointment. Nothing, then, was to be salvaged from this wedding except the wedding itself, which must override the brute facts of nature, must be treated as a successful overture to whatever would come next, and that preferably out of sight. The terrible thought occurred to Mrs May that this interlude might be prolonged, might indeed stretch into infinity, until the Levinsons' fragrant rooms filled with a baby's paraphernalia, until Austin, in his chair, was reduced to groaning over his vanished quietude, until all thoughts of Kitty's maternity were displaced by that of her granddaughter, and the memory of Gerald retreated into oblivion. With Kitty and Austin in place, expectant, there was still room for Gerald. With all the rooms occupied, overflowing, in fact, he might never come home again. And what of Steve? It surely could not be that Steve would want to stay? He had, now that she came to think of it, mentioned the possibility. She would simply have to make it clear to him that this was out of the question. Again, she had no idea how this might be brought about.

At the same time she had to concede that these events exerted a certain fascination, a fascination against which Kitty was completely proof. One more inconvenience was neither here nor there, compared with the onerous task of preparing and organising the wedding. And yet the frown that clouded her still fine features held regret, as well as her habitual exasperation. It was to be hoped that the exasperation would carry her through. Kitty, after all, had a powerful tongue in her head. Kitty would make it clear when her hospitality was no longer available. That they might all be dependent on Kitty to perform this task was undoubtedly unfair, yet the fact remained that only Kitty could see it through. And Kitty's standards, so often invoked in Mrs May's hearing, would hold firm, even if it involved bidding a precipitate goodbye to the long lost granddaughter, so lately arrived. Kitty's standards did not encompass small babies. Voluptuous preparations were one thing, unpleasant surprises quite another. A wedding might just be within Kitty's sights, but nothing else was to be permitted. Even now Mrs May could feel her resolution hardening. And yet the regret was still there, not to be ignored.

A sly girl, thought Mrs May, and one who had learned to deride others for qualities which she herself did not possess. In the broad face she could still see the lineaments of the glum child, but now altered into adult awareness. The dark hair,

once flat, as if reflecting the child's depression, was transformed into a frizzled mop, unsuitable for the large, rather im-
posing figure in her parodic skirt. The mocking smile held
them all to ransom, yet there were traces of disquiet in the fine
eyes, her best feature. Mrs May could see no resemblance to
any of the family, all of whom, in growing older, had seemed
to assume a single expression. Ann must resemble her absent
mother, rather than her equally absent father. Kitty must have
registered this at once; hence her displeasure. Mrs May, who
had known neither of them, merely saw something untidy,
sensual, unfocused. The girl had no looks to speak of, and yet
she gave out an aura of health, hardiness. Above the full throat
the mocking smile came and went, occasionally taking sound-
ings from the silence that had greeted her revelation. In her
boldness Mrs May sensed the child's former antagonism come
to fruition.

'What I don't understand . . .' Austin began, but was interrupted by the sound of the front door opening and closing.
Kitty too had been obliged to hand over keys. The two young
men, in identical sweatshirts and jeans, presented themselves
in the doorway, as if waiting for all to rise.

'Come in,' said Austin heavily. 'Sit down. This is Dorothea,
Henry's wife.'

'Hi there,' said the one who was not Steve. 'Glad to meet
with you, Dorothea. I believe you'll be coming to share witness with us on the big day?'

'How do you do,' responded Mrs May. For a moment or
two she had shared Austin's distrust, for no reason that she
could honestly entertain. It was the smile that dismayed her,
the careful all-purpose smile of the professional well-wisher.
It was also the smile of a man who had nothing to hide. It was
entirely possible, she thought, that this David was what was

commonly understood as a good person. His goodness, however, did not make him attractive. She could not quite understand this, although she could see, in his unvarying smile,
directed at each of them in turn, that he had the awful simplicity of one who had managed to turn his back on life's little illogicalities. Pleasing in appearance—if one liked small
heads and neat beards—he was not quite pleasing in manner.
This, she thought, had something to do with the fact that he
clearly expected to be waited on; in exchange he would offer
his goodwill, and his smile. There was nothing about him of
the prospective bridegroom; indeed he seemed innocent of
sexual impulses. She thought it unlikely that he would have
moved out of his unmarried state by choice, but presented
with the choice by one whose will was stronger than his own
he had judged it prudent to acquiesce. Perhaps he was
shocked, and could not countenance shock. Certainty, however unwillingly arrived at, was more comfortable. And he
had compensated by exhibiting a kind of hospitable passivity.
He was very slightly eery.

It was possible that these two young people were attached
to each other; if so they gave no sign of it. David continued
to exude friendliness, while taking his seat at the table, but it
was clear that he was devoid of curiosity. He might have been
welcoming a congregation, like a vicar at the church door. He
received the cup of tea that Kitty offered him with a well-
bred smile. One would make an effort with this young man,
she reflected, although he seemed equally accessible to all.
One would try very hard to extract from him a sign of spontaneity, to dislodge the smile. There was something adaman-
tine about him that gave the lie to his extreme affability. His
manner towards Kitty was exaggeratedly deferential. It was
clear that he would offer no purchase for her hunger.

Poor Kitty. For Kitty was clearly the loser. Ann had managed to frustrate her advances, yet remained a member of Kitty's family, and thus Kitty's last hope. Mrs May watched her steadily eating and was forced to conclude that Ann was not pleasing. Like David she was jovial, even jocular, but she did not aim to please. In withholding her co-operation she became paradoxically powerful. Negligent in appearance, she gave notice of a lazy will. The child that Mrs May remembered had seemed to be seeking an outlet for her own way. The woman, for she was more woman than girl, seemed to have found it. Of the two of them, David was the innocent. Steve, in neutral, seemed to have no views on this unlikely partnership. Both Steve and David, in their identical sexless clothing, were like members of a youth club. Ann, by contrast, had something of the leader about her.

Mrs May judged it prudent to keep any discussion within the bounds of the immediate family. An argument was clearly on the way.

'I'm sorry to make this meeting rather brief,' she said. 'Kitty, will you excuse me? I hadn't realised how late it was.'

'Steve is staying to dinner, if that's all right, Grandma,' said David.

'Quite all right,' said Kitty, defeated. 'Cold chicken and salads. And apple tart. If you'll wait a moment I'll make some more tea.'

'You see what I mean,' said Austin, accompanying her to the main road. 'You're sure you won't stay, Thea? We see too little of you.'

'No, I won't stay,' she said. 'And yes, I do see what you mean.'

'It's not just that they're strangers. They're *aliens*. They have different customs. When Estrella went in to do Ann's room yesterday she found her still in bed, at half-past ten, reading. She was wearing a T-shirt. Kitty's answer to that was to take her off to the White House and buy her a trousseau. That's how she thinks, poor darling. All leave has been cancelled, of course. No Freshwater, no Bordighera. I must say Molly and Harold have been very supportive, although Kitty can't always talk freely on the telephone.'

'What was she reading? Ann, I mean.'

'I asked her that. I still take an interest.' Austin had been a publisher of trade journals. 'A Holistic Tomorrow. The shout line was "Say no to pharmaceuticals!" '

'If only we could.'

'She'll find out. They all will. Youth is ignorant. That's what makes it so special.'

'We mustn't grudge them their ignorance, Austin.'

'We resent it though, don't we? Old people aren't very nice either. I don't like them myself.'

They came to a stop silently on the street corner, neither of them anxious to go home.

'You'll be a great-grandfather,' she observed.

'Don't. We're old enough already.'

'We are rather old, aren't we? It's such a comfort to be with someone one's own age. That's why I really can't have Steve in the flat. It's not fair to either of us. You remember what I said about the hotel?'

'At least we can send them off on honeymoon. I booked it this morning; Paris, the Royal Monceau Hotel. Kitty and I went there. So did Molly and Harold.'

'Will Steve go with them? I hardly think . . .'

'I booked three air tickets. So you don't have to worry. I doubt if they'll move out, the boys, I mean. Ann would certainly object. She seems to like communal living. Like Gerald,' he added sadly. 'He can eat his dinners with us. Just leave him something for breakfast.'

'It's the daytimes I worry about. I'm usually out for lunch . . .'

'Are you? Good girl. I hope you look after yourself. There's a taxi.' He kissed her firmly on both cheeks and told her to keep in touch. 'It meant a lot to Kitty, your coming all this way. I dare say she'll be on the phone tomorrow. I've enjoyed talking to you; I always do. I'd better get back: Molly and Harold said they'd look in. Take care, Thea.'

The remark was valedictory. Looking out of the taxi's back window she saw him walk dejectedly away and knew that she could not impose further on his attention. The drive back was less enjoyable than the earlier journey had been, although she had a great deal to think about. They were all in this together: that was her conclusion. They were a family, even if she were only an associate rather than a full member. And how confiding Austin had been! She had never heard him talk so freely, on that subject of all subjects. And Kitty had not been on her high horse, had been quite knocked off it, in fact. This equality was temporary, she knew, but was nevertheless timidly appreciated. She was no longer the nervous young wife whom Henry had first introduced to the cousins, young in experience if not in age. Her present age was in some ways more comfortable, certainly more peaceable than the youth of those young people. She had found them unattractive, and this disheartened and puzzled her. Surely they should strike one of her years as beautiful? Unmarked, and therefore beautiful? But perhaps they were beautiful to each other; perhaps the whole thing was a conspiracy to outwit the old. It was typical of Kitty to be thinking of clothes and food, all the rituals of a conventional wedding; it was perhaps natural of Ann to despise her for doing so. Natural, but again not pleasing. She would leave them saddened, unless they took a different line with her. Perhaps the trick was to make a few, a very few concessions, in her case to treat Steve with studied politeness—she could never manage to be impolite—but as a stranger in her house. In that way he might be encouraged to move on, even to go home. Ann and David would go when they were ready; at present they seemed to show no signs of haste. This would present problems. Then she remembered that they were booked to go to Paris, and took heart. Together they must all devise a plan to prevent them from coming back.

She gazed wistfully at the home-going crowds as the taxi moved southwards. So might she once have stood at the bus stop, before being elevated to marriage and affluence. She planned to take a bath as soon as she got in, to spend some time quietly. The evening was, mercifully, taken care of. She was tired, her linen suit a little creased. She wanted to get into a dressing gown, a temptation that must be resisted. As she reached Harcourt Terrace she realised that this journey might have to be repeated, and could not repress a very slight feeling of interest. This was surely the stuff of fiction? A strong plot, unusual characters, a threatened outcome: who could ask for worthier diversion? And she was, after all, an observer. There was some virtue in this, though not as much as others made out. One usually had to keep one's observations to oneself, which halved the pleasure. Not to do so was to court displeasure from all sides.

Her silent street seemed to take on a prelapsarian calm, an embodiment of the quiet life she had so recently interrupted. She welcomed the contrast; it was as if she were coming home after an evening at the theatre. On the corner the honeysuckle gave out its last sweetness. Steve no longer disturbed her. He would move on eventually, and then it might even be pleasant to have her old life back again. In due time she would revert to being the character they all thought they knew. She understood what it was that made people want to change their identity. Even her own identity was threatened by recent events, and yet she might, she reflected, find the change beneficial. It was to be hoped that the others would as well.

The spectacle of the life lived in that flat beguiled her. Kitty and Austin were lovers; they were also conspirators, each devoted to the other's fusses and heartbreaks, genuine and otherwise. Eagerly they worried, consoled, commiserated. No-one could join in: they were an exclusive, and excluding, concern. Any attempt to reassure was shrugged off as irrelevant, of no value. They needed no friends, for what friend could understand them as they understood each other? In this way her role had been defined for her; she was to be respectful of their intimacy, which was indeed worthy of respect.

But now their conspiracy had encountered newcomers who did not know the rules, aliens, as Austin had described them, and respect would no longer be the order of the day. Mrs May had felt little sympathy for the young people, seeing them as predators, ignorant of their own intentions. She suspected, as Austin and Kitty no doubt also suspected, that they despised the values so munificently displayed in the Levinsons' flat, their complacency, their material anxiety, their need for comfort. She herself had always come up against the barriers they erected for themselves against the world, but had seen them for what they were, a defence against fear. David's expansiveness, Ann's insouciance notwithstanding, they too were conspirators. And in any contest between age, which is easily bewildered, and youth, which is scornful, the least prepared were the most at risk.

The real alien, she reflected, was Steve, who had no claim on anyone, unless it were herself. But she was more fortunate than Kitty and Austin, for she had no claim on him. She did not expect him to like her, to be grateful, to be appreciated. His blankness of manner, his lack of affect, made it unlikely that he knew how to pay a compliment. Oddly enough this made him seem vulnerable. Holding him mentally at arm's length she might deal with him in a satisfactory manner. 'Don't get involved' had been Henry's invariable maxim when anyone pressed claims too strongly. Steve, to do him justice, pressed no claims, merely landed weightlessly in other people's lives, expecting to be taken for granted, as a given. She must find a way of dealing with the situation, as speedily as possible. The exercise would be an excellent opportunity to sharpen her wits. I too am old, she thought. But there are times when experience, even assumed, even simulated, counts.

5

He was no trouble. She admitted as much to Molly, who telephoned one morning when Steve was taking one of his lengthy baths. In a whispery confidential voice Molly expressed concern for her sister's health, and solicited Mrs May's views on the matter. This was the usual tenor of her conversations. Devoted to her sister, of whom she was in awe, Molly found it restful to dwell on Kitty's complaints, perhaps because these had no real substance. Of the broken heart she was uneasily aware but did not speak, this being a matter not to be discussed outside the family. What they spoke of in confidence, on one of their stately pilgrimages to Harrods, was also a mystery, though it could perhaps have to do with their husbands, towards whom their innocent yet determined girlhoods had been directed.

Of the two of them Molly retained some vestiges of that earlier self; her nature was placid, yet an unanswered question could still be detected in her round brown eyes. She, the younger of the two, had married first, and had felt apologetic about doing so, yet Kitty's had been the real love match. It may have been some memory of the young Kitty's rage and tears on hearing of that first engagement that had made Molly defer to her ever since. Yet they were close, as close as two sisters ever could be, as close as two girls who had never left home, for the men they had married, and had married for that reason, had never tormented them, had never shocked or challenged them, had acceded with them to married life as if it were merely a superior and agreeable social activity, a stage setting for fine housekeeping and family parties, with access restricted to those similarly endowed. Amiable Austin, amiable Harold, had both chosen and accepted these two handsome sisters, not long back from their Swiss finishing school, and ever since, uncomplainingly, had had their lives prescribed for them. In return for their indulgence they received excellent care, as if they were already in their dotage. There was never a murmur of complaint on either side, or none that reached the outside world.

Yet in Molly's case the doubt that could sometimes be seen in her fine eyes betrayed some uncertainty as to the world's intentions. For this reason she clung to Kitty, knowing her superior strength; indeed it was Kitty's strength that made it so safe an activity to commiserate with her occasional headache or her more habitual exasperation. Mrs May had once seen them out together, arm in arm, walking slowly, as if they were in a foreign city, whereas in fact they were approaching Selfridges. They had not seen her, and she had not made her presence known to them. She had hurried away from such intimacy, from the spectacle of those two heads so close together, and from a conversation which surely no outsider should interrupt. She had felt oddly vulnerable, although Henry was alive at the time and she was going home to him. She had been reminded that she had never shared secrets with anyone, that no-one, not even Henry, would ever engage her in such a conversation. The image of those two sisters, arm in arm, had stayed with her, stayed with her even now. It was yet another sign of their separateness, or of her own.

There were other signs, of course, notably the precautions that had to be observed when addressing them, the sheer difficulty of introducing any information that had nothing to do with their normal concerns. Both claimed to be sensitive, subject to palpitations, attacks of nerves, overwhelming anxiety, justified or justifiable fretfulness. These had to be taken into account before any real conversation could begin. Over the years Mrs May had managed to eclipse herself completely, to engage in an exchange as formal as a Noh play. This was found to be acceptable, as if it were appropriate for her to say so little now that there was no husband to lend weight to her words. Mrs May also knew that it was precisely her widowhood that alienated them, as if it were a fate so terrible that it was not to be contemplated. Outside the married state they would have no further existence, or none that they would recognise. Therefore she played her part, obliterating herself so as not to frighten them. And there was always plenty of information to be received in exchange for her relative silence.

But now that there was something new to discuss she wished that the formalities could be abridged. 'He's no trouble,' she repeated, endeavouring vainly to return to the matter in hand. At the same time it occurred to her to wonder why Molly could not have given Steve houseroom in her capacious mansion flat. She already knew the answer to that one. If Molly's domesticity were no longer a refuge from the threat posed by strangers her position would be untenable. To expropriate her from her chosen way of life was a crime Mrs May could not bring herself to commit. Besides, Steve was no trouble, not at present, not to her, although she was not happy at having an alien presence in the house. But this was nothing to do with Steve, predated Steve, and would no doubt survive him. It was a private fear, one which, not quite identified, hovered on the edge of her consciousness. She wrote it off as one of the fusses that had to do with age, although if she were honest it had been with her for longer, since before her marriage, in fact, when she had first, and how gladly, begun the great adventure of living alone. Now it was no longer an adventure; sometimes she doubted whether it ever had been, whether she would not have done better to share with someone, anyone. So that Steve's presence was both threat and comfort, even justification. But none of this could be expressed.

She reassured Molly that Kitty was bearing up wonderfully, since that was her function, conceded that there were reasons for concern, and resigned herself to a recital of Kitty's difficulties, although she had been able to observe these for herself not three days ago. Kitty's difficulties, which, if confessed, might be genuinely interesting, stemmed from her dislike of her granddaughter and her shame at this discovery. In her scheme of things, not to love a member of one's own family was tantamount to a sin, yet Mrs May had seen for herself that Ann was not necessarily endearing. Why not leave it at that? She had not much liked Ann herself, but had told herself that the girl's appearance was against her: the tight skirt, the untended teeth, the general air of indifference. And in her not unpleasant but undistinguished features Kitty no doubt saw an elusive resemblance to Gerald. Greatly daring, she mentioned this to Molly, who concurred.

'And of course they have nothing in common with David,' Molly went on. 'We were there for dinner last night and he insisted on saying grace both before and after the meal. Apparently he does that every time. And Austin longing to light his cigarette. Harold thought it very insensitive. Harold said, "When in Rome." '

'Did Harold say that to David?' Mrs May asked, interested.

'No, he said it on the way home,' Molly replied. 'I never thought religion went very well with food; silly of me, no doubt. I say my prayers at night, like everyone else. I expect you do too, Thea.'

Mrs May made a noise expressing assent, without engaging in the lie direct.

'But he's quite the opposite,' Molly went on. 'It's Jesus this, Jesus that, as if he knew Him personally.'

'No doubt he thinks he does.'

'I never feel I like to bother God too much: it seems such bad manners. But David speaks as if He's just got off the telephone. I really worry about Kitty. And Austin is not a well man.'

Mrs May recognised this ploy as a return to normal: both sisters routinely pleaded the ill health of their husbands as an alibi for their reluctance to perform unpleasant tasks. At the same time she was aware that she was contributing not only to the conversation in a way that would have been unthinkable a few weeks ago, but to the situation as a whole. The mere fact of taking in Steve had somehow united them, as her solitary unburdened state had never managed to do. It was clear from Molly's confidential tone that she thought that the advent of Steve had turned Mrs May into a normal woman, or almost normal, since she seemed curiously free of the symptoms that afflicted every other woman Molly knew. For this reason, picking up on the lingering sympathy in Molly's voice, she repeated, 'Oh, he's no trouble. No trouble at all.' At this point the bathroom door opened onto a rush of waters,

and she was obliged to send her love to Harold and to promise
to keep in touch.

It was almost true that he was no trouble. Apart from his
frequent baths, and the loading and unloading of the washing
machine, he made no demands on her resources. Indeed she
was pleased that he was so clean, although the crumpled
clothes that he had unpacked from his other nylon holdall, the
one that he had transferred from the Levinsons', had seemed
rather dirty. But he presented himself at the breakfast table
every morning in a spotless T-shirt and jeans, his wet hair
slicked back; and from showing him where everything was
she had progressed to greeting him, to buying a melon and
croissants and honey and free-range eggs, to laying these offerings mutely in front of him before retiring to the terrace
with her own cup of coffee and a slight feeling of accom-
plishment. When she returned to the kitchen he was gone,
and so was all the food. She suspected that he would eat no
lunch, would eat only if food were provided for him, like an
infant. How old was he? Surely old enough to be self-
sufficient. On the third morning, hearing no sound, and wondering whether he had gone out, she had knocked on the
door of his room and looked inside: the room was empty, the
bed made, no trace of occupancy apart from the two nylon
holdalls stacked in the corner. This presumably meant that he
would be gone all day and most of the evening, so that she
could enjoy her freedom once more, or so she told herself.

Except that this was somehow impossible. To begin with
she slept badly, unwilling to relinquish consciousness before
she had heard him come in and lock the front door. She had
to resist the impulse to get up and check that he had secured
the chain, until she reflected that it hardly mattered if he had
failed to do so since she was no longer alone in the flat. There

was the rather worrying fact that they hardly communicated, that despite her readiness to be addressed he had nothing to say to her. From this she deduced that he found her too old to be of interest, felt, if anything, a certain contempt for her grey hair and freckled hands, answered only monosyllabically to her 'Good morning,' and when asked what he planned to do on any particular day, would reply, 'Look around.'

'Where will you do that?' she enquired.

'Soho, I suppose.'

'Why not get out and about a bit more?' she had asked.

'I haven't got a car, have I?' and the familiar spasm of annoyance crossed his neat features, as if constrained by the poor hospitality he was receiving.

Yet she had hardly minded this, feeling sympathy for his smooth face, his moody mouth, his habitually bare feet. Once he had gone out the only evidence of his presence was the heavy smell of his sleep in the bedroom, as if symbolising his discontent. This in turn reminded Mrs May of her father, and her first acquaintance with an odour other than her own. She found this remote association inhospitable, and was newly aware of how prolonged her immaturity had been. Even now she was not quite sure that it had come to an end. A normal woman, she thought, a woman who had brought up a family, would know how to deal with this young man, would not tip-toe round him, laying little offerings on his breakfast table, would rouse him, interrogate him, send him out to do the shopping, generally jolly him along. But she was too shy, and anyway there was no shopping that she could not manage herself. She must remember to cancel the Vietnamese cleaners; once Steve had gone they could put in extra time. She suspected that he did not yet know that he was going to Paris, would be affronted to learn that he was to move on. This was

Austin's master stroke, but Mrs May wondered whether he had considered the possibility that Steve might come back, that they might all come back, having had a taste of London life at its most comfortable, instead of returning to Massachusetts, where Gerald's erstwhile wife Clare lived with her new partner and his children, and where David did his teaching in one of the area schools and Ann relieved the mothers of his charges with herbal tinctures and reassurance. She thought she might leave that outcome to Austin. If they left, of course, as was likely—for what young person would voluntarily keep company with the old?—they would be on their own again. Even Kitty and Austin would feel bereft, object as they may. And Kitty would have fits of tears, and Molly would confide her worries on the telephone, and gradually Mrs May, with no physical complaints to speak of, would drop out, and all would be as before in this empty month of the year, with people still away, and even the traffic in the streets becalmed.

Above all he was no trouble because he relieved her of the obligation to take a summer holiday. This had been an annual problem since Henry's death, had indeed been registered even earlier than that. She had a memory of herself standing forlorn at the school gates on the last day of the summer term, saying goodbye to her friends, all of whom seemed to be going off on expeditions to relatives in the country, such as she had read about in her favourite books. And later, when she was kept at home by ailing parents, the endless month of August was an affair of careful walks and daily visits to the Public Library, until it was time to go home again to read the books she had collected. Matters had eased somewhat when she was on her own and had her salary to herself. Those were the days of careful cultural visits to Paris and Florence and Vienna, but truth to tell they were little more than a repetition of her solitary walks, with the addition of overwhelming scenery and exhausting monuments.

In the Duomo in Florence she had found herself edging closer to a group of English tourists and their guide, if only for a moment's familiarity and relaxation. And when that moment had passed she had gone out, somewhat refreshed, into the blazing sunshine, and not long after had been accosted by a man who grew vituperative when she ignored him and followed her back to her hotel. Unsuitable encounters seemed to blossom in the most unlikely places, in austere cathedral cities, or on buses between remote sites of historical interest. Men similarly obliged to take a solitary holiday attempted further acquaintance; all proposed dinner. One, a representative for a champagne firm, grew insistent. Always, smilingly, she declined, not quite knowing her reasons for doing so. It was all quite innocent, and yet she felt disheartened by the vista of loneliness such encounters seemed to evoke. Yet it was not she who was lonely. The men, particularly the divorced father who had revealed his plight in the course of a journey by bus between Blois and Chambord, had seemed idle, shamefaced. This was not the kind of company she sought, and she intuited that they too were disappointed. She bore her own disappointment stoically; she was not, it seemed, a cowardly woman. She supposed that her expectations, though immense, were too simple, and also too hidden, to allow her to make casual friends.

She longed for a companion, but a companion who would know her instantly, whose face would light up with recognition, who would deliver her from her isolation without a word of explanation being necessary. That was why Henry's two warm hands, raising her to her feet after she had fallen in St James Street, had been just such a magical encounter, after which there was no need to plan or even to think, for matters had been conducted without much volition on her part, so that all she had to do was to follow the way indicated, and for the first time since infancy allow herself to be cared for.

With Henry it had all been so different, yet Henry was in part responsible for the fact that she was now so very much on her own. With marriage she had abandoned, or perhaps relinquished, most of her friends, as if it were now her turn to say goodbye at the school gates. Even Susie Fuller, latterly Meredith, was only remembered at Christmas, and she had been a really good friend, although given to uncomfortably searching questions. 'Good holiday?' she would ask, on the return from Chartres, or the Loire. 'Meet any men?' On hearing Dorothea's polite negative she would click her tongue in exasperation, and for the rest of the morning explode from time to time in a temperamental display that had nothing to do with her own settled expectations, as if she feared something dangerously virginal by contamination. These little outbursts saddened them both, to such an extent that she had been more than willing to listen when Susie Fuller pleaded Henry's cause, on the basis of no more than a single meeting. But that was how other women behaved, she supposed; they took a chance, went ahead, disdained aleatory information. When, on that first evening, Susie had elicited from Henry that he was living with his twin sister, she had earmarked him triumphantly for her equally backward friend. Dorothea had listened to her urgings, knowing that they were largely unnecessary. And something in her quiet nature had flared up and made her behave like other women, women who affected mystery when questioned about their lives but who longed to have their secrets revealed.

And so she had married, and, as she put it privately to herself, joined the ranks. And where was Susie now? A widow, like herself, living in Chippenham, whose accounts of her grandchildren were scrawled on a sentimental Christmas card every year. They met rarely, a fact for which Mrs May continued to blame herself. Those days of complicity were gone, but she felt that to bury memories constituted conduct unbecoming, now more than ever. In old age she had somehow returned to her girlhood, and longed to reassure herself with the sight of remembered faces. But those remembered faces were obscured, not only by the years that had intervened but by their owners' fatalism, so that Mrs May was equally likely to think, Susie Fuller? That girl I used to work with? A perfect dear. I must get in touch. But of course did not.

With Henry, for the first time in her life, she had looked forward to holidays. Because he travelled a great deal for his work—America, Israel—he was unambitious, wanted only peace and quiet and good walking conditions. Every winter they spent two weeks in Nice, as his grandparents had done: she could still see Henry, with his copy of *Nice-Matin,* sitting in a café waiting to be served breakfast, while she walked on a little further to buy a copy of yesterday's *Times.* The companionability of those mornings appeared to her now as a dream from which she had since woken. In the spring or the autumn they might go to Ireland or Switzerland, but as time went on, and Rose's condition became more dependent on Henry's presence, they had not gone away at all. She had willingly made that sacrifice, and when they walked home after their Sunday visits, and sometimes walked as far as the park, she remembered her timid, resolute excursions as an adolescent, and marvelled that the wheel had come full circle, but that she was now no longer alone. Then he had died, quite quickly, in that room that was not their room, the room into

which she never went. When he died, with a look of rumi-
native puzzlement on his face, she had gone to the mirror and
seen an identical expression on her own. The rest was a long
apprenticeship that had not yet reached a conclusion.

Holidays since Henry's death were therefore a major problem, for she was now alone again, restored to a condition
which she had found problematic from the very first. Friends
had urged her to go away, as friends always will, and for five
consecutive years she had obeyed them, had gone to mild, expensive watering places—Vichy, Divonne—had read her
book in public parks and gardens, had conscientiously dressed
for dinner, and had eaten dinner alone. It was on those holidays that she had learned to cultivate sleep, which was now
such a magnificent resource. It was with gratitude that she had
laid down the burden of the day in those hotel rooms, reluctantly had opened her eyes on the following morning, in-
stinctively making plans to return home. To do so was a
defeat, but it was a defeat she had lived with ever since, so that
the whole of August was spent in the same manner: coffee on
the terrace, lunch at the café, the long afternoon spent reading. 'I'm quite happy,' she would say, if anyone asked her. 'My
travelling days are over. I appreciate my home now.' Since
something in her expression forbade further questions she was
usually able to get away with what was, after all, the truth.
Soon she was no longer asked whether she had any plans for
the summer. That was when she was most acutely aware of
defeat.

So that to be able to reply, 'I have a young friend staying
with me,' as if it were the most natural thing in the world, was
a very welcome alternative. But she had to reflect that it was
no sort of summer for a young person, even if that young person were as uncommunicative as Steve. Apart from his non-

existent conversation his body language made him seem unapproachable. He had gone out that morning wearing a T-
shirt inscribed with the words, 'Don't Mess with Texas'. He
tended merely to lift a shoulder in response to her increasingly
anodyne remarks. As far as she knew his activities were entirely innocent. He jogged in the morning—in her mind she
followed him wistfully round the park—and sometimes returned to the flat to spend a silent hour in his room. He left
again before lunch, presumably to go over to the Levinsons'
where he would stay until after dinner. He was as neat and as
anonymous as a midshipman, or a young recruit, treating her
home as if it were just another billet. She knew no more
about him after three days than she had done when he first
arrived.

Yet she sensed that he was lonely, as lonely in his way as she
was in hers, except that her loneliness was the outcome of a
fiercely guarded reclusion, and all that she required to help her
was a deeper sense of reverie. Young people were not given to
reverie, were not particularly articulate, lacked the sort of patience that only the old could command. Seeing him moody
and unoccupied made her feel sympathy for his predicament,
yet she herself could provide few distractions. She pitied his
straitened youth of jogging and rock music, yet on the rare
occasions on which she had heard him speak he appeared to
be educated, even gently bred, but determined to hide the
fact. She had had to come to the conclusion that he preferred
to live as he did, to have no regular employment, to drift into
the company of those who might make his decisions for him.
It was a sadness to her to contemplate such a life. Her own, by
comparison, seemed infinitely rich.

That afternoon, after lunch, she called in at a garage in the
Fulham Road. Her own driving licence had long since ex-

pired, but a kind young man promised to deliver the car within two hours. When the telephone rang she was almost startled to receive news from the wider world: that was the negative result of her quiet days. But she had been drafted into a conglomerate; she had to read the balance sheet. Austin had not mentioned her hotel proposition, for which she felt no surprise; he had always been somewhat lazy, or perhaps merely subject to Kitty's will. Kitty was like the enchantresses of old, those who ruled through fear. In this way she had bewitched her husband into eternal and unwavering sympathy. The alternative would be a *crise de nerfs*. She regarded this—as did Austin—as a legitimate manner of seeing that her wishes were granted. His rewards were also considerable: perfect management of his household, a physical loyalty that soothed and regenerated him. They never argued, or if they did, ended up on the same side.

But on the telephone Kitty's voice was dangerously lofty, hinting that some sort of argument was in train or had already taken place.

'I'm expecting you for dinner on Friday, Thea.' Her characteristic little laugh followed. Dare to refuse, said the laugh.

'That will be very nice, Kitty.'

'I've invited the Goldmarks. They can pick you up.'

'No need. I've hired a car. Steve can drive me over.'

There was a silence. 'I hope you're not making him feel too much at home, Thea. Don't forget they're supposed to be leaving directly after the wedding. In fact the whole thing's been a terrible strain on me. And now Molly's being difficult.' Here an intake of breath presaged an outburst. 'We had words. Too silly. I hate to quarrel with my sister.'

'Is anything wrong? What has happened?'

Kitty's voice now appeared to have modulated without transition into the tearful. Perhaps the tears were always there, threatening to break cover without warning.

'I asked her to take David until the wedding. Of course she said no. I can't blame her for that. But I don't want him either. And he gets on Austin's nerves. It was the least Molly could do . . .'

'Did she agree?'

'Eventually. Oh, I dare say we'll make it up, but it upset me. You know how sensitive I am. And Ann has been quite difficult. I've bought her one or two things, but she takes no interest. Just looks at me with a pitying smile, as if she were doing me a favour. If it were up to her she'd get married in that thing you saw her in.'

'If you have a hand in the wedding it will be beautifully done,' said Mrs May quite sincerely.

'Thank you, Thea. It's nice to receive a little support and encouragement. And how are you getting on?'

'Oh, not too badly. Not too badly at all. But we shall all be pretty tired once they've gone.'

'Austin insists that we go to Freshwater. You wouldn't like to join us, I suppose?'

This invitation, though quite possibly genuine, was couched in a manner and a tone of voice that expected a refusal.

'You know how I enjoy my quiet way of life, Kitty. I don't move far these days.'

'No, you don't, do you?' said Kitty, refreshed by the thought. 'Well, we'll see you on Friday. Seven-thirty. Good-bye, now.'

Mrs May replaced the receiver and was suddenly aware of

a gap in the afternoon. She willed Steve to come back, if only to have a bath before going out again. 'Look out of the window,' she planned to say to him, quite casually. 'I've hired it for you. It will give you a bit more freedom. And perhaps we could go out for a drive? At the weekend? If you're not too busy, of course.'

6

'How's it going, Dorothea?' Steve's taciturnity was somewhat moderated by the sight of the car outside in the street, a fact which, although welcome as a sign of comradeliness, was nevertheless in some ways regrettable. It had suited them both to mount a certain reserve, a reserve made more piquant by a no less certain stealth: each would listen for the other going down the corridor, a metaphorical ear to the door. Now they were obliged to acknowledge proximity, although not as yet intimacy. She felt the weight of his appreciation—for the car, not for her person—in his cheery meaningless salutation, repeated several times a day when they were obliged to meet. He required no answer to his greeting, nor had she—after one fervent, 'Oh, very well, Steve, and you?'—any answer to give him. In fact neither required the other to speak. She intuited that his greeting was defensive, pre-emptive, as though by offering this formula he was at the same time signifying that he was not available for questioning.

She knew nothing about him beyond the fact that he was reasonably tactful; beyond that, and his reclusiveness, which almost matched her own, there was no evidence of nurturing.

It was impossible to imagine him sitting in the same room as a mother or a father, yet she thought she detected a dolefulness in his always retreating figure that made her feel protective. Although he looked like a man he was at pains to conceal a boy's feelings. She admired the set of his features, which gave nothing away, and thought that any girl who set her sights on him would have a hard time. Mrs May doubted whether he had lived at such close quarters with a woman since leaving home: body building seemed to have replaced any interest in the opposite sex in his particular physical economy. Living at such close quarters she had become more readily acquainted with his appearance: the short dark hair, the pleasantly blank smile, the mouth which, when not under strict control, betrayed his dissatisfaction, the neat concentrated body, of average height, that spoke of punishing exercise, the bare feet that rejected shoes until the last minute. She thought too that she detected something disturbingly affectless about him, as if he were some sort of mercenary, home on leave from a distant war zone, scrupulously cleaned up, and all at once bored.

She had no idea what he did with his time. Apart from dinner at the Levinsons his days were unaccounted for. Running served him in lieu of an occupation; she was given to understand that he met David in the park and ran round Kensington Gardens with him. She assumed that they spent the morning together, or part of it, and possibly got themselves something for lunch. She did not know whether he had any money, a matter which tormented her. David, it was clear, at least it was clear to her, came from a comfortable background: he had the expansive manners and comfortable assurance that had apparently attracted the wary Steve in the first place. She thought she could understand that friendship, Steve paying with his silent loyalty for the attention of the other, while

David gained an adherent who absorbed, without a hint of criticism, his evangelical observations. She found David, or what she had seen of him, unattractive, his prospective bride even more so. She sincerely sympathised with Kitty, whose objections to the situation were troubled, imprecise. At the same time she saw in Steve the victim of the others' alliance, the third party unsure of his continued welcome by the other two. With this position she could also sympathise.

Surreptitiously, under cover of preparing more coffee, she watched him eating his breakfast, a breakfast which became more lavish as she was convinced of, or imagined—it came to the same thing—his penury. With breakfast in Fulham and dinner in Hampstead he would not go hungry. Then, safely behind the closed door of her bedroom, she would blush at her folly. As if this young man needed her protection! As if she needed his! Had she not spent fifteen largely successful years on her own, bothering no-one, needing no audience for her occasional fears, no concern for her attacks of breathlessness? Had she not got out of the habit of men, as old women will, and even congratulated herself that there was no longer any one of them to torment her? She had loved Henry, had loved even the trace of his presence—his signet ring left carelessly on the side of the washbasin, the smell of his cigar—yet when she had cleared his room after his death she had felt a sort of elation on realising that in the future she would not be dis-turbed. And she had not been. Living alone, she had discovered, was a stoical enterprise but one that could be rewarding. And now, after only a few days, she was once again anxious, fearful of displeasing this stranger in her house. The date of his departure, fixed for the Wednesday of the following week, when he was supposed to fly to Paris with the newlyweds, struck her as unreal; she was half convinced that at the last moment he would refuse to go. She did not think that she had made him so welcome that he would want to stay with her, although the idea made her blush again. She did not even know whether she would be glad or sorry when or rather if he went. She only knew that clearing up his empty room would not provide that curious relief that she had felt when clearing Henry's room after his death.

This puzzled her. After all she had loved Henry, and by no stretch of the imagination did she love Steve. He was not, she had to admit, immediately lovable, was too stony, too empty, too defiantly solitary. She thought that she had come to terms with childlessness, only very rarely thought how nice it might be to have a daughter, until she realised that any daughter she might have had would perhaps have resented the need to keep her company. She had never really envisaged the possibility of having a son. It was simply that in her case some authentic biological process had been omitted, and try as she may to rid herself of the prejudice, she felt that a son corresponded naturally to that process, gave a truer sense of achievement. So had she avoided joy, as she had in most of her dealings with the world, settling instead for reasonable satisfaction. Yet at this late stage of her life (but was that not the point?) she felt newly vulnerable to the sight of a young man's head moodily bent as he disappeared down the corridor, or the soles of his feet pressed together like a baby's under the breakfast table. He will have to go, she thought, or I shall soon have ruined the habits and the discipline of a lifetime, and it is by those habits, after all, that I'm obliged to live.

She thought of ringing Kitty to ask whether David had had this effect on her, but suppressed the thought as ridiculous. For all her status as a tragic mother, Kitty was not permeable to the simpler affections. Besides, there was no reason why

David should touch a maternal chord. The poor fellow, for some reason, inspired a certain contempt, whether for his easy convictions, or for his hapless good cheer, or for his all-embracing physical and emotional forbearance. Kitty might not be permeable to the simpler affections but she was extremely susceptible to masculine charm, and David possessed none. Even in their short acquaintance Mrs May had felt irritated by his gladness. Kitty probably dismissed him as a sort of eunuch. He had made no effort to tease her, to cajole her, which was what she may have expected; his innocence in this regard compounded his original offence, which lay in his problematic physicality. He had made his fiancée pregnant but seemed strangely removed from the evidence. Kitty would no doubt have appreciated a hint of licence: like many old women she looked to the young to gratify her in this particular way, to remind her of her own youth and its conquests, and of all that she had done to evince a certain reaction from a man, a reaction that David bafflingly refused her, so that she felt slighted, foolish. Dislike came more easily then, and dislike based on disappointment is difficult to dislodge.

From that single encounter over the tea table Mrs May had divined that Kitty felt for her inappropriate granddaughter the same emotion that had overwhelmed her when faced with the refractory child. She herself had felt for the girl a certain distaste which Ann had done nothing to justify. Perhaps it was the lazy turn of the head, a certain sly watchfulness, which may have signalled nothing more than an ability to gauge Kitty's mood, that had awoken in Mrs May an unwelcome reminder of her own girlhood, which had been as innocent of sexual involvement as that of any Victorian maiden. Young men, the brothers of friends, had existed, but on the periphery, while she had sat at home reading *Persuasion*. Like

Anne Elliot she believed that all she had to do was wait, and any slight disappointment she felt, when a belated consciousness of her unsought condition was brought home to her, was compensated by the thought of the lifelong fidelity with which she would reward the man who would eventually awaken her love.

In the meantime she had been the object of a certain lazy scrutiny, not from the brothers of those friends with whom she had once walked home from school, but from the friends themselves. It was the same sly speculative look that she had seen on Ann's face, as if Ann had crossed the line that marked out the experienced from the inexperienced. This was understandable, but nevertheless unwelcome. It was as if the girl took a pride in reminding old women like Kitty, like Mrs May, to whom nothing more could happen in the way of romance, that she at least was sexually active. Mrs May could have told her that her pride was misplaced, that she was in fact deluding herself if she thought she had acquired a singular advantage. Kitty too had felt the weight of that misplaced superiority. Even more than the exasperating David who, by comparison, seemed positively virginal, Ann, once more, had frustrated her. Kitty might have longed to offer advice, not knowing that mothers in these enlightened times frequently took advice from their daughters. Kitty, in short, would have liked to act as a matriarch, as a patroness, graciously revealing a little—but not too much—of that arcane knowledge that only married women possess. Instead of which Ann's almost insolent smile—and it did indeed almost verge on insolence—had relegated her to the sidelines, and worse, had reminded her of her obsolete status, and with it her no doubt imperfect knowledge (for so it was judged) and her redundant maternity. Seeing Austin half lying in his chair, his pills carefully to hand, Ann could not help but revel in her own youth, her own fertility. Even if these were compromised, or at least not particularly well aspected, she had succeeded in exhibiting her trophy, and, young as she was, had thought that sufficient proof of sexual success.

Mrs May could have told her otherwise. There is no longer any rule that states that a woman gains credit from the man with whom she is involved. Perhaps there never was. The beauty of Anne Elliot lay in her spotlessness, a quality in which Mrs May had long desired to believe. Yet in her own experience it was that very spotlessness that called forth that particularly insulting smile from those whom she had thought to be her friends. For too many years she had deliberately maintained her defences until at last she had wearied of them. Timid affections, even infatuations, had left her dismayed: it seemed to her that she was always being introduced to girls flourishing engagement rings, while she was still bewildered by the fact that she had not even been aware of them as rivals. The prestige of engagements in those far-off days! Mrs May thought that no modern relationship could carry the same charge. For years, it seemed to her, she had seen the identical small diamond flourished on the same plump hand, had detected the same degree of satisfaction as her own unpartnered state was revealed. If she were honest—and it was not a matter on which she cared to dwell—it was the superiority of those other girls, her one-time intimates, that had ended her innocence. It was when *Persuasion* no longer had any power to persuade that she had been forced to take matters into her own hands. Since there were no beneficent elders to instruct her, and none even to hold her back, for her equally innocent parents were quite content to keep her at home for as long as she wished, thinking her happy, she had, with uncharacteristic boldness, set about looking for a husband. She had not found one. It seemed that she was too unaware even for that stratagem to succeed. Almost unknowingly she had passed the age of early engagements, early marriages, and had become an old maid. That was what the smiles had forecast for her all along.

Mrs May's lips twisted wryly as she reviewed the facts that no-one had suspected. They were not facts on which she cared to dwell, yet in their way they were relevant to her eventual marriage, to her austere widowhood, even to her present position as Steve's unwilling landlady. It seemed that all it took was that look of veiled derision on Ann's face as she contemplated her grandmother's transparent crossness to send Mrs May, a mere spectator, back to her own past, and the manner in which she had conquered the threat, as she saw it, of female calculation, and allied herself, however temporarily and dangerously, with the world of men. For she had become, for a brief and hallucinatory period, a woman for whom finer considerations were in abeyance, and all that was once signified by the thought of love conspicuously absent. And she had done this deliberately, aware of her fall from virtue, aware that innocence prolonged beyond a certain point can become ignorance, aware that the time had come to shed both. *Persuasion* was removed from her bedside table and put back on the bookshelf. She rather thought she had not taken it down since.

Her attachment to the man who had helped her to form what others no doubt saw as her unattractive reticence was not innocent: that was why reticence was in order. The man in question was so unsuitable as to remove any hopes she might have had for a successful outcome. She had met him at a party to which she had been invited by one of the girls at work, for she had already found the secretarial post from which Henry had rescued her. The attraction was immediate, but on her side the attraction had not turned into liking, rather the opposite, and this dichotomy was her first introduction to complex emotion, a radical departure from her earlier expectations. It was a love affair in all but name, for to name it would have been inappropriate. He was ardent, intemperate; she thought him slightly mad, but his madness was to prove contagious. He drank too much, was feckless, was always short of money, though extravagant, was compromised in some way she could not readily identify, but by the time she knew all this it was too late for her to extricate herself. He had a crumbling mansion flat in Down Street; a good address, he maintained, was essential, though the flat was filthy. She disapproved of him, was even frightened of him, yet in his dingy bedroom had felt differently. For all his shortcomings he was an excellent lover, and she in her turn proved a more than adept pupil. She said little, as did he; words, they both knew, would only divide them.

Their involvement gained an edge from the fact that both knew it to be temporary. It was, she thought at the time, because neither of them had anything to lose: her own folly was surely fatal, and he, Michael, had, ever since their first meeting, maintained that he would die young. This assertion was so much of everything she disliked about him—his neediness, his sentimentality—that she was unprepared for his suicide. The police, it appeared, were interested in his debts, and in certain misappropriations of which she had known nothing. She had read of his death in the evening paper; his family background made this noteworthy. There was nothing to connect her with him; for this reason, and because at heart she despised herself, she was relieved though shocked that it was finished. Shame at her own behaviour crept over her gradually, as if she were implicated in her lover's disgrace, as of course she was. Since that day she had acquired a reputation for being enigmatic. It was a very small advance, but an advance, none the less, on being thought inexperienced.

It was different now, she knew. All sorts of liaisons were accepted, single mothers taken for granted; bishops, preaching about family values, merely sounded foolish. The world of *Persuasion* had been long gone even when she had read it as a girl, believing it to be the norm. Yet Jane Austen had never gone out of fashion; rather the opposite. It was as if those who flouted traditional values longed to be reminded of fine manners, even if they marvelled at them, and made little attempt to emulate them. What marriages were celebrated made news in the papers. In the magazines she picked up at the hairdresser's the brides, ever more elaborately caparisoned, wore the same look of triumph that her erstwhile friends had harboured when flourishing their engagement rings, perhaps with more justification. Men, she thought, had not changed as much as women had. Predators and freebooters still existed, but they could be outmanoeuvred. Many of them subsided into nostalgia, perfected domestic skills, saved their energies for work and sport, while women, who seemed to age much more slowly than in the past, formed more honest friendships. Few of them would accept privation, or exclusion; there were now recognised channels of complaint. Female disorders were accommodated; no-one need suffer. Patience, acceptance of one's lot were devalued. Only the old escaped sexual speculation. The young assumed that they alone had access to what they called commitment, and sometimes let their pity show.

As for herself, she had been marked by her experience, which had been whole-hearted and short-lived. What she had learned about herself had not been welcome. She had shown ruthlessness and deceit, and she was alarmed at her lack of scruple. She had turned away from sex, then, even from affection. No-one had known of her visits to Down Street, but it had taken her several years to delete them from her memory. She had become, in the meantime, an exemplary daughter, an exemplary employee. She went from home to the office, from the office to home. She kept her features impassive. Several times she regretted the fact that her stock of experience was so slender, but did nothing to remedy this state of affairs. Her father died, and then her mother; she bought her flat and moved her belongings and prepared herself for a solitary life. A broken paving stone in St James Street had delivered her, and she discovered that it is sometimes good to awaken envious speculation in others. She considered her own character to be something less than meritorious, but in time she forgot her earlier adventure and became a good wife. She paid for her respectability with her silence, for no-one, not even Henry, certainly not Henry, had known of her past. He had accepted her for what she had become, a quiet, pleasant, rather dull, but infinitely reliable woman who never gave offence. Her new relations saw only the dullness and looked no further.

And now, in old age, the mask had become the face, so that she was rigorously and genuinely dull. But there remained an awareness of more troubled sensations which she tried to metamorphose into detachment; usually she was successful, but for some reason not at present. She had been unprepared for old age to render her so harmless. It was as if her sins had been wiped away, leaving only concealment in their place. She even wondered whether she had in truth been so very remiss. By today's standards she had merely been unwise, had acted out of character. Yet she still felt obliged to make amends. Sometimes, in the very early morning, she had an illumination: none of it matters. But this tended to vanish as the light grew stronger, and the cautious habits of recent years reasserted themselves. In the glass she saw a mild placating expression, unaware that her features were normally set in a forbidding frown. Had she known this she would have attributed the frown to a necessary act of self-censorship.

Nothing had any relevance to the present situation, except that the present was so often chaotic these days, as the power to control it gradually slipped from her loosened grasp. There was no reason why Kitty's granddaughter's engagement should awaken echoes and memories of her own poor amorous record, but that was the way of it in old age, the present merely nudging one back to the past, which was as brightly lit, as inflexibly detailed as it had always been. Why not pursue the thought to the end and imagine that she was jealous of Ann, a girl who had secured for herself both marriage and motherhood: no painful apprenticeship for her. Yet she did not think that this was the case; she simply resented the girl for inflicting complications on her own hard-won quietness, the major complication being Steve. If Steve existed now, in her flat, it was because Ann was in some way responsible. Ann had a certain authority, or perhaps it was immovability: it amounted to the same thing. Ann made decisions. Her sly look at her grandmother rested on a decision already made. Mrs May had no doubt that in a year's time she and David would be back, this time with the baby. 'Your taste is better than mine, Grandma,' Ann would say. And, 'He's growing so fast I can't keep up with him.' And Kitty, shamefaced, would crave the touch of the baby's hands in hers, when all that was required of her was the use of her credit card in Harrods. Mrs May hoped that Steve might have been eclipsed before all this came to pass, and reflected that Ann might dispense with him quite efficiently when the time came. Her own reclusion—or was it entropy?—would prevent her from performing the task herself.

On impulse she went to the telephone and dialled the Levinsons' number. It rang for what seemed a very long time. She was about to give up when Austin answered, sounding distant.

'Austin? It's Thea.'

'Thea?'

'Yes, Thea. Are you all right?'

'What time is it?'

She glanced at her watch. 'Three-thirty.'

'Must have dropped off.'

'Oh, Austin, I'm so sorry. I'll ring back.'

'I expect it was Kitty you wanted. She's out with Ann. Wedding garments, I suppose.' He gave an audible yawn. 'Excuse me. We're all rather tired. At least I am.'

'I really wanted to make sure that Kitty was all right.' For she did wonder, with some fascination, whether Kitty's state of mind were anything like her own.

'Poor darling,' said Austin. 'She's rushed off her feet. I've remonstrated with her, Thea.' As usual his voice warmed into animation as he contemplated his wife's trials. 'I told her, a glass of champagne is all that's needed. Perhaps a few smoked salmon canapés. After all, they're only coming back here after the register office. But no, she wants a proper buffet. That means caterers, florists, the lot. And first of all she wants the flat redecorated. Well, I put a stop to that, as you can imagine.

But she and Estrella have cleaned the place from top to bottom. Nobody's allowed into the drawing room now. I'm in our bedroom, as a matter of fact.'

'I'm so sorry I woke you, Austin. Just give my love to Kitty.'

'Don't go away. I'm quite glad of someone to talk to. I seem to be outnumbered in my own home.'

'And yet it must be easier with David out of the way. How is Molly getting on?'

Austin gave a dry chuckle. 'You'll never believe this, but David is greatly appreciated in Highgate.'

'Really? I rather thought that Molly . . .'

'Oh, not by Molly. By Harold. It seems that David's got him on this macrobiotic diet of his. They spend the afternoon shopping for kelp and beansprouts. Then they spend the rest of the day in the kitchen messing about with them. Molly is bewildered; Harold has always been so keen on his food. But he says he's put on weight since he retired—haven't we all?—and he'll try anything. I have to hand it to David; he's managed to convert the heathen. At least he thinks of us as heathen. "I guide my conduct by the Word," he told me. I said, "So do I, oddly enough." "The Word of Jesus," he went on. Suddenly I felt very tired. I shouldn't have to argue the toss at my time of life. Let Harold do it if he's so fascinated. Made for each other, those two. I'm quite satisfied with the state of my own beliefs, ruined though they are.'

'How interesting that you should say that, Austin. It sometimes seems to me that at our age all we are left with are fragments, remnants, just when we need all the support we can get. We never needed it when we were young, least of all as children.'

'You might have a word with David on that subject, although I'd hardly recommend it. When I tried he smiled patiently and told me that God needed me as much as I needed Him. I said we hadn't been in touch recently. "You will be, Grandpa," he said. He will call me Grandpa. And that smile! He's such a fool I feel almost sorry for him. Terribly hot, isn't it?'

'Is it? I hadn't noticed.'

'Your blood pressure must be better than mine, in that case. Certainly better than Kitty's. To think of her running around in this heat! I tell you, Thea, I'm seriously worried about her.'

'Kitty's not ill?'

'Not yet,' he said cautiously. 'But I'll be glad when I can get her away. I expect you'll be going away yourself?'

'Well, I hadn't thought . . .'

'You can, you know. You'll be rid of that young man by next week. Then you can please yourself.'

But she knew that it would not be as simple as that. After the excitement of the wedding had died down, and they had exhausted the subject with talk, silence would reclaim her once again, and she would, as she must, make the best of it.

'About Friday, Austin. Do you know if Kitty wants me to bring anything?'

'No, no, Kitty wouldn't hear of it. It'll be a scratch meal, I'm afraid: the dining room's about to be commandeered. Aha! I think I hear the car. You'll excuse me, Thea. I'll tell Kitty you rang. More than kind. We'll see you on Friday. See that that young man wears a tie, if you can. All the best.'

The connection was cut off, removing her at a stroke from the normal world, or at least the known world. She walked to the window, aware now of the heat as she had not been before. Beyond the terrace the garden was still, the grass dry and bleached. In a dull sky the sun was veiled, milky, presaging change. The year was moving on; already the evenings were shadowed, and the forecast was of low cloud, although so far no cloud could be seen in the undifferentiated white expanse. She was aware of fatigue, even of discouragement. It seemed to her that some fundamental disjunction had taken place, that she had surrendered her life to amiable insincerities, parodies of concern masking a tiny element of real concern, expressions of regret and anxiety which she hardly felt. Her very early life, until the age of twenty, had been one of untouched simplicity, and even as a girl she had been conscious of the fact, even though she may not have known enough to value it. But she valued it now. Perhaps, she thought, one is only authentic when one leaves one's parents' house, seeking the new but implicit with the old, the inherited. That was when she had last felt truly herself, unwilling to prepare for those alien influences that would change her irrevocably. Even with Henry she had not felt entirely herself, too alert to his moods, in fear of his displeasure. Even his charm had been puzzling to her, that European side of him, lazy, sunny, and melancholy by turns, always more noticeable when he was with his family. 'You've been good for him,' Molly had once remarked. 'Calmed him down. He was in a terrible state when Joy left him.' Joy: that unknown first wife, of whom he never spoke, and whom she imagined as a sort of minor Kitty, all looks and temperament. That was why she was never entirely at ease with any of them, not even Austin. In her own defence she could produce a newly equable Henry, to whom she had given years of peaceful expectation—or was he merely becalmed? She sighed, wishing once again for some ticket of admission to the life other people seemed to live, tears and protests included. And yet Kitty and Austin, Molly and Harold were good people, she reflected. If she were to fall ill they would be sincerely concerned, and Kitty would undoubtedly organise the baked meats after the funeral. For that consideration, even if a little premature, she must play her part, and must do so with a good grace.

The sound of the front door opening and shutting brought her out into the corridor, hungry for another presence. Steve, startled, met her head on. 'All right, Dorothea?' he said. Always the slight movement of recoil before his defences were in place. We are alike, she thought, mindful of his solitude, and of her own.

'I was just going to make myself some tea,' she said. 'Would you like some?'

'I don't much like tea, actually.'

'No, well, young people seem to prefer coffee these days. You know where it's kept, Steve. And there's some raisin bread in the larder. Help yourself.'

'Thanks.'

He disappeared into his room. Later it seemed to her quite natural to take refuge in her own. She listened for him, feeling him listening warily for her. It was not until he went out again, when the colour was already fading from the sky, that she felt able to relax.

7

The Levinsons' scratch meal consisted of cold minted courgette soup, chicken Marengo, and summer pudding. David asked for and received a plate of plain boiled rice. Harold did the same. 'Don't be silly, Harold,' said his wife. By way of compensation David suggested that the following day might be devoted to a fast. 'I'm sure you approve, Dr Goldmark.'

'What's that?' said Monty Goldmark, expert in deflecting requests for medical opinions. Tonight he was deploying his favourite stratagem: an affectation of deafness.

'An occasional fast day is good for the health?'

'If you say so.'

'This is all quite delicious, Kitty,' said Mrs May, anxious to maintain and prolong the pleasant welcome they had all received. 'And such a pretty table.'

Kitty, surveying her family, nodded her acknowledgement. Effusions and explanations would come later, on the telephone, accompanied by an account of her state of health at every stage of the proceedings. This evening, however, she seemed mollified, as did Austin; an illusion of family solidar

ity was fostered, with all the formality of another age. For the
moment the illusion was all.

'You should have brought one of your girlfriends for Steve,'
said Austin, addressing his granddaughter.

'I'm gay,' said Steve. 'And anyway I'm with Dorothea.'

Her heart swelled with pride at this evidence of gallantry,
very little of which came her way in the course of a normal
day. She accepted as her due that the Levinsons had not provided a partner for her, unless Monty Goldmark was to be the
problematic other, an honour of which he appeared to be unaware; despite her marriage and her honourable widowhood
she could tell that she was to be assigned to social oblivion.
She bore this stoically, with a composure perfected through a
thousand solitary meals in public places. This occasion was not
so very different, or would not have been, had it not been for
Steve, neat in his tie and linen jacket, eating his way steadily
through the meal with a detachment that more than matched
her own. They had had their drive through the park, but Mrs
May had not enjoyed it as much as she had imagined she
would: the air was sultry, filled with traffic fumes, and instead
of the submissive home-going crowds with whom she could
so readily identify the streets seemed to be full of young people actively preparing for an evening of pleasure. And then she
had been absurdly anxious; encountered in the flesh, as opposed to at a respectable distance, Kitty made her feel faded,
although she had taken trouble with her appearance, as had
Steve. He had requested the use of an ironing board, and
seemed to have laundered most of his clothes. This evening
his tie was a little too tight, his linen jacket still slightly
creased. Again she worried that he might be short of money.
She knew that once she was at home and lying quietly in bed

she would remember not Kitty's splendid table but that drive through the park. Though it had proved disappointing—for she had expected a more significant reaction, a flood of recovered memory—there had been that oddly stimulating suggestion of exhausted air, combined with a snatch of music from a passing car, that had made her feel that she was at one with the evening, that she too was prepared for pleasure, though even at the time she knew that that pleasure would only properly be savoured in retrospect, one more modest memory to be added to her stock. Living as she did largely in the past, dealing with old age as it dealt with her, undramatically, she nevertheless welcomed new sense impressions, marvelling that the life of the senses struggled to survive, even in circumstances that brought both pleasure and regret.

If she had any misgivings they had to do with the fact that more of Steve's belongings, notably a small radio and a guitar, had come to rest in the flat, and that sad chords could occasionally be heard from behind his door. So irritating were these particular harmonies that the more vigorous beat from the radio was almost welcome. She did not feel that she could object to this, since some residual caution had made her explain that the drawing room, and therefore the television, were out of bounds. He had accepted this more or less philosophically: at least, if he were displeased he gave no sign of being so, hiding whatever irritation he may have felt behind an expression that was tolerant rather than polite. Having in this way conveyed to him that he was confined to his room, Mrs May felt that she ought to be confined to hers. She rarely entered the drawing room when Steve was in the flat, feeling obscurely that it was a matter of the most elementary politeness to observe the same rules. The absence of any strong reaction on his part went some way to convincing her that he was not seriously annoyed. Nevertheless the odd disjunctive sounds of his guitar, just audible through two closed doors, sounded to her guilty ears like a reproach.

'Coffee in the drawing room,' said Kitty, all smiles now. 'And there's a hazelnut cake for later.'

The usual groans of appreciation greeted this announcement, as was intended. Kitty's hospitality was designed to stun. Austin basked in her good humour; they all did. This shed a certain radiance over the table, now empty except for the remains of the wine in the gold-rimmed glasses, a wedding present from long ago. 'Shall we adjourn?' Kitty enquired, and chairs were obediently pushed back, linen napkins thrown aside. In the drawing room they sank gratefully into the softer chairs.

'I haven't quite gathered what you young people do,' said Monty Goldmark, stirring his coffee.

'You could say we're into the mind/body experience,' said David. 'Ann looks after bodies and I look after minds.'

'And how do you do that?' enquired Goldmark amiably. ('No more, Kitty, thank you. Delicious, dear, quite delicious.') 'I'm listening,' he added. 'In fact I'm all ears.'

'Well, we think, Ann and I do, that people's lives are lacking in health, particularly young people's, although Ann extends her care to the not so young. And I try to supply a resource that some people don't even know they need.' He laughed modestly.

'And how do you do that?'

'I run religious encounter groups, I suppose you'd call them, groups of young people reaching out for the unknown and sometimes being visited, you know? By the transcendental.'

'And where do you do all this?'

'This school I teach in has a gym that we use. There's a lot of equipment we need—mainly space, and mats, of course—and a good acoustic for Steve's guitar.'

'Because Steve is involved in all this?'

'Sure. That's how we met.'

'It sounds like one of those films we used to enjoy,' said Molly suddenly. 'You know, "Let's do the show right here, in the gym." '

'We're building on exactly that kind of association, Molly,' said David. 'We aim to bring religion down to an informal level, make it correspond to natural impulses, make it fun. When people realise it can be fun they let God into their lives on a daily basis.'

'I don't agree with any of this,' said Austin. 'By no stretch of the imagination is religion fun. Religion is not a rave, David.'

'It can be,' he replied, almost flirtatiously.

'I thought it was supposed to be a mystery,' said Mrs May, surprised to have spoken out loud.

'We aim to simplify the approaches,' said David, undaunted by their lack of response. 'A little singing, a little dancing . . .'

'Give me strength.'

'Austin,' warned Kitty.

'Maybe strength would flow in if you let it happen, Grandpa.'

' "It"? What is "it"? You make it sound like an orgasm. And don't call me Grandpa.'

'I find all this very interesting,' said Harold. 'I confess David has given me a lot to think about. And this diet he's put me on works wonders. I'm sure Monty would agree.'

'I've been trying to put you on a diet for years, Harold.'

'But this is quite specialised, Monty. You see . . .'

'Monty is not interested in your diet, Harold, and neither am I. I shall be glad when I can get my kitchen to myself again,' said Molly.

The young people on this occasion seemed rather unfairly overshadowed by their elders, no match for their comfortable assurance, their conviviality, their long-established intimacy. They were if anything offended by efforts being made only nominally on their behalf but in fact directed to their own kind. David alone appeared to have some idea that they should make a contribution, but David's particular contribution was falling on deaf ears. How awful if he felt obliged to volunteer it in all circumstances, reflected Mrs May. She noted that Ann made no attempt to help him out, nor did he appear to pay much attention to her. Ann had in fact withdrawn her co operation from the proceedings, although she had made an effort to don some kind of finery, forced into this no doubt by Kitty, who may also have been responsible for the black linen dress and a visit to the hairdresser. The recipient of these attentions was glum, not to say morose. She sat chewing a strand of hair; from time to time she crossed and uncrossed her legs in irritation. Palpably she wished herself elsewhere.

'Ann? All right, dear?' said Austin.

'I'm okay. Got a bit of a headache.'

'Go into the bedroom with Kitty. She'll give you an aspirin. Brandy, Monty? Harold? I won't ask you young people. I'm sure you don't drink.'

'We don't drink and we don't take aspirin.'

'A little eau de cologne, perhaps,' said Mrs May. 'I always find that helps. There's some in my bag, Ann.'

'I'm *okay*.'

'Come with me,' said Kitty. 'You'll feel better when you've freshened up.'

With a violent uncrossing of the legs Ann stood up and followed her out of the room. Without her presence David lapsed into silence, a silence marred by some ostentatious deep breathing.

'Are you all right?' asked Austin.

'Fine, fine. Just repairing the energy levels.'

'You have no stamina, you young people. I never had a headache when I was young, didn't have time. Now, of course, I'm a ruin,' he added cheerfully. 'Monty knows all about that. More brandy? Help yourself.'

'You look rather well, in fact.'

'I put on an act; we all do. Kitty does, bless her. Where is she, by the way?' For the absence of Kitty from the room distracted him, made him uneasy, as if without her he might indeed suffer a reversal. The appetites of the young, who appeared to have little notion of what to do with them, paled into insignificance in the light of Austin's still verdant concern. No doubt they were disgusted, both by the lavishness of the entertainment and by the all too visible evidence of the depredations the entertainment had made on elderly bodies, now relaxed into almost supine postures, at ease with themselves, indifferent to appearances, confident of their acceptance by their peers. It is unequal, thought Mrs May; we are an insult to the young. This is not how they choose to amuse themselves. And they are still intact; they cannot believe that their own muscles will one day relax, so that when they are benevolent they merely look stupid. She readjusted her own expression. In passing she appreciated Steve's neutral demeanour. Although he had scarcely said a word all evening— and perhaps for that very reason—he shone as a model of good behaviour. He replied monosyllabically to Molly's attempt to engage him in conversation. Discouraged, she gave up. In the brief silence that followed Austin stirred.

'Thea, be an angel and go and see what the girls are up to. I don't want Kitty doing too much. She was up at six this morning. Now, David, tell us more. You don't mind, do you, dear?'

Behind her Mrs May could hear the conversation rumbling into life once more. She made her way out of the brightly— too brightly—lit drawing room into a no less brightly lit corridor, and thence, guided by voices, into the main bedroom. Glancing at her watch she saw that it was ten-thirty, at which time she should have been in bed, rejoicing in the great silence that emanated from the garden at night. But this was no longer possible. Her rest, when not disturbed by Steve's radio, was disturbed by the very presence of a stranger in her house. And he was a stranger, she reminded herself, despite the fact that, rather to her surprise, she did not actively disapprove of him. They were all strangers, Kitty, Austin, Molly, Harold, despite the fact that she had known them for thirty years. Briefly and apocalyptically she had a vision of herself as a young girl, walking docilely round the park on a Sunday afternoon, convinced that she was enjoying herself. But in fact she had been enjoying herself, perhaps because there was at that stage of her life no reason to dissemble. She told herself that the time was out of joint, that the occasion was discordant, that it was late, that she was tired, that she needed to be alone. Loneliness is much feared by the gregarious, she reflected, whereas to the solitary the gregarious pose a much greater threat.

From Kitty's voluptuous bedroom, the décor of which paid little heed to Austin's presence, came the sounds of an argument. '. . . beastly to David,' she heard, and the sound of a hard object—a hairbrush, perhaps—being slapped down onto a glass surface. She winced. The girl was upset, no doubt of that. She had been upset all the evening, had sat silent and scowling, overdressed, her hair transformed into a multitude of ringlets, like the up-to-the-minute hairstyling of Albrecht Dürer, whose self-portrait Mrs May had seen on her most wretched holiday, the one taken after Henry's death. She had thought, mistakenly, that a change of scene might be beneficial. She had taken trains, had spent time silently and discreetly in many museums, trying to summon up reactions but experiencing only blankness.

On entering the bedroom she saw Kitty seated on a fragile chair, her eyelids lowered as if in pain. At the dressing table Ann was furiously brushing out her expensive coiffure, anger tightening her mouth. She did not arouse sympathy for her plight. She was too big, too powerful, too unmanageable. Even Kitty was at a loss. The thwarted child had compensated by growing into a giantess.

'. . . beastly to David,' she was saying. 'Bloody rude, in fact. He's been like that ever since we arrived.'

'Please don't speak of your grandfather in that tone of voice.'

'They are only having a discussion,' observed Mrs May pacifically.

'They're having an *argument!*'

'Sometimes a discussion sounds like an argument. I think they are both enjoying themselves, actually.'

'Well, I'm not. And I doubt if David is. He's basically a very shy person.'

'Oh, really? I thought him quite forthcoming. Able to give a good account of himself,' she added hastily, reflecting how many talkative people thought of themselves as shy, positively launching into the fact by way of introduction.

'I know you mean well, Grandma,' said Ann, having dismissed Mrs May's rejoinders as unhelpful. 'But we're simply not on the same wavelength, me and David and you and Grandpa. All you think about is worldly stuff, food and clothes . . .'

'You will have to think about these things too, Ann. And may I remind you that all this is being done for your benefit? We didn't expect you to get married here in London. A girl's mother usually arranges the wedding.'

'Mother hasn't got the means . . .'

'There you have it.' Kitty gave a dry laugh, but Mrs May could see that she was less sure of her position, had in fact become aware that she was being accused of vulgarity, whereas before she would have advanced it as a virtue. Extravagance was her reason for living, her tribute to her husband's financial position, to her own self-respect. That her arrangements might be regarded as crude had not hitherto been apparent to her. Now she wondered how far they had been apparent to everyone else. With strangers she was vulnerable, which was why she stayed so close to home. And this girl had defined herself as a stranger, in which case her efforts had been for nothing.

'You leave my mother out of it.'

'Gladly. We haven't heard from her in years.'

'Or my father, I suppose.'

'Oh, yes.' Kitty gave a wry little laugh. 'We hear from him every Christmas. He sends us a Christmas card. A Christmas card! We only know where he is from the postmark.'

'And where was the last one from?'

'Plymouth.'

'Well, it may interest you to know that David and I are going down there tomorrow.'

'What good will that do? You'll never find him.'

'I have found him! David and I are going to see him this weekend.'

'How did you find him?' asked Mrs May, who thought Kitty unequal to putting the question. Kitty, it was clear, was suffering humiliation, she who only ever dispensed patronage.

'I get a Christmas card too, don't I? And I've got friends, well, a friend, who's been on the road and joined up with his lot a couple of months ago. That's why we're in London, Grandma, if you really want to know. Not because we want a posh wedding, with smoked salmon and florists and relatives . . .'

'And a honeymoon in Paris,' said Kitty quietly. 'And the generosity of all kinds of people. Hélène Goldmark is opening their house in France at this very moment, in case you want to go down there.'

'I wondered why she couldn't come this evening,' said Mrs May.

'I just don't want all these *strangers* . . .'

'One meets a lot of strangers at weddings,' observed Mrs May from the sidelines. 'But they don't matter very much. It is a social occasion after all. One is not getting married to them.'

'You are a silly ungrateful girl, Ann.'

'I don't care. I hate it here.'

'And hate me too, I suppose.'

'I didn't say that.'

There was a brief pause, while each of the combatants reviewed her position. Then, loftily, distantly, expressing only a mild interest, Kitty said, 'So you are going to see Gerald.'

'He is my father, after all.' The tone was now defensive.

'So you say,' said Kitty, as if discounting the connection, even the possibility.

Bad faith rose like a miasma. Bad faith was now seen to have dogged the visit. Kitty's suddenly old face alarmed Mrs May. Kitty was an old lady, she reminded herself. Kitty was seventy-five, nearly seventy-six, Austin a year or two younger. It was vital that they should be kept intact until all this was over, that they should keep their dignity, be seen to triumph. Ann condemns her, she realised. Kitty dislikes Ann, as much for her clumsy appearance as for her graceless manners, but Ann condemns her utterly. Ann sees through the elaborate housekeeping, the invincible chic, sees them for what they are: a defence against extinction, an attempt to console and deny, a refusal to accept defeat. Kitty knows that. But she may not have known that it was quite so evident. So evident that this girl, a virtual stranger, has unmasked the pretence and done irreparable damage.

Her heart ached for Kitty, that proud futile woman, whose absent-minded attention she had loyally translated as kinship. Even now, at the sight of Kitty diminished by Ann's revelations, by the mere introduction of Gerald's name, of his possible presence, when before he had been most vividly and perhaps acceptably present as a ghost, not even a revenant, a person who belonged to the past, to the unimaginable past of a young Kitty, a young Austin, she knew that neither of them would ever forgive Ann, and that they would strive mightily to conceal the fact.

'Powder your face,' said Kitty, with an effort at authority. 'You are being impolite to your guests. They have come to see you, after all.'

'They're not my guests,' the girl said sulkily. But Mrs May could tell that the fight had gone out of her.

'Come, Kitty,' she said, going over to the silent figure. 'A little cologne and you'll be as right as rain.'

'She's going to see Gerald,' stated Kitty without emotion.

'Maybe she'll bring him back with her,' suggested Mrs May, for the benefit of Ann. But Ann's back was turned, as she picked up the hairbrush once again and passed it slowly through her hair.

Kitty looked up. 'I'm too old, Thea,' she said. 'I can't take these shocks. And what about Austin? What will this do to Austin? His angina . . .'

'Come now, Kitty. There may be pleasant surprises ahead, who knows? Now what about a cup of tea? And did you mention a hazelnut cake? Are you ready, Ann?' she said, trying to keep the distaste out of her voice.

Molly appeared in the doorway. 'Is everything all right? Kitty, Ann, are you all right?'

'Put the kettle on, Molly' said Kitty, in her normal voice. 'How are they getting on in there? Is Austin all right?'

For they are united against the world, those two, thought Mrs May, and that will be their salvation.

'Austin is having the time of his life. So is Monty. Your David is certainly giving them a run for their money, Ann. Harold hasn't talked so much for weeks. Months, probably.'

Mrs May watched Kitty restore her face, with the impassive concentrated look of an actress before a first night. Standing, Kitty surveyed her silk-clad form from all angles in the mirror of her dressing table, from which, as of right, Ann had been quite properly displaced. 'We'll join you in a minute, Ann,' she said, a new formality in her tone.

'Well done, Kitty,' murmured Mrs May, taking her arm.

But this was found intrusive. Kitty smiled distantly, disengaging herself. 'You're always so kind, Thea. What should we do without you?'

Maybe it was meant, maybe it contained the same degree of parody as her own expressions of concern for Kitty's welfare, for Austin's welfare. Mrs May no longer knew. She knew that it was very late, too late for further efforts on her part. The lateness of the hour seemed to confer its own solemnity. Almost absently Kitty pulled back the blue silk curtains and opened the windows, as if to banish the memory of earlier dissension. Mrs May was aware of crushing fatigue. She looked at her watch. Just gone eleven.

'Come, Kitty,' she said.

In the drawing room Austin, eyes bright, cheeks flushed, said, 'Where have you girls been? You've missed all the fun. Ah, tea. Molly, how kind of you. Now, David, you can't say I didn't defend my position.'

'Certainly not, Grandpa,' said David, with a thin smile.

'It was a mistake on your part to bring in comparisons. You're on shaky ground there. We're all rooted in the physical, whether you like it or not. You'll discover that when you get older. Young people don't even approach the problem. And Steve, what does Steve think of all this?'

Steve came out of a brief trance. 'I think I ought to take Dorothea home,' he said.

'Oh, not yet. Ann, give your friend his cup of tea. And cake. Perhaps you'd like to pass round the cake. All right, Kitty, my love?'

'Perfectly fine,' said Kitty agreeably, no trace of earlier troubles apparent. Indeed, if anything, both she and Ann seemed somewhat refreshed by their recent altercation.

'It's always nice to be with family,' said innocent Molly.

And Mrs May reflected that at some point all would agree that this was true. When time had done its work, and the visitors were little more than a memory, they would assure themselves and each other that family ties were best, were indeed indissoluble, that all families had their disagreements, but that these were negligible compared with the commonality of interests that bound them together. Even Ann seemed subdued, David mercifully silent. Surveying them, as they drank their tea, Austin was quietly jubilant. 'Now you can't say we haven't had a pleasant evening,' he said. 'No hard feelings, David. I dare say we've both got a lot to learn. If I'm not too old, that is.' He laughed at this possibility, as if it were out of the question. 'Your grandmother's been to a lot of trouble,' he observed to Ann. 'But I think we can all agree that it's worth it. As long as you're happy. That's all that matters.'

8

Various sensations of discomfort, not all of them physical, pursued her through a shorter night than she was used to, leaving her unsettled. Sleep had been difficult after the substantial meal and Austin's excellent wine; she had reached home too tired, so that already regret for lost sleep took the place of the usual pleasant approaches, the ritualistic preparations, the drawing aside of the curtains to let in the night air through the ever open windows. A vague distress had sent her off to her room, after bidding Steve goodnight. She had been anxious to be alone, and not for the first time regretted his presence, although he had retreated behind the door of his own room and need have made no further inroads into her consciousness. She had sat on her bed, fretting, knowing that the family scene had upset her in various ways, yet not understanding why it had left such a residue of unused feeling. Certainly she was unequal to such manifestations of antagonism: quite literally she had no training in such matters. Yet there had been a dreadful sort of excitement in witnessing those two unburdening themselves of their frustrations, even though she knew perfectly well that the breach had been almost instantly repaired, this in its turn a tribute to the marvellous flexibility that those of uncertain temper could command. Yet the fact that both Ann and Kitty had derived a certain pleasure in voicing their objections to one another failed to relieve her: she felt distress, less on their behalf than on her own.

Why this should be so she could not tell. Maybe she lacked the emotional equipment to deal with lightning changes of favour. The fearlessness of Ann and Kitty! Their wholeheartedness, their conviction! She had been reminded of girls at school, best friends who came to blows and swore undying enmity, only to be perceived a few days later, their arms linked, their heads together as usual. Whereas she, timidly welcoming overtures of friendship, considered herself to be party to a contract, one which she would never break, until in the course of events she was left with nothing but her disposition towards fidelity, while alliances shifted all around her, and she learned once again to rely on her own company.

This echo from the past, and the memory of those brazen disaffections and accusations, had so disturbed her that her sleep had been interrupted by dreams of a different order from the ones that usually beguiled her, and even before waking she had felt apprehensive. And this morning the unexamined emotions of her dreams made her alert to change, not only the changes of uncertain favour and disfavour, but to changes in the atmosphere, in this room. She glanced at her clock; it was neither later nor earlier than her usual hour. But it was slightly darker. That was it: the weather had changed. She got out of bed and went to the window. The garden was still sleeping, as were the birds, who had been so active only yesterday. The great sun was on the wane, and the weather was slowly metamorphosing into autumn. She felt a moment of panic at the prospect of months of cloud and dull skies. She remembered a distant holiday in the mountains of Savoy when just such an overnight transformation had taken place. Her one thought, on that occasion, had been 'I must get home', and she had packed her bag and ordered a taxi immediately after breakfast. Now that she was home, and was likely to remain so, her thought was that once again she had missed the summer, had forfeited it for the humble reassurance of sitting on the terrace every morning, conscious of cowardice, or rather of uncertainty, but swiftly, perhaps too swiftly, coming to terms with the fact that such uncertainty was blameless if not particularly noble, and reminding herself once again that she had no accounts to render to anyone, that her obligations were as neatly filed as the receipted bills in the pigeonholes of her desk.

But Kitty knew. Kitty had penetrated her disguise, as had the softer-hearted Molly, who pitied her. Once again she thought of those distant Sunday afternoons, still more vivid than all the expensive holidays that had followed. With Henry there had been no problem: her efforts had been devoted to seeing that he was enjoying himself, that his occasional expression of fretful disappointment was kept at bay. Holidays were what she took after his death, in the immense perplexity of her unpartnered state. She had been astonished and alarmed at her lack of enjoyment, as if in some part of her mind she had expected her undivided and placid childhood to resurface. But it had never come back, and it was only by the most unremitting effort that she had kept it under control ever since, as if she knew that the child she had been might threaten the adult she had become, with all the compromises and the imperfections permanently on hand to render her thoughtful.

Bathed, dressed, she faced the day without expectation of any pleasure from it. There was no sound from Steve's room; maybe he had gone for his run, although she had not heard the front door close. She laid the breakfast table in case he should come back when she was out, then went into her bedroom and stripped the bed. She took clean sheets and towels from the linen cupboard, knocked on Steve's door, and receiving no answer went in. He was still in bed; beside him on the floor was an almost inaudible murmur of pop music from his radio. He sat up defensively. He is afraid of me, she thought sadly, though in fact she was slightly afraid of him. At the same time her heart was softened by the sight of his eyes fixed on her, willing her not to encroach on his liberty. A primitive tenderness warred with her habitual reserve and momentarily overcame it. Her smile was involuntary; any young face moved her. She tended nowadays to smile at young people in the street, whether she knew them or not. All the more reason, then, to take pleasure in this young person under her roof. Nevertheless, he must be made to leave. To allow him to stay would be to court all kinds of danger.

Henry would not approve of this incursion, she reflected. But then in this particular circumstance Henry's opinion was hardly relevant.

'Oh, I'm so sorry,' she said. 'I thought you were out. Here are some clean sheets. Did you sleep well? I expect you want your breakfast. I'll make the coffee; I think I'll have another cup with you. I had a rather disturbed night.'

She had in fact finished her coffee by the time he entered the kitchen, noiselessly as usual, on bare feet. He had washed his face but had not otherwise put himself to rights. His slack moodiness seemed to match the uncertain light of the day. She sighed, empathising with his boredom.

'I think it would be a nice gesture if you were to telephone Mrs Levinson and thank her for dinner last night,' she said. 'She went to a great deal of trouble. I don't expect you'll be seeing her this weekend, if David and Ann are to be away.'

He gave a sour smile. 'Got my marching orders last night,' he said. ' "We shan't expect to see you here before Monday evening, Steve." ' The imitation was not unsuccessful, accompanied as it was by Kitty's imperious turn of the head. This usually preceded what Henry had called Kitty's Aria. 'Life hasn't always been easy. I've had my disappointments like everyone else. But you won't catch me feeling sorry for myself. In fact nobody knows what I'm feeling. I put a bold face on it. And then, you see, I refuse to lower my standards.' Mrs May, who had heard Kitty's tributes to herself on more than one occasion, suppressed a smile. The boy was no fool.

'Did you not want to go to Plymouth with David and Ann?' she asked.

'Got my marching orders there too, didn't I? "This is family business, Steve." Ann was quite rude, really; well, she is rude. Not my type, as I need hardly point out.'

'And David?'

'David's all right.'

'And do you believe in his work? This spreading of the Word, as I suppose we must call it.'

'I do and I don't. Basically I think it's crap, but David's sincere, know what I mean? After all, he gave me house room when he hardly knew me. Christian charity, and all that.'

'Oh, you've been living with him?'

'No, Dorothea. I've been living in his house.'

He grinned. She smiled back at him.

'Where will you go after they're married, those two?'

'Dunno. I'll move on, I suppose.'

'Don't you want to settle down, put down roots? Or is that a silly question? You're maybe too young to think of such things. It's old people like me who want to settle down. Have to, rather.'

'I've got time.'

'I'd rather like to know your plans, Steve. You know that Austin has bought you a plane ticket for Paris? I suppose you will see quite a bit of Ann and David while you're all there. And if they go to the Goldmarks' house at Apt, I suppose you'll go with them?'

'Suppose so.'

'What I'm trying to say, Steve, is that I'm afraid you can't come back here.'

'Can I leave my stuff here?'

'I'd rather you didn't.' This sounded so unkind that she immediately retracted it. 'Are you looking for a place in London, then? Perhaps until you found one . . .'

'Nah. I'll go back to the States with Ann and David. I've got the ticket.'

'But my dear boy, you can't live with them once they're married.'

'I don't see why not. David needs a friend. Ann'll soon get tired of him. And pretty soon she won't need his money if her grandpa coughs up.'

'That's a dreadful thing to say. Surely it can't be true? They are getting married, after all.'

'You're sweet, Dorothea. Too too sweet.'

She wondered where he had heard such suddenly exaggerated diction, such as she had been accustomed to hearing in her youth. She then reflected that she was willing to overlook this moment of mockery in favour of having made it clear that he was to move on. At least, she thought she had made it clear. At least, she had said something to that effect. He was grinning at her, showing his fine teeth.

She rose, collected the dirty dishes. As ever, he had eaten heartily. 'What will you do today?' she asked, a note of formality in her voice.

'Oh, I'll go out, don't you worry.'

'You can eat here this evening, if you've nothing better to do.'

'Thanks, that'd be great.'

'I'm not a cook like Mrs Levinson,' she warned him. 'It'll probably be something from Marks and Spencer. Oh, and you won't forget to ring Mrs Levinson, will you? Just thank her and give her my love. Tell her I'll ring her tomorrow. I expect she's rather tired.'

'No doubt about it.'

She saw that he was about to break into another bout of impersonation, and moved quickly to forestall it.

'Then we'll meet here at seven,' she said. 'Have you got a coat? It looks like rain.'

'No.'

She hesitated. 'There's a jacket of my husband's you could borrow. The only one I kept. You'll take care of it, won't you?'

The jacket, slightly waisted, fitted him perfectly. 'Of course it doesn't look quite right over a T-shirt,' she said. 'Where's that shirt you wore last night?'

'I put it in the washing machine when I took it off. If I do it now it'll be ready for tonight. Must be properly dressed if I'm to dine with you, Dorothea.'

She thought he was probably making fun of her, and felt foolish. Though I don't know why I should, she thought. He is really quite irritating, and after all nothing to do with me. She switched on the washing machine and left the dirty dishes in the sink, as if waiting for Steve to take care of them. When, with a sigh, she ran the taps, she felt a quiver of longing to be on her own again. She put the kitchen to rights, amazed that it still belonged to her. Yet she felt unsettled, and when Steve reappeared wearing Henry's jacket she felt slightly worse. How angry Henry would have been, she thought. The jacket was still redolent of Henry's vanilla cologne, soon to be banished by the young man's alien smell.

Yet, 'You look very nice,' she managed to say.

He put an arm round her shoulders. Henry's ghostly aroma enveloped her more closely.

'You've been a brick,' he said warmly, again with that faintly parodied intonation. 'We could go for a drive tomorrow, if you like. A spin. Out in the country somewhere.'

'That would be delightful,' she said, but her heart leapt. Richmond Park, she thought. And tea at Kew. It was years since she had been there, walking slowly, pensively, as in days of old. 'Don't forget to ring Kitty,' she reminded him. 'Tell her I'll ring her tomorrow.' If I have time, she thought.

Henry had been wearing a soft brown hat when he had raised her to her feet in St James Street. Even in her distress she had been aware of his elegance, as the hat was swept off. She had supposed such suavity to be the outward manifestation of comfortable circumstances. She had always dressed carefully herself, so that her eventual access to those same comfortable circumstances had not made a noticeable difference to her appearance. But initially she had marvelled at the number of suits and shirts that had made their way into the cupboards of her flat. He had liked her home, had not wanted to move. This had surprised her, until she realised that in an odd way he had always regarded it as temporary. Besides, he had been living with Rose, and was thus without a home, having made over his flat in Basil Street to his first wife. Mrs May was prepared to regard herself as a safe haven, as indeed she turned out to be. But she had been unprepared for his fierce devotion to his sister, to the cousins, in whose presence he reverted to a more archaic version of his normal self, relaxing on the soft cushions of their sofas, accepting coffee and cake from Molly or Kitty, a cigar from Austin or Harold. 'They've been through hard times,' he would say as an excuse, though she could see no evidence of hard times in their luxurious appointments. Rose was the only one to whom she had been inclined to make concessions, and those concessions had hardened into an unbreakable routine. 'I didn't know you were so attached to your family' was the only criticism she ventured, after yet another punishing dinner party. 'Well, you wouldn't' had been his reply. 'You're such a solitary. I suppose that's the main difference in our backgrounds.' She had been mortified, thinking that he had been referring to class, whereas all he had in mind was disposition. He was not English, despite his English birth; he did not automatically think in terms of class. And she herself was perfectly civilised. Nevertheless she felt uncomfortable when she remembered that remark of his, for which, if she were honest with herself, she never quite forgave him.

Her bedroom mirror showed a careful, even distinguished woman, in whom she saw all too clearly the lineaments of the studious schoolgirl, and, even more, the faithful employee. 'Dorothea can be relied upon at all times,' her boss, Mr Grindley, had said, perhaps only dimly realising that she had been waiting to be such a paragon for the better part of a lifetime, all the more so because of the assignations in Down Street. She had, even then, been homesick for good behaviour. She smoothed back her still thick but quite grey hair, noticing, as she did so, the veins standing out on the back of her hand. On impulse she telephoned the hairdresser to see if by any chance Jackie were free today instead of Monday, her usual day. Jackie could just fit her in at eleven, if she came promptly. Then a quick lunch, she thought, then the supermarket, although she rarely shopped on a Saturday. No, not the supermarket; the delicatessen in Marylebone High Street, where Kitty occasionally shopped, or where Harold would go, in search of something out of the ordinary. Or perhaps his gourmet habits had been curtailed by David. What did young men eat? Anything, she supposed, as long as it was put down in front of them. But she wanted to do them both credit. And he gave all the signs of harbouring a healthy appetite. She had been impressed by the neat way in which he had disposed of Kitty's meal, leaning back comfortably from the table as he finished his wine.

In the busy salon, above the noise of the dryers, she enquired about Jackie's young man, Neville, and about Neville's difficult mother, with whom they lived. 'What will you do when the baby arrives?' she asked. 'Will you go on working?' She was told that Neville's mother would give up her job at the dry cleaners to look after the baby. 'Early retirement,' explained Jackie. Mrs May thought that Neville's mother might be barely forty. 'Won't she miss the company?' she asked. 'I'm sure I should.' Jackie gave her a swift glance in the mirror: all right for some, said her expression. 'You out tonight?' she asked.

'I have a guest for dinner this evening,' she replied. 'And I shall be out all day tomorrow. So it was kind of you to fit me in.'

'No problem. You'll need a trim next time. Monday week?'

'No. I may be in next Tuesday. I'm going to a wedding.'

In Marylebone High Street she bought a carton of mine-
strone, an onion tart, some salad leaves, a wedge of Dolcelatte,
and six fine peaches. I should do this more often, she thought,
and knew that she would not, for where was the pleasure in
shopping for oneself? It was the need to set one's bounty before another that was so fundamental. Struggling with her
bags she managed to find a taxi just as it was starting to rain.
She got home just after two, almost too late for lunch: a
scrambled egg would do. But she noticed that there was only
one egg left, and consequently none for Steve's breakfast. Although it was now raining quite heavily she went out to the
shop on the corner and bought, in addition to eggs, a packet
of bacon, though she disliked the smell. He is giving up a
whole day for me, she thought; it is the least I can do. And he
should have a decent breakfast if he is to do all the driving.
On further thought she went back to the shop and bought
tomatoes and mushrooms.

Back in the flat she was surprised how dim and cold it felt,
as if it were now truly autumn. The 15th tomorrow: Mother's
birthday. Yet no answering images came. Hardly surprising;
she was now at the age at which her mother had died, although it felt quite different, of a different order of magni-
tude, now that there would be no-one to grieve for her. For
she had grieved for her mother, that quiet modest woman, but
so discreetly that no-one had noticed. The same had been
true of her grief for Henry, but there the shock was greater;
after his death, in the flat, her one wish had been to expunge
every trace of his lingering illness, his relics, the sickroom
odour. Relatives had inevitably arrived, and wept copiously,
while she received them with no noticeable alteration in her
normally self-contained demeanour. She thought that her impassivity, in those crucial days, was the main cause of the faint

disaffection that had sprung up between herself and the
Levinson-Goodman clan, though there had probably been
cause for comment on many previous occasions. She had not
noticed at the time; only now was she aware of incompatibility, and she assumed that it was too late to remedy this. Besides, she had come to tolerate it, as if it were a genuine family
characteristic, the stuff of well-worn discussions. Except that
the discussions went on without her, as she no doubt deserved. After all, she had never truly belonged.

She laid the table in her rarely used dining room, and had
only just put the finishing touches to her appearance when
the front door opened and closed.

'All right if I have a bath, Dorothea?'

'Don't be long,' she warned.

Already the flat was filled with his noise, although initially
he had been as silent as a cat. It was the radio, she supposed,
as she heard it travelling along the corridor with him to the
bathroom, the door of which was never quite closed. Yet
when he reappeared, wearing a shirt and tie and Henry's
jacket, all she said was 'You look very smart.'

'Yeah, it fits, doesn't it?'

'You'd better keep it. Nobody else will wear it.'

'Thanks. Your husband been dead long?'

'Fifteen years. He was older than I was.'

'And you've been alone since then?'

'Yes.'

He whistled. 'Tough. Still, you seem to be making a go of
it. This flat is a veritable pocket of refinement.'

His voice had taken on the exaggerated fluting intonation
that was perhaps his way of paying a compliment. Normally
he was not loquacious, had signally failed to provide much-
needed conversation. I probably strike him as impossibly af-

fected, she thought, yet I was brought up to speak like that. Most people were in those days—not that he knows anything about that. He must have seen old films on television: Ronald Coleman, Leslie Howard. Even I might think them slightly silly nowadays. But it had been Henry's smoothness, no doubt rooted in exactly the same models, that had won her over, as if she were being given access to another world, a semi-fictional world that contained something of the glamour of the films that she and her mother had once faithfully gone to see. Yes, that was it: Henry was glamorous, far more glamorous than she could ever be. And she suspected that he had seen a natural affinity between his restless temperament and her apparent repose, so that he need never be discomfited or challenged by her quieter behaviour, as he had been discomfited, perhaps permanently, by the first wife he never mentioned. Yet she had seen him becalmed by the illness that had killed him, had seen his look of astonishment, as if illness were her domain, the domain of the repressed, and extravagant grief his own prerogative. And the illness that had taken him away had left her intact, and if lonely, at least acquiescent, devoting her energies, or what remained of them, to trying to work out what she should do if she were to encounter grave illness herself before the end. For that reason it would be well to be prepared.

Yet every living fibre protested against such preparation, and the sight of the young face opposite hers reinforced her desire to appropriate a little more of her life while there was still time. Everything is provisional, she thought recklessly. Nothing matters very much. It hardly signifies that this person is here, since sooner or later he will be gone. By the same token I may soon be gone myself; my heart, contrary to Monty's anodyne assurances—not very convincing, now that

I come to think of it—is almost certainly in a state of disrepair. We could all go at any minute, even Kitty, whose calculations do not envisage any such eventuality. Curiously, this idea did not alarm her, alarmed her far less, in fact, than the prospect of more careful uninteresting days spent on unwelcome duties and observances. With the possibility of change before her she felt her spirits lift. There would no longer be any point in cautious husbandry, in the prudent expenditure of time and money. She saw the virtue—and it was a virtue—of living for the moment. She understood how adventurers could justify their actions. She sympathised with predators. Dizzy with this glimpse of freedom she smiled at Steve, for whom she felt a new affection. He had invited her out, as few men of her acquaintance had thought to do since Henry's death. The prospect of her excursion, her interlude, brought a flush to her cheek. She drank her wine gratefully, resolving to do so more often: drinkers had more fun, were more approachable. Perhaps she would take a half of one of her pills tonight, so as to be rested for the following epochal day. All she had needed was a treat, she marvelled, and until now nobody had thought of it. She herself had hardly envisaged the possibility, so remote and impractical it had seemed.

The unlikely agent of her renewal laid down his knife and fork and smiled pleasantly at her, as if she and not he were the guest. He scrubbed his mouth with his napkin, a habit which normally irritated her. However, so indebted to him was she for her change of heart that she merely smiled warmly back.

'Help yourself to bread,' she said, and, following her former train of thought, added, 'My husband and I were complete opposites in many ways. Yet we got on very well. Did you ring Kitty, by the way?'

'Not yet.'

'Neither did I,' she reflected. 'Will you pour me another glass of wine? Do you like it? And the tart? Yes? I'm so glad.'

He was probably bored by now, she reckoned, but she beamed beneficently at him anyway. For he would take her to the park, cancelling a dull Sunday, and she would no longer be alone with her thoughts, and only the prospect of a routine telephone call to break the silence.

9

She woke suddenly, thinking that she had heard Henry call
out to her from his sickroom. Even though she knew that
Henry was dead she was not quite convinced of the fact. Her
heart beat heavily in the dark room while she sought to make
sense of the noise that had woken her. Her inability to do so
alarmed her, as did the torpor that kept her half sitting in the
bed, although it would have made more sense to get up. Gradually she pieced together a few crucial facts. She had, in a
spirit of reckless preparation for the day ahead, taken one of
her pills, rather late, and this, on top of two unaccustomed
glasses of wine, had proved a mistake. I have a hangover, she
thought with horror, though her head was quite clear, and she
was not ill. More facts emerged: it was Sunday. The room was
dark because it was raining. The summer was apparently over.
The sun had gone, and although it might return, might even
return in a day or two, it had taken with it a measure of contentment, a child-like trust in a user-friendly universe, one in
which the days were all alike, with no abrupt reversals, no surprises in reserve. Even, or perhaps especially, in this half-light,
the chill was perceptible. Damp stole through the open win-

dows, and on the terrace rain fell on her abandoned table and chair. She would be obliged to drink her tea indoors, as she had not done for several weeks. This change of habit would be unwelcome: in fact all changes were unwelcome. Her present disarray might even have been a warning to her, as if some sort of general disruption were under way. Such a shame, she thought determinedly; people will be so disappointed to have their Sunday spoiled by bad weather. Fortunately, in the car we shall hardly notice.

A noise again: that was what had roused her. This time she was able to identify it quite prosaically as a knock on the door.

'Come in,' she quavered, in an old woman's voice, the one that was rarely used so early in the morning. Hearing it now, as if for the first time, she was shocked. 'Is that you, Steve? Is anything wrong?'

She could almost see him standing outside her bedroom door. A justifiable recoil would prevent him from entering. She was grateful for this; she was reluctant to be seen before she had bathed and dressed. It must be frightfully late, she thought, and reached for her clock. It was half past seven, two hours past her normal waking time. 'Are you all right?' she called.

'I'm off, Dorothea,' said the voice.

'Where are you going? You're not leaving?'

'I'm going to see my folks. Cheltenham. All right if I take the car? I may stay the night; there's nothing doing here while Ann and David are away. See you tomorrow, then. Okay?'

In the dark room she blushed, as she had blushed when she was a very young girl. 'Fine,' she said. 'Drive carefully.' A constriction in her throat made further comments impossible. She heard a shifting of feet outside in the corridor.

'Until tomorrow, then. Oh, by the way, thanks for the fry-up; it was great.' There was a pause. 'You all right?'

'Yes, of course,' she said. 'You get off. I'll see you when I see you.'

At last the footsteps receded; the front door opened and closed. She sank back onto the pillows, mortified. That was her overriding reaction, one of intense embarrassment that she had so presumed on this young man's indulgence, whereas in all truth he regarded her simply as one to whom he was momentarily obligated, so that a meaningless compliment from time to time might be in order. She had thought that they were getting on rather well, had been approaching a sort of intimacy. In fact, as this event proved, any illusion of friendliness had been simply that, an illusion. Or rather that she had committed her original sin of mistaking friendliness for friendship, as she had on more than one occasion in her early life. She had always had a too ardent desire for closeness, the closeness she had known with her mother, and on which she had relied, or hoped to rely, to see her through whatever difficulties might lie ahead. She had learned, painfully, that no friendship, however well aspected, can protect one in this way, and so had gradually withdrawn her natural desire for affection. She had found that an apparent detachment served her somewhat better than a show of eagerness. Even with Henry she had learned not to show too much zeal, so that concern and care had gradually taken the place of passion. Of passion she had a bad memory. She had taken note of the relief felt on a certain occasion, many years long since, and had resolved there and then never again to be led by her instincts. Even now she had only to visualise that dingy room in Down Street to feel shame, just as now, incredibly, she felt shame at having once more committed an act of misjudgment. She had made an error, and would have to repair it as best she could. Fortunately she was too well trained to voice any objections on her own account. He had simply forgotten, she told herself; it was just as well that she had not reminded him. This was no doubt what the journalists and commentators called a defining moment. She had been passed over, returned to her habitual solitude by someone whose attention she had no right to think focused on herself. In fact nothing had been taken away from her: the bad news was that nothing had been added. And there was a long day ahead, and no help for it. She would simply have to try harder. Yet what she could only experience as Steve's infidelity lingered in her mind. No respect, she thought fretfully, and reproached herself for being old, a failing for which there was no remedy.

It was important to remember that nothing had been taken away; that was the thought to hold on to. In a few minutes she would get up and dress carefully and behave as though nothing untoward had happened, would resume her natural sobriety of demeanour, would make breakfast, and read the newspapers. But she knew that she would gaze unseeingly at the newsprint, would not switch on the radio, since the kindly voices would not be addressing her own predicament, a predicament which she would of course keep to herself. It was only an excursion to the park, she told herself, imagining the smell of the newly wet earth, but instead of an avenue of trees she saw an avenue of desks, the classroom of her secretarial school, and heard the scrape of chairs being pushed back when it was time to go home. It was an image of imprisonment, though she had not thought so at the time: she had been glad of the company of other girls, unwilling to endanger the safety she had known at school. And on Sundays she had walked in the park. That was what Sundays were for. In fact there was nothing to stop her calling a taxi and asking the driver to take her to Richmond. For a second or two she en-

tertained the idea, then dismissed it. The burden of the past
was too heavy; she knew from experience that her exposed
situation would favour further reminiscences, that the day
would be coloured by memory, and that the inner world, in
any contest, would win against the outer. And she had not
telephoned Kitty to thank her for dinner. Kitty would not
take this omission lightly. She would get in touch this evening,
would pretend exhaustion, distress, exactly as Kitty would
have done, had she been so remiss as not to offer thanks on a
similar occasion. She would do all this—after all, she was exhausted, and perhaps not very well—but she would make a
poor job of it, and the offence would remain, would indeed
grow, an occasion for comment in the best family tradition.

The thought of Kitty made her feel worse, especially since
Henry no longer provided support. Curiously, she did not
think of Henry himself, and for a reason which she had long
tried to ignore. It was because with Henry perfect fusion had
never been effected. They had been seen as a devoted couple,
and it was true that they were devoted, devoted to the task of
making up for each other's disappointment. He was a man
whose natural disposition had been towards frivolity, and he
had been permanently cast down by the defection of his first
wife, his childhood sweetheart, whom he had married amid
much splendour, and with family approval. Was she not in fact
a remote relation? Mrs May never enquired, careful of her
own peace of mind. The symbolism of Henry's raising her to
her feet in a busy street was not entirely lost on her. It had
salved his sore spirit to be seen in this act of chivalry. 'But why
did you come back to the office that evening?' she had asked
him. 'I couldn't get your funny little face out of my mind,' he
had replied. 'You looked so woebegone. I felt you needed
looking after.' For this perception—though it had been no

more than a passing remark—she had unstintingly rewarded him. But she had always known that she was not a fit companion for one with his exuberant nature, his moments of fatalism. She was utterly ignorant of the tantrums and stratagems that women used to intrigue or irritate men, and of which he, presumably, entertained a nostalgic memory. She had sensed this disappointment in him, had hoped that it was merely the effect of his age, had hoped that he too would realise that he was no longer the ardent young man of cherished memory, was in fact tired, disheartened. He had seen steadiness, an even temper. To him this had spelled novelty, and, half speculatively, he had succumbed to it.

And she? She had seen her one chance. She had known in her heart of hearts that if she did not seize it she would go through life as an orphan. She possessed nothing but her liberty, was without kinship, attachments. She was not prepared to look beyond this fact: it was Susie Fuller who did that. Susie, with her many boyfriends, was quite simply aghast at the idea that Henry might be relinquished. At one point Mrs May had thought that Susie herself was interested, but was quick enough to see that Susie's boldness put her out of the picture: in Henry's opinion only men were bold, or should be. He was in many ways surprisingly old-fashioned, courtly. It may even have been Susie's cheerfully expressed interest that had brought forth in the normally undemanding Dorothea a faint spirit of rebellion. Thus a friendship had evolved into marriage. And she had appreciated him, and his persistence, until at last they sat, a little dazed, in the living room of the flat that was her pride and joy, and which he found surprisingly to his taste—but always with the unseen proviso that they could move on. Or that he could. Therefore she had made every effort so that he would want to stay.

Now that she had been a widow for so long, the years of her marriage appeared to her as years of normality, but normality as defined by other people. Alone, as she was now, she considered herself to be vaguely at fault, and was confirmed in this view by the attitude of other women, of whom perhaps Susie Fuller was the first. Yet they had been good friends, and Susie had been at her wedding, one lunch hour, in a register office, the awful news to be revealed to his family at a more propitious venue. So many people had had a proprietory interest in Henry that it was difficult for her at that stage to think of herself as his wife. She had felt more like an aspiring candidate for the position, even when she was sitting with him on the terrace of some luxury hotel and he was asking the waiter to bring champagne. Secretly she would have preferred coffee; the thought had made her slightly homesick. Marriage had meant learning new tastes and habits, and she had applied herself to the task. It was strange no longer to have to deal with Henry's volatility, his restlessness. The absence from her life of those qualities meant that her condition was once again like that of an unawakened girl, waiting to be breathed into life by the advent of a stranger, someone by definition remote from her own life and all that she had ever known.

For a moment she contemplated ringing Susie Fuller in Chippenham. Susie had been kind to her after Henry's death, had unhesitatingly put her dogs into kennels and made herself available. Fortunately her stepdaughter lived in London, so that Mrs May had not felt too badly about telling her when she was overcome by tiredness or by that curious dizziness— the first signs, perhaps, of her current malaise—and Susie had been quick to take the hint. Susie Fuller: once Harkness, later

Meredith, and now in widowhood restored to her original status as Susie Fuller, just as Mrs May was again and for evermore Dorothea Jackson. They had had some good times together when they were young, in the office that Susie was in such a hurry to leave. Being assured of an early marriage, to one or other of her boyfriends, she had taken chances, had eaten forbidden snacks at her desk, had no hesitation in trying on the new clothes she bought in her lunch hour. Mrs May remembered a powder-blue sweater being hastily pulled down, a doughnut hastily swept into the drawer containing office supplies, as the door opened behind her and one of the partners came in to request her services, rather urgently, having had no success on the internal telephone, which Susie had assured him was out of order.

She had been a pert strawberry blonde, after the fashion of that time, but when Mrs May had last seen her it was her face that was deeply coloured, and the blonde hair had been too vigorously renewed. Her figure had thickened, but she seemed not to notice her fall from her original prettiness. She lived contentedly, exercising her dogs, not minding too much that she was on her own, since she was still convinced of her own desirability. 'I may take the plunge again,' she had said to Mrs May, stretching her arms luxuriously. They had talked about the past until they had exhausted it. What was it, after all, but an office friendship? Yet had it not been for Susie she would never have married, certainly not have married Henry, who was her opposite in every way. It was simply that she and Susie had been divided by temperament, by custom, and by expectation. Susie was rarely out of the company of men, still had many friends of the opposite sex. Mrs May did not doubt that she had retained her girlhood habits and outlook. Two husbands had left her comfortably off, so that she met men on her own terms, which she saw as advantageous. One would eventually, even now, be tempted.

If she rang Susie it would be to hear how her current affair was progressing, for all the world as if they were still young women in the office, with Susie yawning away the afternoon, until the approach of five-thirty sent her into a frenzy of efficiency, so that her work would always be completed, accurate, and delivered to one or another of the partners' desks with an air of triumph. Don't think you can get the better of me, this efficiency seemed to say. With a little extra effort I can prove that I am owed another week's holiday, and you will not dare to contradict me. And during that extra week the office seemed quite dull, and work proceeded lifelessly. 'Just leave that for Susie,' Mr Grindley or Mr Parsons would say. 'When is she due back?'

Those were the halcyon days of office work, before secretaries were known as personal assistants, with computer skills and an awareness of unfair restrictions, before hurt feelings led to industrial tribunals, before a compliment was perceived as sexual harassment, days when girls were free, outside of office hours, to enjoy their money and their liberty. Mrs May remembered her own liberty as a time of considerable anxiety, for she had just bought her flat with the proceeds of the sale of her parents' house, and was timidly appalled at her audacity in doing so. Her thoughts were never far from the amount of money she seemed to be spending; even now she wondered nervously about money, though she had no reason to do so. What she remembered mostly was the joy of those Saturday afternoons in various antique markets. She had had good if austere taste, and today the flat was just as she had once envisaged it, in those far off days when she had found the round dining table and the ladder-back chairs and the Victorian mirror, which the dealer had told her was Louis-Philippe, though she knew that he was wrong. Nothing had spoiled her pleasure in the flat until now. Now she found it empty, dim, though the Vietnamese kept it in pristine order. When Susie Fuller had given her an Indian rug as a wedding present she had thanked her and put it away in a cupboard, where it remained. Remembering it now, she thought it might do for Steve's room, by his bed. It might as well stay there, for the two or three days until his departure. For now she did not want him to come back.

How could she, a more or less dignified old lady, have thought that she would be fit company for a young man? The wish had been father to the thought, the wish to be driven to the park, to see the occasional yellow leaf fall silently through the windless air. What, after all, would they have talked about? She could hardly espouse his interests, nor would he have cared about hers. She would have lent a complaisant ear; she would have played her part. Only he had not played his, or rather had forgotten that he had a part to play. In all honesty she could not blame him. Only the rain had stopped, and an enticingly fresh smell was making its way through her windows. She shivered. Better to forget, as he had, to retreat into her earlier silence, to treat him as the stranger he still was. Yet even as a stranger he satisfied her hunger for something young. Something young is best, she thought; even armoured Kitty feels that. Although Kitty was not comfortable with her granddaughter, she felt impelled to cherish her, to buy her unsuitable clothes, to argue with her, to be hurt by her, to attempt—fruitlessly—to awaken some love, some response, some return. To get it right for once, and for perhaps the first and last time.

For had it not gone wrong, disastrously wrong? Had the cherished son aroused the same spirit of contention in Kitty, so that her demands and reproaches had put paid to any love he might once have had for her? He had fled, sacrificing the father with whom he may have had more in common. And Kitty, all wide-eyed bewilderment and bitter tears, seeing nothing amiss in her voluptuous hunger for affection, and having no-one appropriate to blame, had lived with a nebulous moral discomfort, a sense of wrong having been done, ever since. There was an innocence in this attitude, the sort of innocence best forsworn. With this Mrs May could sympathise: to surrender any sort of innocence is to abandon part of oneself. She had seen Kitty in this most familiar of situations, her proud stare challenging anyone to say that she was wrong, yet at the back of her eyes, and in her unguarded mouth, lurked the knowledge that something was wrong, very wrong, and yet somehow no-one would tell her what it was.

And in the meantime, in limbo, there were those standards to be kept up, the famous white-gold hair to be burnished, the dressmaker to be visited, the Spanish girl to be supervised. And standards had been kept up, remarkably so. It was just that when Mrs May had caught sight of her that day, walking slowly, arm in arm with her sister, outside Selfridges, the truth had come to light: she was lonely. Few friends came to that house, and when they came they were overwhelmed. In the absence of friends, family had to be relied upon, and that meant Molly and Harold. Molly, with the same blessed or cursed innocence, pitied her sister, respected her for her nervous disposition, but had learned from experience never to refer to the absent Gerald. To do so was to court hauteur.

Hence Mrs May's invaluable but invisible function, for she could be quite openly pitied, without fear of reprisal. She did not grudge Molly or even Kitty the pity they felt for her: was she not more schooled in stoicism than either? For she was not innocent, though she once had been. But in those distant days of her real innocence she would have been of no use to Kitty, who would not even have noticed her. The very real gulf between them had been bridged by her own acquiescence, her own complicity: she had a function, which was to make Kitty feel better about herself, about her standards, though these were never satisfactorily defined. She was a subject of idle conversation, and her duty was to stay symbolically apart, so that any differences of character were to be laid at her door, and her patient attention ascribed to native dullness. 'I can't think what she does with herself all day,' Kitty might say to Molly, having never made the slightest attempt to find out.

Susie Fuller retreated into the past: her task now was to ring Kitty. She glanced at her watch: just after eleven. She dialled the familiar number, wondering which formula to adopt. Too much sympathy would be out of order, an affection of exhaustion unconvincing. Yet she felt some sympathy, and she was exhausted. At the same time she knew that neither excuse would do. She had been discourteous, or if not discourteous, remiss, and this would have been noted, would have roused unfavourable comment, as well it might. With a sigh she prepared to play both cards. The fact that they were authentic would not, she knew, help her in the least.

'Austin? Good morning. I hope I'm not disturbing you?'

'Oh, Thea.'

His voice was flat, toneless. This was a bad sign. He was

normally a civilised if absent-minded man to whom she had
in the past enjoyed talking. His own enthusiasms were hedged
with a saving scepticism; quite possibly he had obtained an accurate reading of his wife's temperament at their first meeting. But Kitty had been beautiful . . .

'I've been terribly remiss, Austin,' she went on, leaping into
the breach. 'I spent so much time reminding Steve to ring
Kitty to thank her for that wonderful meal that I must have
forgotten to thank her myself. What must she think of me?'

'Not like you, Thea.'

She was a little surprised. 'To tell the truth, Austin, I find
having Steve in the flat terribly distracting. He's quite pleasant, of course, but I find the young very disconcerting. They
seem to have no commitments. Yet he's not here today, and
the flat feels quite empty. I believe Ann and David are out too?
You must be quite relieved . . .'

She trailed off. This was tricky. Austin might not know of
the plan to locate Gerald. Alternatively, Austin might know
and not wish Mrs May to know. That was the more likely explanation. Although she had been present at the original altercation, the ranks would now have closed. In time, win or
lose, they would have their explanations ready, but at this
painful juncture they must be left alone to entertain both their
hopes and their deepest fears.

'I hope Kitty will understand . . .'

'I don't want her upset.'

Greatly daring, and enjoying a brief flush of annoyance, she
said, 'I'm sure there's no need.'

She heard a sigh. 'No, you're quite right. All our nerves are
on edge. Kitty's had a terrible headache. The girl upsets her,
Thea.'

'I did think her rather contentious, I must say.'

'And the saddest thing of all is that Kitty was all prepared to love her, which says a lot for Kitty, you must admit. After all, we thought her mother was gravely at fault, abandoning Gerald, just when he needed support.'

'Yes, I do understand.'

'And underneath it all she does love her, although Ann drives her mad. Everything about her: her untidiness, to look no further than that. You should see her room.'

'Yes, I can imagine.'

'It's just that when she's not here, like now, Kitty feels forlorn. She misses her.'

'And you?'

Again the long sigh. 'Oh, I'm a lost cause. I don't care much for the girl and I wish she'd just get married and go away. I've said as much to Kitty, but that upset her too.'

'What will you do today, Austin? You both need a break. You should take advantage of the fact that you're on your own again.'

'Today? Molly has asked us to lunch. Might as well get out of the flat for a bit. Might take a turn on the Heath later.'

'You'll give Kitty my message? My thanks and apologies?'

'She's in the bath. Do you want her to ring you?'

'Oh, no. Besides, I'm going out. I'll talk to her tomorrow.'

'Nice talking to you,' he said, but his heart was not in it.

They had both lacked the energy for their exchange, and perhaps their fundamental politeness towards each other had in some way been undermined. This was disheartening. And Kitty was annoyed with her; at least she had avoided talking to her. And why had she said that she was going out? Some inconvenient moral sense meant that she would now have to go out in order to prove that she had not told a lie. She would be reduced to taking a walk in the damp air. Not that Kitty would ring back; Kitty was offended. Then she remembered that Kitty had other things on her mind and had probably forgotten her altogether. At least there was food in the house. She would go out and buy the *Sunday Times,* although she had not yet so much as glanced through the *Telegraph.* All would be put back in order. Yet, like Austin, she gave a sigh at the prospect.

'Late today,' said the newsagent.

'Yes, I overslept. Strange how it puts one out. I thought I'd get some air.'

He was not interested. 'Clearing up nicely,' he observed, and turned to another customer.

She walked through streets fragrant after rain, the deserted streets of a near-suburban Sunday. There was a certain fragile charm in her surroundings, but also a certain pathos. They were empty of incident, but also of human activity, signs of life. She seemed to have been appointed guardian of this emptiness, a role to which Sundays had accustomed her, and which on the whole she bore uncomplainingly. But it was not an heroic role. Was there not an individual in classical plays who was given the unenviable task of spouting the sort of common sense to which nobody listened? He was usually the hero's friend, even his best friend; she had always thought Horatio a much better person than Hamlet, whom she disliked intensely. Most women did, she believed. All those complaints . . . And inconsolable, despite everybody's best efforts, and credited throughout with the noblest of intentions. Prestigious, of course, though he had not been altogether courteous to his father. Utterly tiresome if encountered in real life, but in tragedy all is forgiven. Look at *Lear.* Aware, belatedly, that she may have been talking to herself, she greeted a neighbour with brilliant cheeriness.

'Just reminding myself to buy some milk,' she explained. 'Quite pleasant now, isn't it? Keeping well? Yes, fine, thank you. Couldn't be better.'

10

And yet the day, as it wound its slow way towards evening, proved to be quite acceptable, neither better nor worse than any other Sunday, and peaceful, as Sundays were supposed to be. Very soon her disappointment was forgotten, and she was even rather glad that the excursion had not taken place. Walking back from the shops she had noticed a new tentativeness in her steps, which she attributed to tiredness, not wishing to attribute it to anything else. Physical decline was not to be contemplated, although it would come, whether she thought of it or not. Back in the flat she felt quite herself again. Nevertheless she looked forward to the time when she could go to bed, as she did more and more these days. They said that the old needed less sleep; what they did not say was that the desire for sleep was incremental.

In bed at last (and it had after all been a long day), it occurred to her that at some time in the future it might be pleasant to renounce her habit of rigorous early rising, to lie back on the pillows and while away a good part of the morning. At the end of this particular road, she knew, lay the ultimate refusal to get up at all, which was why temptation must be fought at all cost. Yet she was always early for everything, a tiresome habit which irritated those who felt more comfortable with lateness. The amount of time she had at her disposal made it difficult for her to be late for anything, even for her own breakfast. And she suspected that even if she were to waste time she would still find a way to be entirely punctual, to the intense annoyance of those who had never mastered the art. For it was an art, less to do with courtesy than with modesty. Only grander personalities could afford to assume that others would wait.

And in the morning she felt uncertain, no longer obedient to her normal promptings. It had been a bad night, that she recognised. After a day which, though idle, had been filled with disconcerting reflections, she had gone to bed early and had slept almost at once, only to wake intermittently from a sequence of dreams which had flowed past her as if they had been projected on a cinema screen. In one of them Susie Fuller, wearing a rather cumbersome tweed suit, had been glimpsed in the doorway of their former office, and when hailed, in an access of fervent friendship which was uncharacteristic of either of them, had said, 'I'm just off to South America. Why don't you go away, Dorothea?'

In the dream Mrs May had experienced confusion: did Susie mean to dismiss her, or was she merely recommending her to take a holiday? Surely the latter, for in another dream, or possibly the same one, there was Henry, in his soft brown hat. 'I'm going to Kitty's,' he said. 'She's been through hard times. It's a pity you can't come with me. I expect it's the difference in our backgrounds.' She had awoken with a sense of horror on hearing those words again, although she knew that she had been dreaming. But she also knew that she had been badly affected by Henry's original remark, even if she had deliberately misinterpreted it. Somehow, with the shadow of the dream upon her, she wondered whether this was in fact the case, whether they had both tacitly agreed to turn a blind eye and a deaf ear to what had in fact been revealing. She had felt foolish at the time, disarmed, unable to defend herself. How did one defend one's birthright? She had never known, had never had to know. She said nothing, careful even then not to offend Henry by pointing out his tactlessness. In the dream she was convinced that he had committed a fault, that he was in fact guilty of extreme indelicacy. Alarm had woken her; only the return to consciousness persuaded her once again that it no longer mattered.

She had settled down once more with an audible sigh, but now her heart was thumping, somewhat out of its normal rhythm, and her hand reached out for her pills before she re-membered their untoward effect. Somehow she slept, but this time it was as if she had taken everyone's advice: 'Why don't you go away?' She was shaking off her immobility, packing up as if for a long journey, but angrily, unwillingly, and yet as if she were not coming back. Huge piles of clothes had to be got into several suitcases, for before leaving on this holiday she had to move house. And there was no-one to lend a helping hand or to offer words of advice or consolation. If others knew of her plans they were discussing them out of earshot, among themselves. That was why she was so angry.

The application of this dream to her actual situation was so easy to understand that she wondered why she had not made it earlier. But she had, she reasoned: she had made it philo-sophically, tolerantly, with as much amusement as she could muster. And all the time she must have felt angry, betrayed. This was unwelcome news. And there was nothing to be done about it. She might as well get up and prepare her breakfast and begin the day with her usual fortitude. 'Be a brave soldier,' her mother had said to her throughout her childhood, when she voiced a complaint. And, 'Be a brave soldier,' she had said at the end, her face white on the pillow, her lips tightening with pain. The implication was clear: there were to be no more complaints. And on the whole she had obeyed her mother's injunction, had made it a point of honour not to weep, just as she made it a point of honour not to be late. But in truth honour belonged to the past, before the demands of society had imposed a measure of concealment, of blandness. Now she merely smiled politely. This perhaps had been the message of her dreams.

But her anger was also significant, revealing more than her conscious mind would have allowed. To travel back down that particular route would be to engage in fruitless recriminations against the very people who had made her what she was: her friend, her husband, even her mother. Her genuine distaste for this kind of investigation proved salutary: in no time at all she was able to remember them with her customary affection. Awake, it was herself she blamed, for not being more demonstrative, for not voicing her own desires more decisively. But in order to do so she would have had to become a different person, and the very people who loved her, or who professed to love her, would not have appreciated such a show of independence. Perhaps her mother might have understood, but even her mother had thought it best to suppress complaint. It was with a powerful urge to live her life more variously that she finally surfaced. The world and all its blandishments beckoned, while her life, her dull steady life, struck her anew as being of no importance. Her attachments were arrived at all too passively, or were imposed on her, like the tiresome Steve, who was so noticeably absent. She almost admired his indifference to her hospitality, which was no more than he had perhaps come to expect. To take what others provided, without expressing gratitude, suddenly seemed to her the height of enlightened behaviour.

These speculations conferred a chill. She was cold, physically cold, and it seemed to her that the weather, or what she could see of it on this overcast morning, was distinctly unseasonable, no weather for a wedding, although Kitty and Austin would manage to create an atmosphere of light and heat. It was their great gift, this natural extravagance. That was why they should be appreciated, should not be criticised for their habitual lack of understanding. One should simply avail oneself of their bounty, which was what they desired and expected one to do. And if one could not repay them in kind, so much the better: it was right that one should be in their debt. This was what they were for. No doubt it mattered more in life to be effective than to be polite, obedient, peaceable, all those admirable negative qualities that somehow did not secure affection. She tried to recapture her recent moment of sympathy with those who broke the rules, but on this damp morning sympathy was lacking. On the contrary, she felt wearied by the depredations of others, feared their intrusion, flinched from bolder temperaments by instinct. Somehow she had condemned herself to a life of self-effacement—or maybe others had done that? The Henry of her dream came back to her but she dismissed him, as she had never done in life. She marvelled at the slyness of the sleeping mind: all she had never dared to feel formulated, as it were, during her absence.

She was aware of various presences, all of them phantasmal. But in the kitchen, very much in the flesh, sat Steve, drinking coffee and reading her discarded *Sunday Times.* 'I thought I heard something,' she said, conscious of her unadorned presence. 'When did you come in?'

'You must have been asleep. I didn't leave Cheltenham till after ten, got here about two. Want some coffee? We're out of marmalade, by the way.'

'I'll get some later. Yes, we ought to think about food. I'm not cooking for you today, Steve.'

'That's okay. I'll go over to Molly's.'

'To Mrs Goodman's.'

He put up his hands in a propitiatory gesture. 'Sorry, sorry.'

'But seriously, Steve, you ought to have some plans of your own.'

'Why? Do I *encroach*?' The tone was camp, inviting her to some craven complicity, and at the same time warning her off.

'Yes, you do rather,' she said calmly, aware of how unseemly an advocate she must be, in her old dressing gown. 'If you're to go off on holiday with Ann and David perhaps it would be best if you took some of your things over to Molly's, to Mrs Goodman's, today.'

'I'll do it tomorrow.'

'I hope I don't sound unreasonable.'

'You? Unreasonable?' He looked waggishly shocked. 'My dear Dorothea, you are reason itself.'

He is impertinent, she thought, vaguely frightened. She moved to the stove to pour herself some coffee, aware of him, not moving, behind her.

'And how were your parents?' she asked, sitting down at the table as if this were an ordinary morning.

'Bizarre, as usual.'

'But very pleased to see you, I'm sure.'

'Possibly.'

'How did you spend the day?'

'Crashed out. Did the family lunch bit. My sister and her husband came over for tea, by which time I'd had enough.'

'Yet you didn't leave until ten.'

'They had to give me the benefit of their advice, didn't they? That took a couple of hours.'

'They must be worried about you.'

'I don't see why. I'm not worried about them.'

'But they haven't seen you for quite some time . . .'

'I rang them once or twice from David's place. They just don't accept that we've nothing in common. I feel more at home when I'm away from them. That's what they don't understand.'

'And do you? Understand, that is?'

'Look, Dorothea, I just want to get on with my life.'

'Of course you do. I suppose all I'm trying to say is that it gets harder as you go on. That's why it's not wise to get rid of too many people. You seem to rely on David and Ann rather a lot, if you don't mind my saying so.'

'And?'

'I don't want to criticise your friendship, Steve. I just want to warn you that friendship does not automatically mean love and support. Friends do not always have your welfare at heart. That's what your family is there for.'

'Or not, in my case.'

But she was no longer interested in him, being transported back in time to the old house, to her quiet parents and their total acceptance of her. It was the last occasion on which she was conscious of security, the real thing, not the poor substitute she cultivated in these straitened times. She wondered if she were unnatural in thinking so much of her parents and so little of her husband, until she reflected that she was old, that she was allowed to think as she pleased, that perhaps all women thought in these terms towards the end of their lives, that perhaps time itself was circular, returning her to the beginning. Perhaps it had not even been as idyllic as she remembered it: she had felt symbiosis rather than extravagant love. They had not been a demonstrative family, and she had had few conversations of any depth with her father. He had died first, in the street, of a massive heart attack, while her mother, at home, waiting to pour his tea, wondered what was keeping him. In some ways it was an acceptable death, causing no embarrassment, unlike her poor mother's face on the hospital pillow. A brave woman, following her own advice. Henry had not been brave, though suffering from the same illness. Why should he be? His was not a reticent nature. Even at the very end his expression had been one of bafflement, as if some injustice had been done, as if he should have been spared this final indignity, as if, for a man with his natural flair, this death was altogether too plebeian.

There was one more death to come, her own. That should be instructive, she thought wryly. But there will be no witnesses, no attendants. Maybe that was the message of that last dream, the packing up. Those dreams were not about other people. Those dreams were about herself, and they were terminal.

'I'm off, then,' said Steve, offended by her sudden indifference.

'What? Of course, you're going to see David.'

'I'll probably eat there,' he warned her, offering her a chance to make amends.

'Yes, I think that would be best. Tell Molly—'

'Mrs Goodman.'

'Tell her I'll ring her later. I imagine there are things we

ought to discuss, about the wedding, and so on. You'll all be
going to Paris later that same day, I take it?'

'I'm leaving that side of things to David.'

'Remember what I said about friendship, Steve. David will
have a wife to look after.'

'I get on all right with Ann.'

'You must do. You've known her how long?'

'About a year.'

'Well, I should just think of the whole thing as a holiday, an
extravaganza, if you like.'

'We'll work something out.'

She had annoyed him, she knew. But then she was unlikely
to do anything else in her present guise, old, unkempt,
unlovely. Her fantasy of being driven round Richmond Park
now appeared to her as no more than that: a fantasy, and an
unambitious fantasy at that. Just as well it had remained one,
she thought. At some point there might have been some show
of antagonism, the same antagonism as was palpable across the
kitchen table. She got up abruptly, scraping her chair back.
Moral discomfort invariably made her physically clumsy. Presumably his parents had given him some money. Nevertheless
she asked, 'Was there anything else you wanted? Besides the
marmalade, I mean?'

'No, thank you,' he said, disappointed. But they were both
disappointed, she reflected, turning the hot tap onto the
breakfast dishes, disappointed in each other. Because this
made her genuinely sad she did not turn round again until she
heard the front door close behind him.

She bathed and dressed hurriedly, ashamed of her earlier
unpreparedness. Although she was only going to the shops she
put on her good linen suit and a superior pair of shoes to the
ones she normally wore. Then she sat down suddenly, her

hands idle. She was filled with shame that she had not handled the situation better. What could she tell this young man of love and friendship? The subject was too vast, and she felt herself to be too ignorant, even after a lifetime of what now appeared to her as studious application. And something in her had wanted to win him over, to get behind the defensive smile and the intermittent mockery. For he thought her ridiculous, that was clear. There was no instinctive sympathy between them, and yet she wanted there to be. This was strange: he was hardly appealing, was far too cold for such a young person. In fact the three of them, Ann, David, Steve, made little attempt to come close. That was what was so shocking about them. Yet, despite her wish for harmony, she thought she could understand their reluctance.

David, if anything, was even more enigmatic than Steve, with whom she still wanted to be on good terms. For what reason? His approval was irrelevant to her life, just as David was oddly irrelevant to the matter in hand: his wedding. They seemed furiously passive, that couple, contributing their bad behaviour as evidence of integrity. They objected proudly to the blandishments being offered, thereby making it possible to accept—negligently—the goods and services that had accrued. In this attitude, as in all other matters, Ann was the leader. Ann's motives were imprecise. Perhaps she wanted to impress the wealthy David that she had family resources of her own. She had by now seen the error of her ways, since David, for all his faults, seemed genuinely unworldly, unlikely to be impressed by evidence of the Levinsons' wealth, indeed dismayed by it. And what Ann had gained was the burden of family life, the meals, the arguments, the conversation, and above all the propinquity. It was the propinquity that was making her so bad-tempered, dealing with the presence of old people with whom she was forced to exist at close quarters. A young person's objections to the old were likely to be over-whelmingly physical, as well as moral. Ann saw Kitty as Kitty never saw herself, stout, highly coloured, overdressed, and be-yond that complicated, self-centered, self-important. She was all of those things, of course. But to her granddaughter's un-adorned state she opposed a certain knowledge, that nature must be cajoled, subdued, above all disguised. To Ann, Kitty was artful, with all that that implied to one of her scornful na-ture.

In fact they were all subject to the scorn of these young people, and it was proving an uncomfortable experience. After fifteen years of more or less peaceful solitude Mrs May was now being called to account, for no particular fault that she could think of, unless it were for not being racier, more complicit. It was not that Steve had overstepped the mark in any way, although he was beginning to show signs of wanting to. The fact that they were doomed to disagree pained her, as if all she had ever wanted was some kind of endorsement that had so far been lacking.

But why did they fail so abysmally, she wondered. Were they too selfish, too set in their ways, or were they simply hurt that these children had no need of them and made this fact so plain? Were they, Ann in particular, only too aware of their age, their uselessness? In that case why did they avail them-selves so freely of what was on offer? No doubt the clean linen and the soft beds spelt out a message to them of bourgeois vanity, and they were on the defensive, knowing that they had nothing to give in return except their love, which they with-held. They were determined to move on intact, uncompro-mised. And that was what they would do, leaving behind a sense of anticlimax, of disappointment. And no doubt long

after they had gone Kitty and Austin would be discussing their
visit as if it were a landmark, even a success. In retrospect it
would be seen as a success, for the young people would move
on, with an agreeable sense of having bestowed their company where it was most needed. They were undoubtedly
graceless, yet if time were to prove kind they would become
endowed with a grace which they possessed only by virtue of
their youth. And those who had been their unwilling hosts
would discuss them endlessly, as if they were interesting. In
that way they would wrest a sort of success from what was,
after all, a fairly routine incompatibility.

She stirred and sighed. She must do two things. She must
go out and buy marmalade—and bread and butter, and eggs,
and perhaps some apricots: would he like stewed apricots for
his breakfast? And she must ring Molly, not because she had
anything to say to her but because she had told Steve that she
would. With a start she noticed that it was almost half-past ten
and that she had idled away half the morning. She dialled the
Goodmans' number. She had always liked Molly, a softer creature than her powerful sister, less intelligent, more approachable. She was likable chiefly because she gave out an engaging
aura of contentment, even of happiness. Peacefully married to
her plump little estate agent of a husband, she seemed fulfilled
in her not very demanding role. Like Kitty she was an excellent housewife, paid attention to her appearance, and, according to Henry, who teased her, was known to spend whole
afternoons on her sofa, waiting for visitors, so that she could
make a fuss of them. She was tearful and feminine, utterly
lacking in curiosity, and possessed of a simplicity which enabled her to breach normal conversational conventions. She
found it natural to speak of her feelings in any company, too
guileless to expect embarrassment, too guiltless to feel it. The

wide ardent eyes begged indulgence, and normally received it. Her husband, with something of the same simplicity, or as much as a life in the property business had allowed him, protected her, as of right. Mrs May had a vision of them on their annual holiday, sitting on the terrace of their hotel in Bordighera, and homesick for Highgate. And in a week or two they would be there, as they were every year, although this year was different from most. This year, more than ever, they would seek the haven of each other's presence after the departure of their unbidden guest.

'Molly? It's Thea. How are you?'

'We're very well, thank you, Thea. And yourself?'

'Oh, I'm fine. Has my young man shown up yet? He said he was on his way to you.'

She wondered why she used this uncharacteristically arch locution, and concluded that she and Steve were simply not on terms other than the most uneasy intimacy.

'He's gone out with David and Harold. They've gone to the health food shop, although I've got salmon steaks for lunch. Will he eat salmon, do you think? Only David and Harold will only want a salad, so that will be salmon for Steve and myself . . .'

'Don't spoil him, Molly. He won't want to leave.'

'Frankly, Thea, we shall miss David. He's been so good to Harold, seeing that he takes exercise, and so on. And Harold says they have such interesting discussions.'

'What about?'

'Oh, I didn't ask, dear. Religion, I suppose. Funny, because Harold's never been particularly inclined that way.'

'You're not too tired? With all the extra work?'

'Oh, no, not at all.' There was a brief silence. 'Of course, it's not the same as if he were our own, but he is part of the family, isn't he? Harold minded more than I did, our not having children. Well, I minded, of course I minded, but I didn't want him to see me grieving. No regrets, I said to him. And when I see him with David, I know he minds . . .'

'Don't upset yourself, Molly.'

'No, no, it's nothing,' she sighed. 'It's just that Harold will miss him when he goes.'

'We're all a bit unsettled, I suppose.'

'It's Kitty I worry about. She's overdoing it, as usual.'

Mrs May sighed too. There was a very brief pause while she hunted for words of concern and reassurance.

'If you could just give her a ring, Thea? She looks up to you, you know. "Thea has inner strength," she says. If you could prevail on her not to make herself ill . . .'

'Was there anything in particular?' she enquired. 'Has anything happened?'

'She's very disappointed in Ann, between ourselves.' Molly's voice was lowered as she uttered what was to her a recently discovered fact.

'We must remember that they'll all be gone by the end of the week.'

'If you could just have a word with Kitty, then. I don't want it to end badly. And don't worry about Steve. He'll be fine with us.'

Mrs May replaced the receiver thoughtfully. So her energies were to be invoked once again for the task of appeasing Kitty. Yet here she was, dressed and ready to go out, and it seemed suddenly that only a trip to the local shops would free her mind from pondering these twisted alliances. A pleasant normal activity—and how blessedly normal it seemed!—would restore the illusion that her life was her own, if only by virtue of old age. Old age should be a time of great and significant self-indulgence, she thought: otherwise it is too bitter. At the same time she wondered how she would put up with her daily routine once all the visitors had gone, and the task of talking about them—of reconstructing them, in fact—was not yet fully engaged.

She was half way out of the door when the telephone rang. 'Kitty here.'

'Good morning, Kitty. How are you?'

Was it her imagination that Kitty's breathing sounded more laboured, bringing her splendidly upholstered form most vividly to mind?

'I need your help, Thea. Could you possibly come over?'

'What's wrong? Is it Austin?'

'No, it's not Austin. It's Ann. She won't get out of bed.'

'Is she ill?'

'She says she doesn't want to get married. She won't talk to me; just pulls the covers over her face. I'm afraid we had a silly argument. Do you think you could have a word with her?'

This was new. Kitty frequently had arguments, but not, according to her, silly ones.

'Of course,' she said.

'Thank you, Thea. We'll expect you for tea.'

11

'Well, Ann,' she said, closing the door of the bedroom behind her. 'We haven't had much of a chance to talk, have we?'

She glanced round the room unhurriedly, and in doing so caught the momentary gleam of an eyeball from the motionless figure in the bed. Sleep was not easily simulated, she thought; there was always something tense in the impersonation that was absent from the natural condition. She thought of her own bed, in her own quiet room, and wished she were back there. Her heart had behaved uncomfortably in the taxi and she rather wondered whether she had the energy to convert this recalcitrant girl to a course of action in which she could see no merit. Kitty's peace of mind, of course, must be restored, but for the moment she was more interested in her own. She thought of home most lovingly, as it had been before the arrival of Steve; she saw herself moving through her shadowy rooms undisturbed, as though she were her own ghost. And this room, in which she was most reluctantly seated, beside a crumpled bed, was too bright, too eager, too obviously Gerald's room, kept pristine in case he should decide to come home and behave as if he had never been away, which was Kitty's obvious wish. Austin, she knew, was more philosophical: Austin did his duty, although publicly he might deride the fact that he did so. What he had against David was the ostentatious nature of his goodness, an affront to one of his sly and sorrowful nature. Austin knew that all was vanity, whereas David appeared to be convinced that salvation was available to those of a sunny disposition. They were aspirational, the young, she reflected; what a pity it was that they must be disillusioned.

But she was here to deal with a crisis, and she must be sympathetic, although it was difficult to feel much sympathy for the figure in the bed, her hair flattened, her cheek creased by the pillow. She was with Kitty in this, perhaps by virtue of her age. Older women felt an instinctive impatience when the young squandered their endowment. She sat up straighter, smoothing her linen skirt. 'Won't you talk to me?' she said. 'I have come rather a long way to see you, and I don't suppose we shall meet again. I remember you as a little girl, you know. You were unhappy even then. I remember your dark eyes repudiating everyone and everything. I had hoped you were happier now that you are going to be married . . .'

The figure reared up in the bed. 'I don't want to get married.'

'But why not? It's very pleasant. On the whole I enjoyed it, although I didn't marry until I was quite old.'

There was no answer. 'What do you want to do?' she enquired in her mildest tone.

'I want to go home.'

'And where is home?'

'America.'

'But I thought you were going back anyway, after you are married.'

'I want to go *home*. I don't want to be here, with all this fuss, all this *furniture*.'

Mrs May contemplated the dusky cheeks, now red with anger and unhappiness, the round accusing eyes, the plump chin, and thought that if Ann put her mind to it she could be to a certain extent attractive. She would not put the estimate higher than that. There was a lack of intelligence in the mere fact that she was so deliberately unadorned, so dishevelled, although the bright light of day outside the window should have alerted her to the fact that there was a time to present oneself properly, just as there was a time for every other societal act. This indifference was what drove Kitty mad. Or was it more than that? It took a measure of insolence to ignore the proper rules of engagement, particularly if one were under another's roof. Yet she felt some sympathy for the downcast head, the dark uncombed hair, the womanly breasts under the crumpled T-shirt. She felt sorry for the child still visible in the woebegone face, just as she had felt sorry for the real child all those years ago. Then she had empathised with any child condemned to this milieu of ardent disappointed adults. No doubt there would have been tears, adult tears, and not quite adequately disguised frustration. The child, then, had remained implacably tearless, as if in contempt for Kitty's hysteria. Henry had been sent for to smooth things over after some such battle of wills and had devoted his energies to comforting Kitty. Mrs May had wanted to approach the child, but a glance had told her that the child was quite literally unapproachable. The cheeks then had been the same alarming red as she triumphantly stood her ground, uncomforted. What rage she must have felt! For her status as a child was not being respected: it was the older woman who was weeping.

It was the same entrenched resentment that had been revived by the wedding preparations. For it was, if anything, to be Kitty's wedding, and Mrs May had inherited Henry's obligation to pacify. Her efforts had been momentarily redirected, but only in order to put Kitty's mind at rest before the inevitable outburst. The poor girl had learnt nothing beyond what she had known as a child: contempt. Had she been more worldly she would have perfected a whole repertoire of smiles, attitudes, disclaimers, which would have held condemnation at bay. But this was beyond her, in the same way that truly adult opposition was beyond her. What was called for was selfishness, but to be effective selfishness must be deployed with charm. Ann lacked charm, was not likely to acquire it. Mrs May watched as the fiery cheeks faded and the downturned mouth became rueful. Only the round dark eyes still looked out accusingly, although the gaze was merely directed towards the opposite wall, which a fitful shaft of sunlight had transformed into the purest yellow. Such a pity to be indoors, wasting this brief interlude of bright weather. Surely it was in everyone's interest to be up and about, in the beneficent air, the fugitive sun, instead of settling into this miasma of primitive feelings? Mrs May felt a nostalgia, little more than a memory, for her terrace, for silence, for the simple act of contemplation. A bird on the lawn—even a crow, a magpie— was all she needed in the way of incident. With an effort she addressed her mind once more to the matter in hand.

'Tell me about your home,' she said.

'I suppose it's poor by your standards. Frank, that's mother's boyfriend, has a garage. There's nothing fancy, not like here . . .'

'Your grandmother tries too hard, I know. But you see she still grieves for your father. Did you find him, by the way?' She asked this question as casually as she was able to manage, although her heart, which had been quiescent, was beating irregularly once again.

'It was easy.'

'It can't have been.'

'It was. I had his phone number, didn't I? You've heard of mobile phones, I take it? Of course we had a bit of a job finding this place in Somerset where he lives. It's a camp, sort of.' She wrinkled her nose in distaste. Perhaps she was not Kitty's granddaughter for nothing. 'Lots of little kids running around, and dogs.'

'So Plymouth was just to put us all off the scent?'

'I think he's got a bank account there. Of course they don't use money, but I reckon he's got some. I thought he might like to shell out for me, but he said it would all be needed to buy more land. They own this piece of land, you see; they do a bit of farming, sell apples, and so on.'

'How did he look?'

'Old. Dirty. Cheerful. I hated him, Dorothea. And I wanted to get to know him, but by the time we got there it was nearly dark and we had to come back. And he didn't want to know about me or about grandma or any of us.'

For it was 'us' now, Mrs May noted.

'Did you tell him about the wedding?'

'Yeah. He said it was a bourgeois custom, which it is. That's why I don't want to go through with it.'

'Though if you changed your mind I'm sure Gerald could be persuaded to be present. You could ring him on his mobile,' she suggested idly. 'Keep the whole thing up your sleeve until the last moment. Wouldn't that be rather amusing?'

The girl smiled reluctantly. 'You mean not tell Grandma?'

'Well, of course, you'd have to tell her at some point. But it would all be your doing, wouldn't it?'

There was a silence while this idea was being digested.

'David seems a very genuine sort of person,' Mrs May observed, again in an idle, only half interested tone.

'David's all right. I don't know why everyone's so beastly to him.'

Mrs May smiled. 'We are too old for you,' she said, acknowledging the truth of this remark. 'Old people don't want to be converted, particularly not to a young man's way of thinking. Austin may have been through it all before on his own account. Have you thought of that? Young people are aware of endless possibilities, either in this world or the next. Except that they are nowhere near the next: that is the difference. When you get old you realise how limited those possibilities really were, and you regret the fact that you made so little of them. And really, there's no harm in a discussion, you know; most people get good value from a discussion about religion. I expect Austin is genuinely sorry that his faith has gone. That's why he teases David a bit.' She paused. 'I expect you tease him too sometimes.'

'I can't say I agree with him on everything, though I admire him for what he does, of course. It's just that I don't want to spend the rest of my life surrounded by guitars and cheering.'

'Cheering?'

'They cheer when they hear the name of Jesus,' the girl said glumly.

'And that's why you don't want to get married?'

'I'd be quite happy to live with him for the time being.' For as long as it suits me, they both understood.

'Then why don't you do that?'

'He's religious, isn't he? He won't.'

'But the baby?'

'That was the one and only time I got him to do something I wanted. He didn't want to, really. That's what put me off.'

'Just the one time?'

'Yeah. Well, twice, actually.'

'I wouldn't recommend abortion,' Mrs May said. 'It can leave such sadness behind, and I doubt if one recovers very quickly. I should go through with it, if I were you. David is nice-looking, well-meaning. He will change, you know, lose that optimism of his that annoys Austin so much. Why did you agree to marry him in the first place? You must have been a little in love with him.'

'You just don't understand, do you?' Ann said wearily. 'David's well-off, and I'm not. Do you think I'd marry him if I had money of my own?'

'Is that why you're here? And why you went to see your father?'

'Partly.'

Rather more than that, thought Mrs May, whose initial antagonism had quite dissolved. As a novice wife she too had been oppressed by the wealth of the cousins, and even of Henry himself, had been embarrassed by their unembarrassed enjoyment of the fact. The girls, Kitty and Molly, had been substantially well-off even before they married. There was a carelessness about them, an indifference to thrift which would disgust a young person, particularly a young person with no resources of her own.

'I dare say you will be quite wealthy one day,' she observed. 'But wealth doesn't enable you automatically to do as you please. That is how the poor think, and it is not true. The poor think that wealth confers irresponsibility. But my dear Ann, nothing confers irresponsibility. Each of us is bound by duty, and I think you know that. If I were you I'd go through with it, get married, have the baby, grow as a family. And there are good times to be had, you know. You will always have a companion; you can travel together. Believe me it's no fun travelling on your own . . .' She checked herself here; her own solitude had nothing to do with the matter in hand. Or had it? She remembered the last holiday she had taken with her mother, after her father's death and before the sale of the house. Her mother was already ill but did not yet know the nature or extent of her illness. They had gone to Rottingdean, out of season, at the beginning of autumn. To her mother it was an escape from the dark house, although she was uncertain in a different setting. Every morning they took a careful walk through the quiet streets, and every afternoon her mother rested. Mrs May could still see the yellow leaves on the lawn outside the dining room of their modest hotel. She had felt acutely aware of distant horizons forbidden to her by her mother's failing health. She had felt a desperate need for a miracle, or the appearance of a stranger who would mysteriously take care of them both. But of course no stranger appeared until many years had passed. And on her honeymoon that was how she thought of him: as the stranger who would henceforth keep her company.

'I could get my head round it if it weren't for the fuss,' Ann went on. 'Caterers. Paris. I don't want to go to Paris.'

'Why ever not? Paris is marvellous. You probably think all this is very conventional. Well, of course it is. But you can still enjoy it, you know.'

There was a knock on the door, which Mrs May got up to open. Kitty stood there, a petitioner, a tray in her hands.

'I brought you a poached egg, dear,' she said. 'You didn't

have any lunch. At least, I didn't want to get you out of bed.
You must have got back very late?'

'Latish, yes.'

They watched her humbly as she ate the egg and the slices
of toast. Trimmed of their crusts, Mrs May noted. Poor Kitty.

'You know what I think?' she said. 'I think Ann needs a new
haircut. Really short and simple. She's got such a pretty face,
and—I don't know if you were going to wear a hat for the
wedding, Ann?' She flashed the girl a look of the keenest intelligence, which was at the same time a kind of complicity.

'Would you like that, darling?' asked Kitty eagerly. 'I could
ring up and make an appointment for this afternoon.'

'If I had short hair need I wear a hat?' asked Ann, in whom
a kind of slow acquiescence was dawning.

'No, of course not, you must please yourself,' said Kitty, and
to Mrs May, 'The dress is divine, very plain, you know, a simple shift. But the colour!'

'Then a hat would certainly not be needed. Let the old
people dress up; that's why they enjoy weddings so much. Perhaps we should leave you to get up,' she said. 'Something short
and feathery, I think, don't you? Ring the hairdresser, Kitty.
And perhaps you'd give me a cup of tea before I make my way
home. I've hardly had a word with Austin.'

She left Kitty on the telephone to the hairdresser and made
her way back to the drawing room. Her part in these revels
was now ended, apart from one crucial detail. She sat down
beside Austin, who raised a hand in greeting. They sat silent,
listening to Kitty's excited voice in the other room.

'She has a telephone number for Gerald,' she said quietly.

'I know that,' he said, just as quietly. 'I have it myself.'

'But how?'

'Ever since we got that Christmas card with a Plymouth postmark I've had a man on the job, tracing him.'

'A private detective?'

He shrugged. 'Just a man I used to use when I wanted to check someone out. Credit worthiness, mostly. Don't look like that, Thea. You're not going to tax me with underhand-edness, I hope.'

'But Ann said he was in Somerset.'

'Plymouth was an accommodation address. He had had a room there at some point. I put my solicitor onto it, arranged a bank account.' He smiled faintly. 'The account has been drawn upon.'

'But you didn't get in touch with him yourself?'

'He broke Kitty's heart. I can't forgive him for that.'

'Then Kitty doesn't know?'

'She only knows what I've told her, which is that he's farm-ing with a group of friends.'

'So he is, I suppose.'

'He is forty-eight years old, Thea, and he's a hippy. My son.'

She put a hand over his. 'Don't upset yourself, Austin. Do you want one of your pills?'

Her hand lay on his, ignored. She left it there.

'She drove him away, of course. Now she's doing the same thing with Ann. They sense it, you know, that will of hers. Al-ways criticizing, demanding, calling to account. I put up with it because I love her. Everything I've ever done has been for her protection. "Let him be a farmer if he wants to," I told her. "He's not like us. We've got each other." She can't even see that he married just to get away from her. I thought he'd have a breakdown, and he did. That's when she agreed to let him go away for a bit. The doctor backed him up—not Monty; I didn't want him involved. It was either that or a mental hospital. So he went, abandoning his wife—not that we cared for her, but that's by the way—and his child. And never came back. I understand that, in a way. His equilibrium depends on his freedom. I'm willing for him to have it. Kitty isn't.' He sighed heavily. 'It's been the subject of a good few arguments, I can tell you. And then I went to see him and had that bad attack, and she got frightened. That's when we stopped discussing it. You'll keep this to yourself?'

She patted his hand, much moved. Then she put both hands in her lap, so that she looked quite composed when Kitty bustled in with a tray of tea.

'You don't mind if I leave you to pour out, do you, Thea? I'm taking Ann to the hairdresser. Daniel said he could fit us in. I know he's doing it as a favour to me, but anyway I want to tell him about the arrangements. Molly and I will go tomorrow. Between you and me I want to see what he's doing. Left to himself he'll probably be too radical. I'll be back about five. I hope you'll stay and have a bite of supper with us? Austin? Are you all right?'

'Perfectly all right, darling. You go. Thea will keep me company.'

They were silent until they heard the front door close. Austin raised his teacup to his lips with a hand that shook slightly.

'What will happen to her when I've gone, Thea? Who will protect her then? She'll be looked after, of course; I've seen to all that . . .'

'Austin, are you telling me you're not well?'

He sighed. 'I'm as well as I'll ever be. I should never have retired, of course. I did that to please Kitty. We're both too old for more heartbreak, Thea. I just want this wedding to be over, and nothing to go wrong. It would kill Kitty, if anything went wrong. And I'm not as robust as I once was.'

'I remember you swimming at Freshwater.'

He smiled. 'I was better-looking in those days.'

'You look just the same to me.'

'You're a good woman, Thea. I nearly said "girl". But we're not young any more.'

'Not any more, no.' She placed her cup tidily in its saucer and stood up. 'I won't wait for Kitty. Tell her to ring me if she wants a chat. And that will give you time to have a rest before they get back.'

'I love her so much, Thea.'

'I know, dear.'

All the way down the hill she wondered at this perfect love, then raised her head and saw that the sun was quite strong. The extreme tiredness that she now felt had to do less with the afternoon's exchanges than with the knowledge that time had passed, taking them all—Kitty, Austin, herself—with it, and that nothing she had said to Ann, or could say to her, would change that fact. At the same time she felt a new compassion for the poor bewildered girl, schooled against her will for an inappropriate wedding—and it was a wedding rather than a marriage, she reflected. What was still disconcerting was Ann's absolute lack of curiosity. Not once had she asked a single concerned question, of the sort that Kitty, preoccupied though she was, never failed to ask. How had Thea got to Hampstead? Had she had trouble finding a taxi? And Austin would go out with her when it was time to leave. But today Austin had not had the heart to do what he always did, and truth to tell, she was glad to be alone. These small cherished attentions had little to do with the activities of the young, could be seen as archaic, out of place. Fussy, as Ann would have said, a word conveying maximum condemnation. Her language was opaque, as was Steve's: David's partook of the higher opacity. And even Ann, in her moment of truth, gave evidence of all manner of unclear thinking. She might do well to marry that young man, Mrs May reflected. He had been open enough to ask her, although their testing time was still to come. Eventually David would encounter arguments subtler than his own and be forced to think a little harder. And perhaps that might make a man of him, and thus enable him to make a woman of his wife. In that way they might make some sort of a life for their child, or children. For whom Kitty would yearn. But of course Kitty would be dead, and Austin too, and she no doubt with them. That was the awful truth that Ann had not approached. Perhaps no young person could.

She also realised that she felt a new affection for her puta-tive family, perhaps more than she had previously felt throughout her married life. She had always made an auto-matic distinction between her real family and the families of others, had thought of her silent, stoical, and almost wordless parents whenever the subject of Henry's family was raised, as it so often was. During those afternoons with Rose she liked to think that she had played her part willingly, had felt noth-ing so patronising as pity, had even loved Rose, and loved Henry for his devotion, but at the same time had felt herself to be cut from radically different cloth. It was no accident that the image of her mother at Rottingdean had come to mind: there were no accidents. Her mother, puzzled by her tired-ness, had gone up to the room they shared for her rest, leav-ing her to contemplate the yellow leaves on a lawn sparkling from a recent shower. And now she was as old as her mother had been, and had been a widow for longer. 'Be a brave soldier,' her mother had whispered through her pain, and she had run in terror for the nurse. But that was all over, the lingering illness, the final days, her own helplessness. The wisdom of age decreed that she forget, that she cleave to those who would be her companions in this shipwreck. It was true that Kitty and Austin had each other, but this would not guarantee them a merciful outcome. In fact their hold on life was as frail as her own, more so, for if one went the other would follow.

She caught a bus, eager for faces. The confinement of a taxi would not answer her present mood. A woman with two shopping bags made room for her and smiled cheerfully as she did so. 'Awful the evenings getting dark again,' the woman remarked, though it was still brilliantly light. 'Autumn in the air,' she obliged, and remembered that she had not done any shopping. 'What time does Selfridges close?' she asked her new friend. 'Oh, you'll just make it,' said the woman. 'Mind how you go.' For she must look as old to others as she felt herself to be. The facts were ineluctable.

She bought her marmalade and her apricots, a rye loaf, some French butter, and half a dozen eggs, then, tired, took a taxi home. The flat seemed strange to her; she was rarely away from it for so long. She looked at herself in the bedroom mirror, appraised her drawn mouth, tired eyes. She presumed that Steve would make his own arrangements for dinner, or that Molly would make them for him. David too would eat his boiled rice at Molly's table. Ann would be fed, by force, if necessary, if only to satisfy Kitty's hunger. How vulnerable Kitty was if one did not love her extravagantly, unconditionally! With her moderate pleasantries maybe she herself had done too little in that regard, had ignored the human frailty below the surface. Austin could be relied upon to supply that

love, to protect and to cherish. But Austin might not always
be there . . .

Since for the moment she had an hour or two at her disposal she wandered out onto the terrace, which was now in
shadow, the sun, in a late burst of activity, shedding a hectic
radiance on the windows of the houses opposite. There was
nothing more to be gained from the garden this evening. In
the drawing room she picked up the book she had abandoned
when Steve had first taken up residence, but it was not so
much the book she had abandoned as the drawing room, reluctant to open more of the flat to Steve than the rooms he
had already colonised. She had hardly read more than a few
pages recently, alert to the opening and closing of the door,
which preoccupied her throughout her increasingly disturbed
nights, and now in the daytime as well. She settled down in
her chair, with Inspector Maigret for company, but the former
fascination was gone; she no longer found the images on the
page persuasive. No book would hold her interest on this particular evening, when she had images of her own to distract
her. She felt keenly for Ann, not because of her confusion, but
because those flaring cheeks and bleak set lips seemed em-
blematic of the fate of those constrained by powerful elders.
As a far from young bride she had felt equally beleaguered in
the Levinsons' company. The awkward moments had passed,
but the feeling of oppression had taken longer to disperse.

Ann could not be divided from her family; no act of will,
however determined, could quite manage that. But she could
be offered an alternative view of family life. It need not necessarily be subversive; it could be merely detached. And in offering it, as she had this afternoon, her own role—her
presence, even—might come to be appreciated. She smiled
tentatively at the thought. To be identified with, yet apart

from, the family seemed to her a long overdue rationalisation of a position which until now had been improperly interpreted. She began to look forward to receiving the girl for tea in this very flat, to hearing her grievances, to patiently pointing the way to more mature pleasures. This would be a legitimate role, one she could inhabit without prejudice. Not exactly collusion—never that—but certainly dialogue. And it had been so long since she had had any proper conversation!

She was boiling herself an egg when the telephone rang.

'Kitty here. Thea, you've worked a miracle. That suggestion of yours about the hairdresser was a stroke of genius. No trace of sulks now: she was just having a silly fit. And you should see how pretty she looks! Well, you will see, of course. So clever of you. I'm sorry you couldn't wait, but it won't be long now, will it? Goodbye, and thank you so much for coming over. I expect we shall all be busy tomorrow, but I look forward to seeing you at the wedding. Twelve o'clock here, the day after tomorrow.' She laughed. 'I can't tell you how excited I am.'

12

'Let's face it, Dorothea,' said Steve. 'The middle classes are ridiculously mollycoddled.'

'If you say so, Steve.'

'I mean, look at this flat. Two families could live here.'

'I know what brought this on,' she said, stacking the dishes. 'It's because it's time for you to go.'

'I don't have to.'

'But I'm afraid you do. I have other commitments.'

She could hardly blame him for his look of undisguised scepticism. They both knew that she had no commitments, as he had been able to observe. Nor did she feel sufficiently defensive about her life in order to mount a case. She was idle, it was true, but she had earned her idleness. All her life she had worked, or so it had seemed, not only at her job, but for her mother, for Henry. There stole into her mind at this forbidden crossroads the temptation she had entertained earlier, of relaxing in her bed long past her waking hour, of wasting time in a way she had never done before, of that long and easeful preparation for the final sleep. It was her secret, one of the many she had learned to keep to herself. To one of his ceaseless, even pointless activity, reclusion was an unknown quantity. If it were to be made known to him he would have been puzzled, even derisive. More, he would have perceived it as an excuse, which in part it was.

There was another, more phantasmal reason, unconnected with the first, which made her anxious for his departure. This was both frightening and unjustifiable, issuing from some shadowy depth normally dispersed by the light of day. It was an image, a presence, rather than a threat, the potency of which she was able to gauge by the fact that it had been with her for as long as she could remember. She thought of it as a not quite mythical embodiment, which she had privately christened the Intruder. The aim of the Intruder was to dispossess her. Even as a child she had been unable to take her home for granted. Returning from school it daily occurred to her that her parents might have been turned out in her absence. Their mild smiles of welcome had just as regularly reassured her, and yet the following day would see a return of the same fear. Paradoxically adolescence and adulthood had put an end to this particular ordeal, which made a return of the fear, when she was of an age to conquer her demons, all the more alarming.

For the Intruder was tenacious. The Intruder was a smiling creature, invariably a friend, or a stranger with a friendly face. Despite her longing for company—also phantasmal—she would be aware that the Intruder had an eye on her belongings, and was only waiting for a moment of inattention on her part to take possession. This image had been particularly strong just after she had bought the flat, when she had contact with solicitors, surveyors, workmen. As they cast a knowing eye over her property she could imagine them earmarking it for future use. The builder whom she had employed to make some minor internal adjustments showed a tendency to linger, indicating that it was time for her to make him more tea, appropriating a chair, and rolling another cigarette. In a sly way he had flirted with her, emphasising the obnoxious character of this flirtation by the way he appraised her slight, tense figure, in which his practised eye could discern anxiety. The anxiety, however, was not sexual but territorial. Willing him to drink his tea and leave (but he was in no hurry) she bore as best she could the accusation of spinsterhood in his increasingly jocular remarks, knowing that no woman was safe from this particular menace. Even after the front door had shut behind him there was no relief, for he would be back again the next day, a bulky jovial figure, like a child's idea of Santa Claus, and in his shrewd eyes an ability to search out weakness and to take advantage.

And lately she had had a more urgent worry. At her age it was natural to think in terms of strange doctors, Social Services. Indeed she had no doctor, since Monty Goldmark had retired. What if some newly appointed person came to examine her circumstances, liked the look of the flat, which was in fact desirable, and after having explained to her that she would be better off somewhere smaller, moved in and changed the locks? This was not entirely inconceivable. Only recently she had read of old people forced to sell their homes in order to pay for residential care. It was within the realms of possibility, or at least it was to her, that those designated to assess old people's circumstances might have an eye for a bargain, and in the most opportunistic way possible might avail themselves of a pleasant property without the bother of going through the usual wearisome procedures. And they would smile, would prove to her that she had no future need, or indeed entitlement, would become severe if she put up even a token resistance . . .

Of course Steve was nothing like as menacing as the creatures she had no trouble in imagining. The similarity resided in the fact that he had assessed her circumstances, had seen that there was room for him, had seen above all that there was no argument she could convincingly muster to stop him from putting down roots in her home. There was, in fact, no way in which she could get rid of him if he had no wish to leave. Her heart beat strongly, sickeningly, as she realised this. She told herself not to be a fool, dried the dishes, and folded her teatowel with a hand that shook only slightly. When he returned to the kitchen with an armful of dirty clothes, she merely said, 'I expect you'll want to spend the day with David. I'll leave some food if you want to eat here tonight. But don't forget that the car goes back tomorrow, first thing. I shall want your car keys and your front door keys on the kitchen table by ten o'clock at the latest. That will give you time to get to the garage and back. I'll order a cab to take us to the wedding.'

He said nothing, his head in the washing machine.

'Or perhaps you'd like to take David out for a meal this evening. That might be more amusing for you. But whatever you do I want to see those keys tomorrow morning.'

'Can't wait to get rid of me, can you?'

'But you always knew that this was temporary. And besides, you're going to Paris. Don't you want to go to Paris? And to Apt? I believe it's very beautiful down there, although I don't know the house.'

'I could have spent more time here.'

'But that's not possible. I've told you that.' The washing machine roared into life. 'I know you think I'm a selfish old woman: I can see it in your face. And I'm certainly not going to defend myself to you: I'm sure it would be a waste of time. But if you're going to make a habit of this sort of thing, Steve, you must know when to make a graceful exit. I've rather enjoyed your being here, but that is coming to an end. Now have I your word that you will do what I ask?'

'No need to get uptight about it.'

'Your word, Steve.'

'Yeah, okay.'

'I wonder you can stand living in other people's houses. It would drive me mad.' For it was another nightmare, somehow connected with the first. She would be a timid lodger in a small dark room, her brutal landlord waiting for her to die so that he could install a new victim. Or she would be a prisoner in her own flat, subject to another's will. 'I wonder that you're not more positive about your life. Don't you want to go to university, for instance?'

'I've been, haven't I?'

'Oh?' She was surprised.

'Bristol. Drama.'

'Really? I had no idea. You look so young . . .'

'I'm twenty-two.'

'Then this year in America—are you looking for work there?'

'I'm not actually looking for anything, Dorothea. I'm passing through.'

The question of money returned to haunt her. What if he were poor? What, on the other hand, if he were comfortably off, was supplied regularly with funds by his family? He had made no contribution towards household expenses, had not, now that she came to think of it, expressed appreciation for her hospitality, yet she did not hold that against him. Rather, she admired his freedom, his refusal to make concessions, seeing no need for concessions to be made. The three of them, Steve, David, and Ann, were cuckoos in the nest, but of them all Steve had the requisite air of insouciance. He was indeed a free spirit, so free that he would not even pretend to like her. To be fair she had given no evidence of liking for him. On that basis they had got on remarkably well. She might even miss him. Once more she faced the possibility that he might not go. But now she rather thought that in some mysterious way she had gained the upper hand. Never would it have occurred to her that this was a simple procedure. Even one as untrammelled by correct manners as Steve had conceded the victory. More important, there had been no real resentment. That would come later, she knew, when he was obliged to pack his bags, make provision for his guitar, his radio. She rather thought that most of his impedimenta would of necessity be taken care of by David. For she did not doubt that Steve had become rather practised in precisely this situation.

'Are you going to iron those things before you go out for the day?' she asked. 'For the day' struck the right note, she thought.

'I'll do them tonight. I've got to wear them tomorrow, haven't I?'

'Just for once, Steve, for this last time, I'll do them for you. They ought to be hung up, anyway.'

'You're a brick, Dorothea.' Again the intonation from a wartime film. 'Darling, tell me I'm forgiven.' This time the voice was fruity, actorish.

'All right, Steve, that will do.' But she was smiling. And who would make her smile when he was gone?

He left, whistling; even the whistling was parodic. In the silence that followed his departure she knew that there would be no telephone calls that day. Kitty would be busy, Molly had no need of her, and already Austin must regret taking her into his confidence, sharing with her information that he had not shared with his wife. This left her almost as she had been before Steve had arrived. She went back into her bedroom, surveyed her empire, hers alone since Henry's death. He had professed a liking for the flat the first time he had seen it, but had never come near her deep possessive love for the first and only home she had ever owned. It had seemed a natural progression to move from the tall narrow house in the farthest reaches of New Kings Road closer to what was always referred to as the centre of town by her mother, who rarely went there. Armed with the knowledge of money in the bank, she had looked at several flats, as of right, and yet was appalled at her audacity. To be treated as a potential home owner was a new experience for her, and everyone except herself seemed to think that it was in order for her to do so. Gradually her timorousness had given way to pleasure. She had spent more money, for the delight of having a new kitchen, had not really relished possession until Henry moved in. Then, strangely, it became just another flat, no longer hers by right. She had achieved marriage in exchange for sole ownership.

She had been puzzled by Henry's alacrity in moving in, until she had met Rose and understood the restrictions of living with her. And he was in a hurry to find a home, one ready to receive him. His funds were constrained by his obligations to his first wife, and continued to be so until she remarried. He had still seemed comfortably off to the new Mrs May. She never enquired into his finances, secretly relieved that the mortgage was paid off (he had insisted on that) and trusting him implicitly with the day-to-day running of their lives. In

time the intense pride of ownership had faded, only to return
after his death. But that too did not last. She had been unprepared for inactivity, for silence. When she thought of Henry
it was of someone in another room, laughing, talking on the
telephone: she could almost smell the fragrant smoke of his
cigar. Although he was so gregarious and she so solitary they
had been good friends. Perhaps it was easier for her to make
adjustments, concessions: she was of an obedient disposition.

She had coped quite well with bereavement. What else was
she to do? Yet sometimes she confessed to herself that the days
were too long and the nights all too short. And if she were not
very vigilant she might seek to extend those nights until there
were less and less of the days to manage. She thought that she
had behaved with a certain courage at critical moments in her
life. But it was the sort of courage that was not visible to outsiders, scarcely detectable to herself until some great fatigue
signalled the discharge of a duty, a task completed. She did not
invite sympathy and received none. To outsiders she was a
typical English widow, dignified, uncomplaining, comfortable
in her mind, no longer visited by unseemly thoughts. She did
not languish: that was the characteristic by which she was
recognised. To do so would be to entertain various forbidden
possibilities, to remember her early licence, and the man to
whom she no longer gave a name. That humiliation had
taught her caution, impassivity, but also shame, a cold distaste
that was a regrettable after-image of the whole affair. Her
amorous history was not flattering; had it not been for Henry
it would have been disastrous. And imperceptibly she had
grown into someone who needed to keep her own counsel,
so that any enquiry seemed like a violation.

And yet, she thought wonderingly, she had tolerated Steve
about the place. Even more remarkably, she had found the

courage to tell him to leave. This cheered her somewhat, until she reflected that she had always made a good job of endings. Since that afternoon in the hotel in Rottingdean, when she had gone up to their room and contemplated her mother sleeping with a kind of greediness, a desperation that could be read in her grimacing features, she had known that she must rise to whatever terrible occasion was in store, and in so doing would pass some test that not all are required to take. She put it down to what she called the sadness gene, a pathogen which had perhaps been there from birth. Nature rather than nurture had given her this disposition, for she had loved her kindly parents and even now commended their values, although she was to outward appearance more fortunately situated than they had ever been. If she missed anyone these days she missed her mother, a fact which struck her as infinitely sad. But she had read of men wounded in battle crying for their mothers, and she assumed that the most unlikely people were similarly affected. Those who loudly bewailed their unhappy childhoods were spared that, at least.

Her task now was to disguise this uninteresting elderly person as someone agreeable, someone who must prepare for a social occasion, someone who would be called on to display a certain artfulness, in the best of all possible causes. She hated to be unaccompanied at a wedding, one to which Kitty was sure to invite a hundred or so of her closest friends. But art: she was with Kitty on that matter. On went the palimpsest of colour beneath which the naked face was temporarily concealed; after various dabbings, smoothings, and brushings she looked quite creditable, rather better in fact than she had done twenty years ago. Some essential acceptance had taken place; the features had gained in definition. The docile appearance had taken on a certain decisiveness. This was not easy, but she had learned from others that it could be managed, had seen that brief flicker of respect in unknown passers-by. She thought that this was on account of her straight back, her upright head, unaware of the fixity of her expression. And yes, she had dealt with that young man quite satisfactorily. Nevertheless she would buy him something nice for his supper. For it was important that her hospitality was not seen to be at fault.

In her dreams the Intruder came, and took up residence: she merely smiled politely and left home, taking enough money to enable her to start again elsewhere. Except that she never did, or rather that this part of the dream was quite unclear to her. What was clear was that she never put up a fight, because it was quite impossible that she could ever win. And this morning, in her own kitchen, she had come as near as possible to the worst happening, the endgame, and the surprising thing was that she had not given in, had stood her ground, had stated her requirements calmly and without a fuss. She could not remember this ever having happened before. Of course her relief might prove illusory: the keys might not appear on the table, as prescribed. But the fact that for the first time in her life she had managed to convince herself of her rights might embolden her to assert her wishes again. She saw only one occasion on which this might happen, a further confrontation with Steve, but she had also perceived a certain weakness in her opponent, a certain frivolousness. It would not amuse him to persecute her if there were other distractions to be exploited. She rather thought that it might be David who would have to confront the continuing dilemma of Steve as a perpetual houseguest. Or perhaps it flattered David to have Steve as page to his squire. Even David could not be without some vestige of human vanity. On the other hand, if matters were to turn unpleasant, David would have the spiritual resources for a contest of wills, could indeed invoke higher powers, though she suspected that Steve, if he had a mind to, could mount a quite sophisticated defence. That, however, would be nothing to do with her. Her own involvement would be ended; all that was required now was to draw a neat line under the whole episode.

The memory of her victory, and the sight of her disguised face in the mirror, momentarily cheered her. She decided to go out, although it was too early for her hair appointment. She needed air: the flat had too recently been a battleground. She would shop for Steve, hang up his clothes, and perhaps put some money in an envelope and leave it in one of his nylon bags. That way at least he could enjoy a little temporary independence, although she thought it was rather dependence that he preferred. He is not charming enough, she thought cruelly; if he were he would have far less trouble getting his own way. For people of her own generation charm was a considerable attribute; a woman got nowhere without charm. Yet Ann yesterday, Steve today, David presumably always, were completely untouched by it, saw no need to cultivate it, found it suspect, akin to dishonesty. Yet their raw charmlessness was an impediment to their desires, could they but see it; they scorned, as inauthentic, the delicate manipulations of which a woman like Kitty was such a mistress. Not that Kitty was delicate, but she knew how to handle a man. She could, on occasion, be endearing, and she always got her own way. Women were rather good at getting their own way in those far-off days before sexual equality. But the young would hardly understand their largely innocent ploys. Their values were no doubt exemplary, but their methods were dishearteningly crude.

After a night of rain the weather in the streets was cool, with a promise of more rain to come. The smell from the saturated gardens was welcome, invigorating. The brilliant and exceptional summer had justified her inactivity; now the darker days would begin, confining everyone to home. She thought that she would no longer seek a brief distraction in foreign towns, and the knowledge saddened her. She had not enjoyed those solitary holidays but they had added to her brief stock of independence: that was her reason for undertaking them. And then there was always the alibi to offer the neighbours, should they ask her. The question was customary at this season of the year. 'Good holiday?' was the greeting acquaintances offered each other, momentarily revived by the presence of familiar faces after sojourn abroad. She had nothing to exchange except the presence of a 'young friend', though no-one yet had given her an opportunity to offer him to the general public. Nevertheless he would serve during the long dark months ahead. 'No, I didn't go away this year,' she would say. 'I had a young friend staying with me,' and they would be mildly intrigued, having been so used to seeing her careful solitary figure and assuming, correctly, that she had no attachments.

But perhaps nobody would enquire; she thought that more likely. Only her immediate neighbour, Mrs Baird, might possibly be interested, yet Mrs Baird was a world traveller, given to trekking in Nepal, despite her age. A putative young friend would be of no interest to Mrs Baird, who could even now be seen at the end of the street, her wheeled basket clattering behind her. Mrs May marvelled at the purposeful progress of this rather stout woman, who, under guise of perfect suburban conformity, might even now be contemplating a visit to the temples of South-East Asia. I could have done that, she thought; all it takes is a little courage. But it was the sort of courage she signally lacked. Courage to live alone, yes, and to die alone when the time came; courage to meet the empty day formally dressed and scented; courage to confront long endless Sundays, sustained only by a diet of newspapers and walks round the garden, the latter curtailed in case she was observed by idlers at their windows. What was missing was the courage that would enable her to put long distances between herself and her home, her bed. Even when married to Henry, and genuinely enjoying their excursions, she had been homesick, although at that stage, she remembered, her home was not entirely her own, so that the homesickness was very slightly mitigated. And she had only to feel Henry's arm in hers, when he was beginning to be ill, to know that her duty was no longer to herself, that home was to be his refuge, no longer hers.

She bought smoked trout, potatoes and spring onions for a potato salad, blackberries, and Greek yoghourt. She took her shopping bag home, emptied the washing machine, and hung up his clothes to air; she would iron them this afternoon while waiting for the potatoes to boil. There was just time to fit in her hair appointment, although she had almost lost sight of the wedding in the light of the greater drama of her moral struggle with Steve. That was how she continued to think of it, and to marvel at the simplicity of her victory. Of course he could still overturn it, could transform victory into catastrophic defeat. This could still happen. Against this was the ticket to Paris, the return ticket to the States, already paid for. And anyway she bored him. Reduced to her sole company— for Kitty and Molly would prove inhospitable—he would soon want to look farther afield. She hoped that this could be managed without more delay, by the morning of the following day, in fact. All depended on the presence of his keys on the kitchen table. She thought she had it in her to demand them, hand outstretched, if necessary. It was simply a question of confidence, and in this matter she had already proved herself.

While Jackie tended her hair she saw her polite face wearing an expression of abstracted thought, and realised that despite her resolution it would be difficult for her to resume her normal life. The previous week had brought a certain excitement, a certain amount of company. All this would now vanish, and her part in the proceedings would be overlooked, for after all what had she done? She had allowed herself to be made useful; she had not volunteered for active service, even though circumstances had drafted her into it. In the mirror she saw a woman behind her receiving the attentions of the manicurist, then hanging her little red claws over the arms of her chair to dry. That is all we are good for, she thought: to keep up appearances and thus avoid giving offence. It was the young who must not be offended by the sight of mad old people with wild hair and bad feet. The irony was—and it was a remarkable sign of sophistication on God's part—that they in turn would give offence and not entertain the slightest idea that they were doing so.

At home, her chores completed, she sat and proceeded with her daily exercise, which she thought of as the reckoning. This was essential if she were to retain any semblance of self-mastery. Today the results were as good as could be expected: health more or less unchanged, eyes no worse but liable to tire if she read for more than an hour, heart giving its usual warnings. It might be sensible to find a local doctor, in case of emergencies. Monty Goldmark might exceptionally still visit, but this could be inconvenient for both of them.

Suddenly she was swept by a great wave of grief. What was she doing here, in this flat which she purported to love, which she did love, completely unoccupied, in the middle of a weekday afternoon, with only the sound of a car passing on a wet road to keep her company? And it would always be like this. Perhaps if Steve were to stay, she thought, I might be spared these moments when my nerve fails. But after she had laid the kitchen table for him, she wrote a note, reluctantly, and with a curious sadness: 'Steve. Don't forget to leave me your keys. D.M.'

13

'Do I look all right?' she asked him, as they left the flat.

'Very nice,' he replied, stowing his bags in the front of the taxi.

He was annoyed with her, but she had expected that. Her blue silk suit was too thin for such a cool day, but she was relieved to see that she was wearing it. The previous night she had dreamed that she had set out for the wedding in a dress of pale yellow crêpe, and a yellow pillbox hat; she was a good half hour late, but seemed indifferent to this aspect of the affair, was in fact bubbling over with high spirits, until the tube train in which she was travelling drew up outside Goodwood race course. By this stage she had acquired an assistant, to whom she was entrusting a rather precious piece of research. The wedding had quite receded from her mind, until she looked at her watch and discovered that it must be over by this time, that the newly married couple had already left, and that Kitty would never forgive her.

She had woken in a panic, reaching for her pills, and then relinquishing them. Tense, in the dark, she strained her ears to listen for Steve, either closing the front door or going into the kitchen. She even persuaded herself that if she were very attentive she might hear the clink of the keys being dropped. But all was silent, and the only sound she could discern was the crepitation of the rain on the leaves outside in the garden beyond her window. She saw that it was just before five o'clock. She had not dared to sleep again, bethought herself briefly of the long lazy mornings she was keeping in reserve, and shortly after seven had eased herself quietly out of bed and gone to make a cup of tea. On the kitchen table the smoked trout and potato salad were untouched. She took an apple for her breakfast—for she would keep out of the kitchen until well into the morning—and went back to her room.

As usual when there was disagreement in the air she felt at fault. She tried to exculpate herself from what was after all a purely subjective impression, but without success. The early hour, the uncertain light, a natural apprehension with regard to the day's events, all conspired to produce a sinking feeling of withdrawal. It was impossible to return to bed, and in any case she felt too restless and uncomfortable, distracted by the sound of dripping leaves. This was no weather for a wedding, yet the forecast had only referred to bright periods. After waiting tensely for half an hour she ran her bath; though it was still too early she made up her face and prepared her wedding outfit. She discarded Henry's dressing gown, retrieved a scarcely worn housecoat from the wardrobe, and sat down until she judged it an appropriate time to enter her own kitchen.

In the dream she had been frivolous, uncaring, dressed like a character in one of the American films that she and her mother had so enjoyed, films that supplied them with their very small stock of worldly wisdom. Yet both she and her mother had been too grave by nature to profit from the example of those flighty flirtatious girls, all of whom treated life as a series of delightful opportunities; and now age had reinforced that gravity, so that every small trial was a moral test. Somewhere, in another part of the flat, Steve was either preparing to return the car or deciding to keep it. She could hear nothing; perhaps there was nothing to hear. She opened the window wider, inhaled the poignant smell of wet earth. If she had been on her own she would have walked into the garden, broken off a few stems to put in a water glass, just in order to bring the outdoors in with her. The day would have been empty, but she would have been free. Instead she sighed, smoothed down the skirts of her housecoat, and prepared to confront the enemy.

She had anticipated an unpleasant interview over the breakfast table, but as soon as she came into the room he put the keys down and waited for her to pour his coffee. He was formally, even smartly dressed, and already he seemed a stranger. Seeing his intransigence she felt moved to make amends, although there was nothing for which she need apologise; at least that was what she told herself, remembering the envelope she had placed in his holdall. The uneaten food went into the bin.

'Are you looking forward to going to Paris?' she asked at last.

'Yeah. Yeah, I am. Might hang around a bit. Establish a few contacts.'

She recognised this for the bravado that it was. She said nothing, busied herself with the washing up. 'You sit down,' she said, 'since you're already dressed. I've ordered the taxi for eleven-thirty. I'll get dressed myself, and then we'll have another cup of coffee. Why not sit in your room, make sure you've got everything?'

For she was suddenly ashamed of herself, of her fussy housecoat, of her tired eyes, of her anxiety to see this day over and done with. Once again the wedding receded in importance: all she knew was that she would be required to stand for a long time in a hot noisy room among strangers before she could come home and be on her own again. And even before that ordeal—for it was an ordeal—she must oversee Steve's departure, must be vigilant until he was actually beside her in the taxi, his bags finally removed from the spare room. And all through the reception she must keep an eye on him in order to make sure that he left with David and Ann, which meant that she must stay to the very end. And then, when she finally came home, she must sit down and write to Kitty to congratulate her on a marvellous success. She would write because the idea of saying all this on the telephone made her feel quite faint. The telephone call could wait until the weekend, by which time she would hope to have recovered her composure. And even if she did not, as she hoped, recover her composure, at least there would be no witnesses to point out any discrepancies in appearance or behaviour. She would contact the cleaning agency, go back to the Italian café for her solitary lunches. It will all be as before, she told herself, but she knew that this was not true.

Their departure from the flat took place in silence. In the park the rain was bringing to patchy life the grass left piebald by the summer's heat. Surreptitiously she felt in her bag for the keys, while pretending to look out of the window. Steve pretended to look out of his.

'Write to me if you think of coming back to London,' she said, as casually as possible.

'I might,' he said, after a pause.

'Come, come, Steve, don't let us part on bad terms. You've

had a pleasant break and now you're off to Paris. You said you were looking forward to going.'

'And?'

'Well, then.'

There was no more to be said. She was in disgrace. At that point a spark of irritation, ignited by his mulish silence, but rather more by the weather and the unsuitability of her thin silk jacket, inspired her to say, 'I hope you will not be ungracious at Kitty's. She's had a lot to put up with this past week. And you'll remember to thank Molly, of course.' If she had hoped that he would thank her she hoped in vain. In a way she could appreciate his obstinacy. She was obstinate herself, when there was nobody to object. And it was very tiresome when others impeded one's will, particularly when one was young and had no others to consult. She saw all this, but was too exasperated to make further concessions. They sat in silence.

'Here we are,' she said finally.

Outside the Levinsons' block of flats several expensive cars and a camper van were drawn up. They joined a rustling throng of highly groomed highly coloured women and acquiescent husbands, looking forward to a chat among themselves. In the hallway, at regular intervals, stood large gilt baskets filled with lilies.

'Kitty pushing the boat out, as usual,' murmured one lacquered matron to another.

'I wonder the girl's mother didn't do all this,' her friend replied.

'Said she had to stay at home with the younger children. Not married, of course. If you ask me there's no love lost between her and Kitty.'

'Wasn't there a divorce?'

'The son. A bad business.' An electric smile lit up her features. 'Kitty, darling, how lovely all this is. And how lovely you look. We'll go through, shall we? I must congratulate the bride. Where is she?'

Ann was easy to locate: she was the tallest person in the room. She looked not unattractive in her lavender shift, her now neat head bent as she inclined an ear to Molly. David had been appropriated by Harold for a final consultation: dietary instructions, she surmised, were being issued. Both young people looked mystified and bored. Maids darted across the room with trays of champagne and plates of canapés. Mrs May felt her head begin to ache. She had lost Steve and did not know anyone else. For a moment she wondered if she might leave, might creep down the hill in her silk suit and find a taxi—or a bus! A bus filled with ordinary people!—and go home. But Kitty, resplendent in bronze grosgrain, was pushing her way through the crowd towards her, holding on to the arm of a stoutish man with a beard, dressed in an old-fashioned three-piece suit. 'And of course you know Gerald,' she was saying, to people who could not conceivably ever have met him. 'My son.' For he was her son, and hers only. Her face glowed with a supernatural flush of youth. She was a woman in love.

Across the room Mrs May caught a glimpse of Austin dabbing his eyes. 'Wonderful, wonderful,' he was saying, to no-one in particular. 'You know my son, do you? Come over, I'll introduce you.'

Mrs May moved across to Harold, who also looked much moved.

'How did they do it?' she enquired, in as low a voice as the buzz of conversation would permit.

'David did it. He had a word with him, man to man. I tell

you, Thea, that boy is a marvel. He has unusual powers of persuasion. He just came straight out with it. "Dad," he said. "I
think you should come to the wedding." I'm going to miss
him, Thea. He looks well, doesn't he? Gerald, I mean.'

'That's his van outside, I suppose.'

'Yes, he drove himself here. Well, it's his home, after all. Not
that he'll stay. But he's made contact, that's the main thing.
And you can see what it's done for Kitty and Austin.'

'So this was your secret, Harold? Yours and David's?'

Harold blushed. 'I didn't even tell Molly. Well, if I'd done
that I might as well have told Kitty, or rather Molly would
have done. Who do you think he looks like?'

He looked like no-one. He looked like a not very prosper-
ous country cousin, flexing his all but obsolete social muscles.
Beside the radiant Kitty he appeared extinguished. This must
be difficult for him, she thought; he must be on the defensive,
nerving himself to reject his mother all over again. But in fact
she could see no signs of psychic upheaval in his pleasant
rather nondescript face. He seemed if anything indifferent,
stood absently with a glass of champagne in his hand, surrounded by strangers, patiently offering himself to be shown
off by Kitty, on whom, from time to time, he shed a puzzled
smile. Beside him, clutching his arm, Kitty looked like a tem-
ple houri.

'Congratulations, Kitty,' Mrs May shouted in her ear.

'Oh, Thea, do go and have a word with Bessie Millington.
She's over there, by the fireplace. You've met Gerald, haven't
you?'

'How do you do?'

Gerald gave her an affable if bemused smile. 'Over here,'
shouted Molly, who had produced a camera. 'One with Kitty.'

The bride and groom, overshadowed, stood at the bar, each

with a carefully chosen plate of hors d'oeuvres. They appeared at last to be having a conversation with each other, possibly reckoning up the rewards of their activities. No, that was unfair, Mrs May reproached herself. They were simply bored with the whole thing. And Paris would be quite the wrong choice for them. They were naif and strong-willed: they should be in the country, or back home in America, where they belonged. Payment would no doubt have been made: Austin and Harold would have seen to that. So presumably everyone was satisfied. She craned her head, searching for Steve, but he was nowhere to be seen.

'Bessie Millington,' Kitty instructed her, nodding in the direction of the fireplace before moving off, Gerald in tow. 'All alone, poor soul. Do have a word.'

Bessie Millington was a very old lady, so old that Mrs May thought she must have been brought along by a nurse, who would have the task of returning her to whatever retirement home had booked her out that morning. She wore a well-preserved hat of coq feathers, at least forty years out of date, and a dress of printed silk, the bodice of which, tactfully draped, could not quite conceal her completely flat chest. In contrast to her shrivelled body her hands were massive, the knuckles swollen by arthritis. Several fine rings were buried in the interstices. Around her tortoise neck hung a gold lorgnon.

'Good afternoon,' said Mrs May, raising her voice against the surrounding hubbub. She could not hear herself speak but presumed that she had done so. 'Can I get you something to eat?' Wrinkled eyelids were momentarily raised. 'A glass of champagne?' she enquired at the top of her voice.

The ancient lips moved. When the words came out they sounded as if they had issued from a cavern.

'What is on offer?'

'Well, there's smoked salmon, asparagus rolls, caviare, cheese puffs, oh, and wait, the maids are bringing out some hot savouries.'

'I should like some caviare.'

'I'll be back in a minute,' she said, suddenly aware that she was rather hungry herself. Breakfast had been a distracted affair, largely unregarded. She put caviare and crackers onto a plate, added some cheese puffs, and shouldered her way back. She found a small table and arranged it in front of Bessie Millington, then snatched a glass of champagne from a passing tray.

One should not watch the old eating, she thought, should not imagine the mouthfuls travelling down those aged throats. Impervious, crumbs clinging to her withered lips, Bessie Millington seemed neither satisfied nor dissatisfied with her part in the celebrations. She might have been seated in a restaurant, Mrs May thought. Here was one person to whom Gerald's presence was a matter of complete indifference, if indeed she knew who he was, who any of them were.

'If you'll excuse me,' she said. 'I'd like to have a word with the bride, before she goes to change.' For surely this cannot last much longer, she thought. They have a plane to catch.

'Who did you say you were?' asked Bessie Millington, lighting a cigarette with a large trembling hand.

'Thea. Thea May. Shall I take that plate?'

'You married Henry, didn't you?'

'Yes, that's right.'

'The second wife.'

'Yes, yes, the second wife.'

'I knew the first one,' said Bessie Millington, taking in a lungful of smoke. 'Terrible little bitch.'

'Oh, really?' Mrs May felt a warm surge of appreciation for Bessie Millington. 'I never met her.'

'Little gold digger.' She inhaled again, deeply. 'Men are so cheap,' she added. 'I should know. Three husbands, all dead. How old would you say I was?'

'Eighty?'

'Eighty-six,' she said, disappointed. 'You seem a sensible woman. He was lucky to find you. Or were you on the look-out too?'

'No, no, I wasn't. We were very happy.'

Bessie Millington gave a cunning smile. 'That's what they all say. But you're an improvement on the first one, I'll give you that. Women always spoiled Henry. Is there any coffee?'

'I'll ask,' she said. 'And I'll just have a word with the bride, if you'll excuse me. I'll bring you some coffee, if there is any.'

If I were at home I could be having a rest, she thought, as she fought her way, smiling, through the crowd. The disturb- ing dream of the previous night had left her anxious, as if even now she might be forced to undertake some task for which she was unprepared. The Bessie Millingtons of this world were an easy proposition, but she dreaded what was to come: Kitty's triumph, to which she would never oppose the truth of Gerald's indifference, of Ann's antagonism. Again she would be called upon to play her part, but it would be a lowly one; she would despise herself for the appreciation which it would be her duty to offer. But what else were they to do? They were all old, must cling to evidence of affection, even if they had to beg for it. Kitty's armoured carapace had been pierced by the sight of Gerald, and to judge from his expres- sion Austin's cynicism had quite deserted him. If they were very careful there need be no damage. If Kitty would let Ger- ald go, without extracting promises from him, if Austin were to behave in a suitably grandfatherly manner, they might be encouraged to remember this as a happy family occasion. Even Mrs May would be invited to do this; indeed she would be the ideal audience. And Kitty would feel more kindly towards all those friends whom she had mystified with stories of the absent Gerald's well-being: present, he had justified all her untruths. And she would have witnesses to acknowledge the fact that he existed, as many had begun to doubt. 'I assumed he was in prison,' one man was overheard to say, before being silenced by his wife. Gerald was thus doubly successful; he was both son and attribute. But Mrs May had seen his cautious smile dull from time to time, and his glance turn towards the door. She silently urged him to be patient, for it would soon be over for all of them.

She edged her way into the bedroom, where Ann was athletically divesting herself of her wedding dress. 'Aren't you going to take that with you?' she asked. 'I could pack it for you if you like.'

'No way. As soon as I get out of that'—she gestured to the pink suit laid out on the bed—'I'll be back in my jeans. What a farce. I'll tell you one thing, Dorothea. If we don't like Paris we'll be on the next plane home. We've got our return tickets, remember.'

'And Austin has no doubt been generous.'

'Not bad. I still think he's a mean old sod, though.'

'Oh, do be kind,' she said. 'After all we shan't see you again. Give Kitty a big hug. And thank Austin nicely. Then it will all end happily. They do want you to be happy, you know.'

'They expect us to thank them all the time, don't they? We're here, aren't we? We've gone through it all, haven't we? What more do they want?'

'They want you to love them,' said Mrs May sadly.

There was a silence, while Ann zipped her skirt over her substantial hips. 'You've been okay,' she said finally.

If it were to end now, it would be all right, she thought. If I could simply walk out of this room, smile my goodbyes and go home, I should be quite happy. But it was the goodbyes, the leaving, that would be the problem, and of course the empty flat. Henry and she had married soberly and gone away unnoticed. Susie Fuller had thrown confetti, and they were embarrassed. In fact they had been embarrassed with each other, with what they had done. It was better when they got to the South of France, but then everything was better in the sun. And she had appreciated male company. But she could not ignore his own difficulty: he was a man recovering from an unhappy love affair. Once she had understood that, she was in a position to care for him, which she had done wholeheartedly. She was seen as Henry's comforter, rather than as his lover. No-one knew of her lost ardour, of which there was no trace.

'They're leaving!' The cry went up as she returned to the drawing room, where husbands had drawn up gilt chairs, and, legs crossed, were enjoying a discussion among themselves, free of their wives, who, although still professionally animated, had also lapsed into normal conversation. Rallied by the appearance of Ann in her pink suit they resumed their fervent expressions. Maids were already clearing away dirty plates, removing ashtrays. Ann seemed empowered by the prospect of release. They followed her out onto the pavement. A brief hectic sun sparkled on wet leaves, on Gerald's van, now decorated with white ribbons. 'Harold did that,' Molly murmured to her. 'Wasn't it clever of him? It was to be a surprise. Gerald's driving them to the airport.'

'And then driving on, I suppose? Not coming back here?'

'We didn't like to ask him. Mind you, it's just as well. Kitty looks exhausted. We shall all need a rest, after the excitement. We'll miss him, you know. David, I mean. Harold has got so attached to him. They had such long talks. He needs a man to talk to, especially since leaving the office. He'll be depressed. He won't want to upset me, but I think he'll be lonely.'

'You must book your holiday, Molly. He'll be all right, once you're away.'

'Will he?' Molly smiled sadly. 'We'll miss him,' she repeated.

'Goodbye, goodbye,' they cried. 'Dorothea, come and say goodbye.'

'Well done, David,' she said, pressing his arm. 'You did really well.' He flashed her a genuine smile, the first she had seen. 'And Ann.' She kissed her. 'Godspeed. Don't forget us! Steve?' Steve was already opening the doors of the van. His cheeks were flushed, his expression hilarious. 'Good luck, Steve.'

'Yes, good luck, Steve,' someone shouted amiably behind her.

He came round the side of the van to where she stood, a little apart from the crowd.

'Take it easy, Dorothea,' he said. 'Stay cool.' And bending her backwards he enfolded her in an elaborate Hollywood embrace. Cheers went up. She blushed.

And then they were gone. Those who were left trooped back slowly inside, for coats, for hats. In the great silence left by their eventual departure Mrs May had time to notice a couple of cheese puffs trodden into the carpet. Slowly, very slowly, Bessie Millington emerged from the cloakroom, an antique mink stole draped round her shoulders. 'Goodbye, my dear,' she said to Mrs May. 'I have enjoyed talking to you.' She made her way out, her stick flicking a forgotten glove out of her path, without further acknowledgement of the occasion. 'Margot's glove,' said Kitty absently. 'I must ring her up.' But her mind was clearly elsewhere.

'A great success, Kitty,' said Mrs May.

'It did go well, didn't it? Did you manage to have a word with Gerald?'

'Gerald was surrounded,' she said, smiling.

'He looked well, didn't he?' queried Austin, wiping his eyes again. Mrs May thought how old he looked. They both looked old, drawn.

'I'll leave you to rest,' she told them. 'You'll have plenty to talk about. I'll be in touch, of course.'

'Goodbye, Thea,' said Kitty, with a poor smile. 'Did you enjoy yourself? You don't mind if Austin doesn't come out, do you? He's awfully tired. Austin? Don't cry, darling. Come and lie down. You're tired. It's all right, dear. Kitty's here.'

Mrs May found her way down the hill to the bus stop, careless of the last raindrops falling from the trees onto her blue suit. How pleasant it was, out in the air, away from them all. Yet she was touched, perhaps more than touched. And she would play her part, as she always had, would add her voice to the long appreciation of Gerald's *acte de présence,* as they expected her to. And she would find it in her to be genuine with them, at long last. And maybe the silence of the flat would once again be welcome. A wedding stirs up all kinds of emotions, she thought, feeling the moisture in her own eyes. It was a success. Even those young people were a success. What more could they have done? A 74 bus reared out of the sun just as she reached the stop. They might perhaps appreciate a telephone call this evening. And on Sunday, of course. Of the intervening days she did not think; they would be filled somehow.

206 / Anita Brookner

'All right, love?' asked the conductress, a hand under her elbow.

'Yes, thank you,' she said. 'Just a little tired. I've been looking after a young friend.'

'They take it out of you, don't they? Kids?'

'They do, rather. But they make up for it, don't they?'

Men have feelings too, she reasoned, as the bus approached Baker Street. Quite enlightening, those remarks of Bessie Millington. And that kiss of Steve's, ridiculous, but all the same . . . Quite all right to have an early night tonight. Quite safe to take a pill. Their plane will just have taken off. I shall never see Paris again. Once more she felt a pressure behind her eyelids, as memory furnished her with images of her first rapt visit to Paris. She had quickly tired of churches and museums, had gravitated towards the humblest of little squares, in streets far from the centre, had eaten a sandwich for her lunch, had dared only later to ask for a coffee, sitting in the farthest corner of the café in order to watch the people. She had walked all the afternoon, for the sheer pleasure of seeing the lights come on at dusk, for feeling herself to be at one with the workers going home. And she had slept as she had not slept since, without those dreams, those half imagined interruptions that thronged her nights, just when she had always imagined herself to be safe.

Her street, just as she turned the corner from the main road, was, as always, sedately silent, as if no-one lived there. Though the silence should have been welcome after the crowded afternoon, she found it slightly sinister. In her mind she was still in a Paris square, watching a dog drinking from an iron fountain, hearing the splash of the water, waiting for the children to arrive, as they sometimes did, to play in the little sandpit. Instead she was all too soon at her front door, and not a soul in sight. It was her youth that she missed, when pleasures could be guaranteed to please. In the kitchen she filled the kettle, then sat down at the table. The flat was empty, of that there was no doubt, and she was alone as she had wished. When the kettle boiled she made tea and poured herself a cup, which she did not drink. As if through a camera obscura she saw the young people preparing to defend themselves against the enticements of Paris, or indeed enquiring whether there were seats on the night flight to New York. They too would be affected by their brief stay in London, would feel unprotected, undirected for a while. In that way they might learn a valuable lesson: namely that it is prudent to seek cover. Not courageous, but prudent. This was a lesson that most adults knew, that most families knew. Mrs May bowed her head, recognising her unenviable courage. She hoped that those young people were not too offended by the lights of Paris, and not too lonely, out there, unprotected, on their own.

14

That night, in her dreams, she had a vision of what she understood to be Heaven, or the next world. It took the shape of a field full of folk, some sauntering absent-mindedly, some merely taking the air, on a sunless afternoon. The light disappointed her: she would have expected splendour, but here everything was reassuringly banal. The setting appeared to be Hyde Park, although there were factory chimneys in the distance. This latter detail, and the self-absorption of the walkers, were faintly reminiscent of a painting by Lowry, although as far as she could see no work was being done. This was leisure, not the leisure of the unemployed but of the pensioned class, enjoying its eternal rest. She recognised no-one, although a man in the foreground, wearing a raglan overcoat and a tweed cap, was vaguely familiar. There were few women: she understood that the women were in another place. The area was fairly thickly populated, but by people on their own; no-one walked with a companion. And their walking was purposeful, as it would have to be in this dull light, in this absence of obvious attractions. There was no sign of Henry: perhaps he too had gone to another place, a more vivid and spectacular place better suited to one of his temperament. His relations would also be in that place, leaving her free once more to savour the sort of Sunday afternoon which she had once enjoyed. But faced with the prospect of enjoying it throughout eternity she wondered how it had ever convinced her of its desirability.

And yet there was an air of camaraderie in this version of Heaven: one would not fear introductions. And that sauntering strolling silent crowd was one in which she could easily mingle; she would be accepted. It seemed to her that there was a faint questing smile on her face as she prepared to step from solid ground into this slow-moving throng, relieved that there was to be no entrance examination, no stern scrutiny, no tiresome dissection of past misdemeanours. The absence of judgment convinced her that this was indeed Heaven, a place of easy access, and thus a jealously guarded secret.

She returned to this vision or apparition several times in the course of the morning, astonished that it was still so present in her mind's eye. She could not see that it was overwhelmingly attractive: its main advantage was its specificity. She had found the lack of obvious glory extremely persuasive; as she had always thought, there were to be no angels, no saints, no apotheoses, no Christmas card fantasies. Presumably the saints had already gone to the same glum place, or to whatever equivalent their peculiar make-up dictated. By the same token there were no rewards, an important consideration to be borne in mind, and undoubtedly no punishments either. One abided by the rules because of some innate disposition towards them, not in the hope of compensation. This left a tricky question mark over those who claimed divine sacrifice. Might not the truth lie elsewhere?

There had undoubtedly been an impression of truthfulness,

of almost unavoidable dullness, about her glimpse of Heaven. It was the dullness that made it convincing. It was an English Heaven, framed precisely to satisfy the expectations of those who had grown up in a Welfare State, sparse decent people who wore hats and took healthy walks. It was a Heaven for those who remembered the Fifties, as she herself did, as a time of peace and order. So that this was a retrospective vision, dating back to an era when hospitals were reassuring and songs intelligible. The one necessary qualification for entry was obedience, which was, after all, the defining characteristic of the 1950s. She herself was defined by it. So that all she could look forward to was a return to more innocent times, or perhaps to her own more innocent times.

She had perhaps been unprepared for such tedium as she had identified in the Lowry-like setting. Looking back on it—and the details were still astonishingly clear—she gave more prominence to the factory chimneys in the background. This was above all a workers' paradise. It was a place of modest weekend pleasures, of a Sunday walk in the park. It bore a moral resemblance to Seurat's great picture of a summer Sunday afternoon: bodies unveiled and exhibited to the white sky, cautious immersion in the river, and on the horizon the sugar refinery bearing witness to the inevitable Monday morning return to work.

So that perhaps her eventual arrival in this place was not inevitable. It may be, she thought, with a slightly quickening pulse, that this was a warning, that this was what awaited her if she continued to live so unadventurously. Were it not for the fact that she felt some affection for the man in the raglan overcoat and the tweed cap, who was probably a half-remembered neighbour from far-off days, she would have dismissed the whole thing out of hand, together with the business of obedience and its increasingly problematic morality. She was aware, as perhaps never before, that alternative deaths might be available, that one might progress to a cheerful and inconvenient old age somewhere in the sun, instead of putting up with that resigned half light. Old people in the south, good wine assisting, relied more on being obstreperous than on being polite. She had seen ancient women in Italy, in Spain, in Greece, their legs bowed, their faces deeply wrinkled, rocking along sun-struck streets with a sort of gaiety, raising their sticks in greeting, laughing at babies in their new innocence, babies themselves in the immediacy of their sensations. These people too lived modestly, making do with small rooms, with pensions, having happily divested themselves of most of their worldly goods. They were returning to nature, which was perhaps a lesson worth learning. The revelation—for it was nothing less—was that one did not have to sit down and wait to be transformed. One could, and should, go out to meet nature half way.

She remembered Venice, and the old lady encountered every morning at a bar near the hotel. She wore a shapeless dress and her legs were bare. She drank her coffee black, and exchanged sharp pleasantries with the waiter before ambling off to buy her lunch. And there had been one other old lady in Paris who ate at the same table in the same restaurant every day, and who proclaimed that the stairs to her attic room were extremely troublesome but that once at home she had the same view as Diderot had once had. This particular old girl was loquacious, and in the young Mrs May had found a willing audience. Even Henry was charmed, and had flattered her; his compliments brought out the flirt not yet dormant in the more or less shapeless figure, with her scarves and her hat, her mouth gleaming from her *poireaux vinaigrette.* They had kept her company for a week, until they were due home; on their last day they had shaken hands and said goodbye. The woman had given Henry a dazzling smile, but to Mrs May she had said, *'Que tous vos rêves se réalisent,'* as if she knew that the story was not yet over. Her secret message—that dreams could yet come true—had been disregarded, confounded with the amiable aspect of Paris as a whole. Henry had cheerfully forgotten the encounter. Yet she remembered it, as she remembered the old lady, wishing somehow to be taken under her wing, or to be admitted to the company of such astute and self-sufficient elders as she represented.

And now she herself was an old lady, living in fairly gracious circumstances which were suddenly intolerable to her. The flat in which she had once taken such a pride seemed to her now like a prison. She had, as far as she could see, two choices. She could either continue to live as she had always lived, and thus accede to that bleak Heaven of her dream, or she could do something entirely uncharacteristic. What this might be she did not yet know: she rather thought it might involve taking a few risks. Curiously, the dream had had another effect; it had removed all fear of death. If the next world were to be as homely as her half-remembered girlhood there was no cause for fear or alarm. If she wished for anything more enriching she must go out and find it. That was the dream's secondary and more important message. It was time to take flight.

Moving effortlessly through the day, as if already in that so clearly defined limbo, she concluded that it would be unnecessary to take a walk, since if she believed in dreams and portents (and she now did) she was condemned to walk through all eternity. Something further was called for. She had as yet no idea what this might be, but found herself thinking insistently of the old lady in the Paris restaurant, quite inexpensive, her gracious manners so at odds with her battered appearance, her shrewd eyes taking in the ill-matched couple, and whom she alone perhaps perceived as ill-matched, the bon viveur and his inexperienced companion, draining her glass of red wine and calling for a large black coffee: '*Un double!*' Henry had appreciated the young woman buried in the old woman's tired flesh; she in her turn had responded to his gallantry. Mrs May had wondered what she did with the rest of her day before descending once more from her attic room for dinner. On the lookout even in those happy circumstances for hidden or suppressed feelings, she imagined solitary afternoons with only Diderot's view for distraction. She felt an imaginative sympathy which, she knew, would be repulsed with hauteur, her relative youth dismissed as mere ignorance.

Now an old lady herself, her reaction was one of grim amusement, as if it were no longer necessary to show mercy, pity, even sympathy, as if it were in order to be sharp and realistic. Even her stance was deferential, she thought, catching sight of herself in the glass, her invariably blue-clad figure concealed by suitable clothing, her grey hair tactfully groomed, even her lipstick an inoffensive pastel. And the hard thinking that even her modest appearance entailed! Whereas that old girl, who was clearly well educated and might even have been well born, was slightly dirty, decidedly badly put together. Her ancient black coat had seen better days, her hat, which she knocked back impatiently from time to time, was quite shapeless. She represented freedom from the desire to please, and was for that reason infinitely attractive to one of Mrs May's hesitant disposition. Even then, with Henry beside her, she had felt a faint envy. Now the envy was no longer faint, but it had metamorphosed into something more benevolent. What she felt now was appreciation.

Before making any decisions as to her future conduct she had an immediate problem: she had taken the last of her pills on returning from the wedding and now needed a new prescription. The logical thing was to ring Monty Goldmark, but this she shrank from doing. It was not simply that Monty was retired; it was rather that she had never quite trusted him. He had been in a state of semi-retirement for so long that any service he performed was viewed as a favour, not least by Monty himself. He had dealt gracefully with Henry's last illness by not pretending that treatment would be useful, and for this they had been grateful; his manner, half cajoling, half fatalistic, had, on this occasion at least, been appropriate. But she had encountered him too often at Kitty's dinner table to feel entirely frank with him. In society he was heartfelt and weary, as if burdened with the world's illnesses, whereas he went to his rooms in Harley Street on only two days a week, and rarely, if ever, made house calls. His energies came into play when he flirted with Kitty, as if this were an old-fashioned doctor's proper function. Excessive if mocking sympathy was expressed; nothing was taken seriously. This was his main therapeutic tool: his conviction, invariably imparted to the patient, that his services were not really required. Hands were patted; an arm was put round a shoulder: Kitty was mollified, and the consultation was concluded. 'Doing too much' was his diagnosis, entirely reassuring, and, more important, carrying no threat of morbidity.

This approach did not satisfy Mrs May; nor, to be fair, was it offered to her with any conviction, as if her lack of flesh made her an unsuitable patient. In addition she was wary of his physical aspect, which was corpulent and suffused, bathed in a cologne which did not quite cover his hoary breath. She thought of him as an eighteenth century abbé, not the nimble darting aphoristic type, but slack, watchful, corrupt, a kind of informer at court, soon to be swept away with the rest of the *ancien régime*. He had married well. His wife, a Frenchwoman of good family, was hesitant, bewildered by his lack of sexuality, his devotion to a small circle of old friends, his professional slackness. When forced into attendance at Kitty's, Hélène Goldmark was regularly and routinely overwhelmed, as if Kitty were still trying to demonstrate prior claims. Hélène, watching her husband succumb to Kitty's attentions, was too well bred to show contempt. Nevertheless she allowed herself to feel irony for these two flirtatious but mysteriously tragic creatures, so alike in temperament as to seem too closely related. More time was spent with her family in France: the house in Apt, to which the young people had been invited, was technically hers. Monty went there infrequently. Hélène's relations, some of whom were medical men, made him feel uneasy, whereas his own rare patients never did. If she consulted him, Mrs May knew what the diagnosis would be: 'Doing too much', or even, 'Doing too much, as usual', and the treatment another prescription. And the pills were too strong, of that there was no doubt, and not really suitable. The solution—and it was timely—was a second opinion, and although this might in itself have unforeseen consequences, it might at the same time be preferable to a further encounter with a man whom, she now realised, she had never really liked.

Indeed the atmosphere at Kitty's, too fervent, too disappointed, encouraged the likes of Monty Goldmark (who may even have been genuinely saddened over his lack of intellectual honesty) while discouraging his wife. But Hélène Gold-mark had a family of her own to reinforce her; if she fell ill she would make straight for home. It was probably her lack of confidence in him as a doctor which made Monty so resigned and cynical. He did no harm; on the other hand he plainly ex-pected to see no progress. Henry's account of his courtship had been entirely partisan. 'Madly in love,' he said, shaking his head. 'Couldn't see that she was unsuitable. Quite cold, really. And he's such an affectionate chap. Well, you can see for your-self.' But in Hélène Goldmark Mrs May had simply seen a very conventional woman, never entirely taken in by her suitor's emotionalism and entirely disillusioned by his short-lived ardour. What was extraordinary, even at this distance, was the strength of Kitty's trade union, or rather her court, in any event a conjunction of the like-minded. One of the conven-tions governing those who remained loyal was a willingness to shake heads over the fate of those who did not.

Those extravagant and disheartened people no longer an-swered a need, however faint that need had become. Indeed the need was theirs, as were all needs, for love, for comfort, for support, for reassurance. It was in the face of such neediness that others took flight; it was of extreme distaste to the young, who could not altogether be blamed for their refusal to enter into the loving symbiosis that was required of them. Gerald had been the first victim, had been seen as a lifelong partner in commiseration, until he had shown the courage to make the break. The flaw was that the courage had not taken him very far, had not led him into a productive adult way of life. His vague expression at the wedding betokened a refusal to engage with anyone, even a fear of being reabsorbed, as if his mother were a gigantic sea anemone waiting to envelop him. What courage it must have taken to resist her hand on his

arm! By the same token the bride and bridegroom had remained suspicious to the end, had escaped intact but not perhaps unaffected . . . Ann had thought to extract a favour, or
favours, unaware that the favour was in fact a bargain, an exchange. She had been visibly irritated by her grandmother's
demands, yet had not known how to deal with them. For
Kitty's needs were stronger than Ann's refusal to meet them,
and she was not sufficiently skilled to turn them aside. Who
was?

Mrs May found that she did not miss the young people, not
even Steve. With her new old woman's perceptions she saw
them as crude, affectless. She was willing to concede that they
felt affronted by their enforced contact with Kitty, with Molly,
with herself, but at the same time she saw little evidence of
wit or charm. Charm alone would have done, she thought,
but they had not mastered the art. Worse, they were unaware
that it was recommended. They were of course entirely correct in seeing the necessity of escape: it was just regrettable
that their escape was so precipitate, so heartfelt. They were
barbarians, but that did not make them unfit objects of desire.
And now, as in the aftermath of any unsatisfactory love affair,
their would-be patrons felt fatigue, disaffection, even something of the distaste of which they had been the original re-
cipients. What love survived, as it would do in the hearts of
Kitty and Molly, would be tinged not just with disappointment but with reluctance. The original wounds had been re-
opened. Childlessness was once again their portion.

Mrs May tore herself away from contemplation of this state
of affairs and tried to concentrate on her own discoveries, the
details of which were fast fading from her memory. Certain
constants remained: the sun as opposed to the sunlessness of
the dream, harsh vivacity as opposed to well-mannered ac-

quiescence, shamelessness as opposed to supine adherence to a group. She had left it too late: these options should have been taken up much earlier. What was not in doubt was the strength of her refusal to continue in the old ways. The sight of the terrace, with its table and chair, no longer charmed her, nor was she tempted to step out into the garden. The fact that she felt cold might indeed have something to do with the temperature rather than her psychic state; she thought of switching on the heating, and stopped herself as her hand reached out to the radiator. To make herself more comfortable would be to settle down. There would be time enough for that. When I am back, she thought, although until that moment she had not been aware that she was moving away. Matters seemed to be taking shape without her direct intervention. Her behaviour seemed to her imprecise but powerfully influenced, as if her dream life were still in control. This was presumably why worshippers made reference to guardian angels. The dream had revealed the mundane origin of such apparitions, just as it had demystified the world to come, which she now saw as a ragbag of sense impressions and reminiscences. Art came into it somewhere, perhaps merely the memory of a postcard once received. She was glad of this. A life without transcendence seemed to her infinitely preferable to an infinity of promises.

The weather in the street confirmed her impression that it was colder, or did she merely imagine that the mild sun had a frosty aura? She had come out without any determined action in mind, but turned, as if by instinct, to a house which bore on its railings a brass plate proclaiming, 'Dr Peter Noble. General Practitioner'. She had visited the house three years ago with a damaged wrist, had been obliged to, since it was on the icy pavement opposite that she had slipped and twisted her arm. The accident made little impression and was soon forgotten: a kind young man had applied a tubular bandage and given her some painkillers. But it was a different young man emerging from the door who immediately said, 'I'm afraid the surgery's closed. I'm just going out. I'd advise you to come back at three.' He hesitated, expecting her to retreat with an apology, as all patients were now supposed to do. Or were they all consumers now?

'This won't take a minute,' she said calmly. 'I only want a repeat prescription. And I can't come back. I'm going away.'

It was, surprisingly, he who retreated. In the surgery, in which she noticed a multitude of leaflets with advice on Aids and Sexually Transmitted Diseases, and a notice which read, 'Don't blame the receptionist!', she handed over her empty bottle and said, 'I think I need some more of these.'

'What do you take them for?'

'My heart.'

He shifted his long legs irritably. 'These are sedatives. Rather strong ones. Have you a history of heart disease?'

'It beats rather irregularly at times. And I'm not aware of any history.'

'I'd better examine you, though this is rather inconvenient.'

'Yes, I'm sure it is, but since I am here I should be obliged . . .'

As she bared her chest to the cold of the room—for since he had been going out he seemed disinclined to switch on the fire—she looked him over gravely, assessing him as yet another specimen of that unknown race, the young. It was he who seemed embarrassed, by her seventy-year-old frame and its inevitable fall from grace. He was so evidently healthy himself that it was probable that all illness struck him as unusual: he was no doubt more at home with sports injuries, or with the stress of which one heard so much.

'I am not particularly stressed,' she observed, though he had not asked her.

'Then you are the first person today who isn't,' he said. 'I note a slight arrhythmia. I'll have to have an ECG, of course. Call back later; my nurse will make an appointment.'

'I'm going away, you see. If you could just give me a mild palliative, until I get back . . .'

'When might that be?'

'I'm not sure.'

He looked at her narrowly. 'I can give you something to put under your tongue if you have an episode. I take it there have been one or two?'

'Just a little breathlessness. That would be most kind. And perhaps a mild sedative?'

'It doesn't do to get into the habit of such things.'

'At my age there can't be much harm.'

He was already writing the prescription, his stomach rumbling. She thought that had she come earlier he might have proved more recalcitrant.

'Is it dangerous?' she thought to ask.

He looked up, but not directly at her. 'No more than anything else,' he said. And then revised his remark. 'No more dangerous than crossing the road.'

It was what they said to people of her age. She understood that they were both glad that this particular consultation was so briefly concluded.

'Of course this is irregular,' he said, straightening up. 'I should want the results of tests . . .'

'I do understand. But as I am going away . . . And you must be very busy. I won't delay you any further.'

'I like to get in a game of squash,' he explained. 'Even medicine is stressful these days. And you say you don't suffer from it. Extraordinary.'

He accompanied her to the door. 'Come and see me after your holiday,' he said. 'Where are you off to? Spain? Majorca?'

'South Africa,' she said at a venture.

'Oh, right. Well, take care, Mrs . . . Mrs May?'

'Dorothea May, yes. And thank you so much, doctor.' For it hardly mattered what his name was, 'doctor' being a generic mode of address. The whole exchange had taken fifteen minutes.

The doctors of her youth had been grave, attentive, sympathetic, certainly less informed than the present generation. For all his faults Monty had been of that number, so resolutely on the side of the patient that he was almost a patient himself. Whereas this young man, even now loping rapidly down the road, would hand her over to the hospital. She had no intention of allowing this. She would take her chance, accept whatever was in store for her. And if she weakened, and found herself in need of just that missing sympathy, she might put through a call to Monty after all. As he had proved in Henry's case, he knew how to take care of a death. And naturally he would inform the others. That too had to be taken into account.

By the end of the afternoon she was surprised how much had happened, none of it willed. And now began the difficult part, the hours to be filled. She took up her book, but Maigret, Lucas, and Lapointe had lost their power to divert her. And she felt idle, sitting in her peaceful room while others worked, though no doubt hard-pressed workers would envy her her leisure. Had she been more active, less reclusive, she would have gone out into the streets to lose herself in some sort of company, have made the pretext of buying an evening paper an opportunity to chat to the newsagent, but she rejected such stratagems, seeing them for what they were. It had been decreed that she was to be solitary, and somehow she had always known this. Once she had left her parents' house all friendships had seemed provisional; even marriage had not changed that. Yet now, when she was most truly alone, she felt the need to reach out to such friends of her youth who were still alive. She sat down at her desk, and wrote, 'Dear Susie, I thought I would not wait until Christmas to give you my news. I may be going away for a while. I have no particular destination in mind, but I think it is time to'—Here she broke off; time to do what? '. . . time to see more of the world before it is too late. I will let you know where I end up. If you ever think of joining me do let me know. It would be great fun. And you were always such good company. Do you remember how you virtually ran that office? And how you encouraged Henry? I have a lot to thank you for. Do let me know if you would like a break, and if so where we might meet. I feel quite nostalgic these days about the past, when we were young. With best wishes and love to you, as always, Dorothea.'

She did not write, 'Dear Susie, I have a heart condition which may kill me.' Such news was not for long-lost friends, or were they merely acquaintances? At this distance it was difficult to tell. She sealed her envelope and stamped it; now she had a reason for going out. She walked swiftly in the direction opposite to the one she had taken that morning, in case she encountered the doctor and prompted second thoughts.

There was no hesitation in her steps, none of the awkwardness she had noticed on that previous awful Sunday, but the motor now was fear, fear of the decisions to be taken. These seemed ineluctable, though there was no-one to reproach her should she stay quietly and secretly at home. Indeed that was where most people expected to find her, should they come looking. But if, as was likely, no-one should come looking, how could she bear to sit in her flat, undiscovered, for ever?

A child ran towards her, cheeks aflame. To be able to run like that again! 'Bobby, Bobby,' called his mother. 'Wait for me. Don't cross the road.' He looked back, laughing, and then ran on again. The mother smiled her excuses and hastened her step. But Mrs May silently willed the child forward, as if his unbroken stride, his flaring colour, were a portent, and when the dull sky briefly brightened she thought how fitting it was that speed and light should be celebrated, and the long evening kept at bay.

15

'Kitty? It's Thea. How are you?'

'Thea.' The tone was distant.

'I'm not disturbing you, I hope?'

'No, no. There's nothing much to disturb us now that everything's over.'

'I hope you've managed to rest a bit. Will you go away now?'

'To tell you the truth, Thea, I don't feel much like going away.'

'There's nothing wrong, is there?'

'I'm not easy in my mind. I'm worried about Austin.'

'Is he unwell?'

'He thinks I don't notice, but I know him. I heard him get up in the night. In the morning he said he was fine, but I'm not so sure. He's pining. And so am I, to be honest. I miss the children. The flat seems so quiet. She looked lovely, didn't she?'

'She looked very good, yes. It was a great success.'

'Yes, I think it was. It's just that it's all left us rather down, you know?'

Here the voice broke, as it was bound to do. Kitty's tears, never far from the surface, did not despise the use of the telephone to relay their message.

'Is it Austin you're worried about?'

'Well, of course. But I don't want him to see I'm upset. Let's talk about something else. How are you? I expect you're quite pleased to have the flat to yourself again?'

'I've hardly had time to notice. I should have thought I'd be relieved, but now I find it rather empty.'

To her surprise, as she said these words she knew them to be true. Steve, whom she had hardly liked, and whom she liked even less in retrospect, had obliged her to live in the present and to combat her tendency to introspection. It was true that he had agitated her, that every day she had to convince herself that there was no harm in him, that she had lain awake for the sound of his key in the door, but in fact the agitation had had a tonic effect. Even her dreams had benefited, revealing to her past anomalies, delivering true verdicts, restoring to her lost names and faces. Even the warnings of ill health had been without foundation, or so she cared to think; the knowledge that there was a doctor at the end of the street gave her new confidence. Not that she would ever call him, she told herself; she would manage on her own. Or hoped she would.

And then there were the plans to turn herself into a quite different person, a cranky old woman with bare legs and a formidable tongue, living in a stone house somewhere in the south. Surely Steve was in some part responsible for this upheaval in her thinking? At the same time she knew that she could not bear for him to come back, that there was a danger in leaving the flat empty for any length of time. Resourceful as he was, he would soon find a way of getting in. And once in he would be excessively difficult to dislodge.

All this passed rapidly through her mind as she listened to Kitty composing herself. At least she imagined the deployment of the snowy handkerchief, having witnessed this scene many times. The heartache, she reflected, was genuine. Or maybe it was a form of homesickness. This was not entirely paradoxical. Although exile was distant by two generations, the family had always seemed in need of a security that was not quite within its grasp. Even Henry had felt this. She saw suddenly that her value to Henry was as a safe haven, not simply from the bruising effects of his divorce, but from uneasiness, from a lack of weight, from the menace of underlying tears. Kitty's tears had merely served to emphasise this occasional piercing bewilderment, as if to ask, 'Where am I?' And all relationships, which were intended to serve as ballast, revealed their essential fragility at unexpected moments, so that Kitty, and Henry, and even Austin, chose to stay close to home, cocooned in stifling physical comfort, ingesting frequent meals, loving anxiously, easily disappointed, fearing abandonment or dispossession.

She felt an overwhelming pity for these people who, in the light of their own essential needs, had almost inevitably shut her out. It was not that she was inimical to them: it was simply that they were preternaturally alert to the threat of otherness. And with her thin frame and her meek but decided presence she had represented a majority to which they could never belong. She saw suddenly that she had made them feel uncomfortable, that Henry had in a sense betrayed them by marrying her, that the first wife, however hysterical and difficult, had been more easily understood, and that she herself had always paid the penalty for being so contained and unemotional. They had sensed a criticism, where no criticism was intended: reticence was not a faculty they possessed, yet they possessed many others. They were passionate people, but at the same time they were inept. The children of such people were bound to suffer, as indeed they had done. Yet even Gerald, even Ann, would carry within themselves some atavistic memory of raw emotion, and although they would do their best to ignore it, would, she knew, fly to Kitty's deathbed when the time came, and in one long heartfelt outburst confess their love.

It would be too late, for them, not for Kitty, who had always solicited such an outpouring. And no doubt she herself would be there, assisting, and aware as never before of the differences they had managed to contain throughout their long association. For now she saw that they were menaced, and that she was still intact, that it was up to her to make provision for the future, that they knew this and regretted it. Her task was not an easy one. She must be present and absent at the same time, available, but not for that reason cherished. She would not be able to allay their fears, but perhaps those fears were irreducible, and the task of allaying them not in anyone's gift. Not in this world, certainly, and as Austin had comfortably announced, they were in no need of the next. This was true: they wanted their needs met in this world, not quite understanding that the world was indifferent.

'Are you there, Kitty?'

There were a few final sniffs. 'Yes, I'm here.'

'I thought I'd better tell you: I'm going away.'

'Oh, yes? Where are you going? Portugal?'

Portugal was another of the Levinsons' fiefdoms, together with the house in Freshwater and the Royal Monceau Hotel.

'No, not Portugal. I haven't quite decided.'

'But Thea, that's not like you.'

'I feel like a change,' she said weakly.

'But supposing we wanted to get in touch with you? We shouldn't know where you were. After all, we're not young any more. It's important that we stick together.' Here the voice was lowered. 'To tell the truth, I'm concerned about Austin.'

'Has he seen a doctor?'

'Monty was here last night. Monty said he's been doing too much, that we all had, Molly too. It's just that they've left such a gap, the children, I mean. If I feel better tomorrow I'll go out and buy Ann a few things. A couple of blouses, perhaps a skirt or two . . .'

'They wear jeans, Kitty.'

Again the heartfelt sigh. 'You think I'm silly, no doubt.'

'No, no, I don't. I think I know how you feel. Young people are precious, even if they're not quite as one would want them to be.'

'Exactly. How did you think Gerald looked?'

'He looked fine to me.'

'He looked like my father did at his age. You've seen the photographs.'

'He did rather. Don't fret, Kitty. They will all come home in the end.'

The starkness of what she was saying appalled her, yet false comfort was not within her gift, and maybe never had been. That was another factor that marked her out as alien. But in fact she was anxious to move forward from this position into that mythical future in the sun. For a moment she saw herself quite clearly, transformed. She was wearing an old black dress, unbelted, and she was hurling the contents of a bucket of dirty water onto the cobblestones in front of her house. Dogs barked at her; children made fun of her. She saw the mocking faces of the children, and all at once the fantasy evaporated. There would be no transformation, no apotheosis. At her age, with her constitution and temperament, she was unlikely to become a wizened hag, however wistfully she desired such a protective carapace. She was too polite, too accommodating to disenfranchise herself; she was too dependent on home comforts, though at present she found more desolation than comfort at home.

'Just a few days,' she told Kitty. 'Perhaps a week.'

'You'll let us know?'

'Yes, of course. Don't worry. I shan't be far away.'

She could sense a certain relief at the other end of the line. To her surprise she felt a measure of relief herself, together with a sharp sense of anticlimax. It was like waking after a particularly enthralling dream, to find that her course of action was not to be dictated by magical thinking but was circumscribed by mundane reality, and that instead of encountering and overcoming mythical obstacles she had merely to take her shopping basket and mingle with the other suburban ladies at the supermarket. And that instead of that doorway in the sun there would be the spectacle of old Mario, with his carafe of wine and his mimed greeting, at the Italian café, where once again she would resume her custom. And all would go on as before, or almost. Perhaps the fantasy had wrought some infinitesimal change, revealing the nature of her ordinary life to her. But she looked down at her neat figure, at her narrow feet in their sensible shoes, and knew that reality was not easily traduced, that, like fate or heredity, it would impose itself even on the most cherished imaginings. Indeed it was the peculiar gift of imagination to provide a respite from reality, the reality that even now was breathing audibly down her ear. Surely Kitty was not her usual self, had, however briefly, lost her power to dominate?

'We'll talk on Sunday, as usual,' she said.

'Very well, dear. And maybe we'll see something of you.'

After replacing the receiver she was thoughtful. Kitty's re-mark had signified a return to normality, or rather to the *sta-tus quo ante*. She was to be an adjunct, but not necessarily an intimate, admitted to certain colloquies but not to others, her status as family member once more to be negotiated. She felt a certain sadness on understanding this, even a certain loneli-ness. Then she braced herself to meet the day, took her shop-ping basket, and went out, greeting one or two neighbours as she walked carefully down her familiar street. Now that the world had shrunk again she forced herself to appreciate the modest nature of her surroundings, all pleasant, all subdued, all seasonal: the honeysuckle at the corner, now drooping, a few early yellow leaves on the pavement, the first of the sea-son's apples on display at the greengrocer's. The Indian newsagent raised a dignified hand in greeting as she passed. Yes, it was all quite bearable.

Some days later—but where had the time gone?—a letter and a postcard arrived. The letter was from Austin. 'Dear Thea,' it read. 'Quite in order to take a holiday, but don't aban-don us! We are rather sad at the moment, as you can imagine. The sight of Gerald quite upset me, although I wouldn't have missed it for the world. Between ourselves I have not been feeling too good; of course I haven't said a word to Kitty. She has had enough to put up with, one way and another, and you know how careful one has to be with high blood pressure. I am very anxious that she take it easy, so I doubt if we shall go away this year. I just wanted to say how much I had enjoyed talking to you, and how much I look forward to turning things over with you again. I know that Kitty feels the same. They say the Alfonso XIII at Seville is a good hotel, but of course you won't want to go that far. You know that the house at Freshwater is always at your disposal, even when we're not there. Forgive this long letter. Kitty says I think too much. Perhaps she's right. Yours, as ever, Austin.'

The letter was typed on an ancient machine whose irregular 'e's and 't's seemed to give an all too graphic impression of Austin's erratic heartbeat. Or maybe it was his nervous system that was affected. The thought of the two of them, hiding the extent of their ailments from each other, was a sad reminder of their collective age, a fact that could not be dismissed. Imagination was of no help in this particular circumstance.

The postcard, which was of the Eiffel Tower, read 'Having a great time. Going south tomorrow' and was signed 'Ann, David, Steve'. So they do not miss us, she thought. Yet they had each signed their name. This fact cheered her immeasurably.

She searched through her address book for the number of Henry's solicitor, Zerber, now, she supposed, her solicitor as well. She had had no contact with him since Henry's death, when he had sorted out Henry's affairs and told her that ample provision had been made for her. He had urged her at the time to make a will and had shown her a disheartening list of various charities—for the blind, the disabled, the mentally handicapped—that would in due course benefit from the quite substantial monies she left behind. A female voice informed her that Mr Zerber had passed away five years previously, and that he had been succeeded by his nephew, young Mr Zerber. She made an appointment to see him, for she supposed it hardly mattered that they were strangers to each other, and found herself regretting the original Zerber, tiny, shrewd, even then shrunken, his head barely rising from his shoulders. He too was one of what Henry designated as 'the old crowd', which meant that Zerber's father, or possibly his grandfather, had been known to some ancestor of the May family, and thus indirectly to Kitty and Molly, their mother having been born a May, or rather a Meyer. This gave Zerber the stamp of authenticity, something akin to a royal appointment, and she could imagine the dismay his death would have occasioned. It would have been one more intimation of the indifferent world beyond their deliberate confines: having to deal with strangers was avoided as much as possible. Yet for what she had to do a stranger was entirely appropriate. She was given an appointment for that afternoon, for which she was grateful; she was anxious not to give herself time to change her mind.

She would have liked to take a bus to Southampton Street, to immerse herself in a crowd. But any putative crowd was also illusory, and she merely picked up a taxi in the main road. Everything was proving both easier and more difficult than she had imagined from the silence of her flat, nor was she cheered by familiar landmarks. What she had to do was simply a formality, and yet it took precedence over all her other activities. Those activities were so habitual that they were automatic and gave her no trouble; by the same token those streets could now be taken for granted. She thought briefly of that other landscape, the one she had so recently conjured up, and was surprised that the details had slipped from her mind. She remembered a shapeless black dress, but could not now have said why this should ever have been attractive. She was, however, keenly aware of the ridicule she might have caused, in this or any other garb, and resolved to be more circumspect and to submit her imaginings to ordinary daylight whenever she was threatened by what was after all a very normal ennui. She could begin with the task in hand.

'I want to make a new will,' she said to the young Mr Zerber, who was about fifty, but who had none of his uncle's *grav-
itas*. The old man had worn striped trousers and a black jacket,
admittedly sprinkled with dandruff. Young Mr Zerber was in
a canary yellow waistcoat and blue shirt sleeves, at which she
found herself staring rather fixedly.

'It's the new informality,' he explained, smiling. 'For the
weekend, you know. It is Friday,' he reminded her.

'Is it really? Yes, I suppose it is. Then I won't delay you. I'm
sure you're anxious to get away.'

'Your will is what? Fifteen years old?'

'Yes, and there have been some changes. Family changes,
you know. I want to leave my flat to my . . . To my niece,' she
said firmly. 'Ann Newhouse. Ann Levinson Newhouse.'

This was her great decision, and it had been easily made.
Ann could have the flat, and David could have it too, if he
were still around. There was no need to make provision for
Steve. Steve would come along as the lodger. Eventually, no
doubt, if Ann and David decided to move on, Steve would
become the sitting tenant. But that would no longer be her
problem.

Out in the street the sun hectically shone, as if congratulat-
ing her on her modest resolve. She walked towards Gower
Street and the bus stop, reluctant to reach home too early. She
now regretted her letter to Susie Fuller: it would be necessary
to follow it up in some way. She looked back in amazement
at the image of herself that had taken shape, only to disappear
as fitfully as it had arrived. Yet it had been strong, and as such
welcome, although it was of course a fiction. That woman in
the shapeless black dress was not herself but someone else,
someone she might have encountered in a book. But books,

she had found, were too powerful, and invariably misleading. The novels she had read in her studious girlhood all ended with a marriage, for that was how the reader wanted them to end, believing that marriage was the conclusion of the story. They gave no instructions on how to spend the time once the marriage was a thing of the past. And yet she would not have it otherwise. Those who survived and grew old were in a country without maps: she knew that. All that was left to them was to find some middle way, between acceptance and defeat. When grace was gone only usefulness remained. How could she have envisaged that curious adventure and become the woman in the black dress? Yet some details of that woman's appearance were still vivid in her mind, her bare feet, the arc of water thrown from the bucket. A plate-glass window showed her a neat, careful, and unmistakably elderly woman: herself. Perhaps she would write again to Susie suggesting a package tour at some unspecified date in the future. This might even come about, though she had no enthusiasm for the idea. 'Kept at home unexpectedly by family matters,' she would explain, wondering why this did not feel like a lie.

As she got off the bus she remembered: Austin and Kitty's fiftieth wedding anniversary fell at the end of the month. And she had thought to be away! They had not mentioned it, and had no doubt been hurt that she had forgotten. Once again she had been saved from folly. And although her absence might have been insignificant (as no doubt her presence would be), it was essential that she should join in the celebrations. For this was the measure of her usefulness. She would be present for Kitty, but rather more for Austin, whom she imagined to be low in spirits, undermined as if by some Jamesian vastation. There would be tears, of course, though she would shed none. She would smile her admiration, and at some point that admiration would become entirely genuine. Then she would retire gracefully, not forgetting to telephone the following day with further appreciation. By that time the smile would be fixed, but they would not know that. It was like a novel, one of the novels that ended with a wedding. And in Kitty's case—though Kitty never read novels—fiction would have delivered its promise. So that in a sense, and for some if not for others, the stories were true.

She thought of the children, as they had become, on their way to the south. But the immediacy of their recent visit was lost. She knew, or thought she knew, that she would never see them again. This she did not regret. They had been so ungainly, so rebarbative! And yet she followed them in her thoughts, as they grew ever smaller in the mind's eye. Theirs was the sun, the heat. What they would make of their experience she could not imagine. Their remaining virtue was the memory they left behind. 'It was when the children were here,' those who had never moved would say. And Kitty would invariably remark, 'Didn't she look lovely? And didn't Gerald look well? Not that I ever thought he wouldn't come.' And the photographs would come out again, and be passed from hand to hand. And the truth would once more be put in its place, somewhere between desire and regret. She did not see how this could be avoided.

Between acceptance and defeat lay the middle way, which must be negotiated. But it must be negotiated without assistance: that was the rule. Her street, when she reached it, was empty, devoid of answers. She would have wished some sort of presence, even the sight of a woman like herself (and all her neighbours, she supposed, were like herself) on her way to the shops for some forgotten purchase. She knew, or thought she knew, those stratagems for filling the day, although so far she had not made use of them. She knew, quite calmly, that her days were empty, as the flat, which she now entered, was empty, with an emptiness she had not quite anticipated. She had thought to enjoy her solitude, but in fact she found herself listening for another's presence, however fleeting, however indifferent. She would have welcomed a stranger, for now she knew that this was possible.

She had not felt this when she was first widowed. Then the relief of clearing away the reminders of sickness had been too great. She had sat for hours, dazed, not quite believing that there would be no more calls from Henry's room, or the nervous cough, almost constant, that had afflicted him at the end. The sight of his own sorrow had put paid to any self-pity she might have felt. In his eyes, grown huge, sat incomprehension; he was absorbed in the drama of his own passing. She had sat with him and held his hand, but he had seemed not to notice, as if she herself were a shade. When the others visited, fearfully, with defensive badinage, he had responded with a careful smile very remote from his usual caressing manner. They had left, duty done, and the silence once more descended. She had refused Monty's offer of a nurse, knowing that if she assumed this task her conscience would be clear. Somewhere in her mind she knew that she would have earned her freedom. And in a sense she had appreciated that freedom. But now, with no-one to mourn, she felt no such release and could not rid herself of an alertness which, though irksome, served in some capacity to remind her of her obligations.

'Dear Susie,' she wrote. 'Ignore my previous letter, which I sent you without first consulting my diary. Plans are, for the moment, in abeyance. I have a family function at the end of the month, which means that I must be here. Perhaps I wrote too hastily: I had nowhere specific in mind, simply some place in the sun which I should have recognised if I had ever found it. No doubt you have plans of your own, and may in fact be away already. But perhaps we could undertake some sort of holiday in the future? I say "undertake" because that is the reality at our age. And remember if you ever want to spend some time in London I have a spare room'—these last words were uncomfortable to write—'which is not being used at the moment. So let us look forward to seeing each other in the not too distant future. With love, as always, Dorothea.'

On re-reading the letter she found it weak and unconvincing, though every word of it was true, and she rather thought that Susie would not bother to reply. It was entirely possible, and more than likely, that Susie would not be tempted by the idea of an old ladies' shared holiday, for Susie might have become one of those women of whom it is remarked that they have not changed. In a way it was true: Susie was loyal, as witnessed by the Christmas cards, but she had always been easily bored. She had too readily seen others as a foil for her own vivacity, and Mrs May had on more than one occasion been conscious of filling this role. In a sense they had both been conscious of it, which removed the threat of incompatibility. Her true good nature had been revealed when Henry arrived on the scene; she had been generous, although she had not been entirely able to stop herself flirting with him. No resentment had been felt on either side, and this she reckoned to be a proof of true friendship. And although, if she and Susie were to spend time together now, they might find themselves at odds, or have little to say to each other, she knew that their past friendship held good. She also knew that it would be pointless to try to revive it. Which left her without even the saving grace of illusion.

She lingered at her desk, wondering why she bothered to

make telephone calls when writing was so much easier. 'Dear Molly,' she wrote. 'I haven't forgotten the fiftieth wedding anniversary celebrations, although Kitty and Austin think that I have. Do you have any idea of a suitable gift? I know what they really want, but we can't count on Gerald, I fear. In fact it is a great pity that the children will miss it, though of course it is hardly to their taste, and in any event they know nothing about it. And yet I find myself wishing that they could be here, and that they could rise to the occasion. Do you think they enjoyed their stay? I sometimes wonder. I even think that although they undoubtedly found us tiresome we may have made some sort of impression.' (She would not send this letter, she decided, but she went on writing.) 'When dealing with the young at our age we forget our own youth. Not that mine would have been much use to me in the present circumstances. I clung to my parents, and they to me, whereas Ann seemed to be without parents altogether. One could see that David had been properly cared for—one does not come by that sort of assurance in any other way—but Steve seemed like a foundling. That was part of his appeal, I suppose: he was like one of those sly characters in a fairy tale. At least that was how he struck me. Was it for that reason that I found him so'—she hesitated—'amusing?

'They seemed so rude, didn't they? Yet that was the only way in which they could assert their independence. I wish they could have stayed a little longer, so that I could have got to know them. Which is more than they would have done. In many ways they rejected us, and we had no experience of having done this ourselves, though I suppose we must have done so at some stage. My own parents never reproached me, nor I them. This now strikes me as extraordinary.

'I hope David's departure has not left you too sad. I know

that both you and Harold were prepared to love him. Being prepared to love is in truth a very dangerous condition. One cannot always find the right object, and one is always, as it were, the subject, one's own preferences not consulted.

'I also hope that you have not cancelled your plans to go to Bordighera as usual. You know of course that they will not come back. Unless . . . Unless by some miracle they miss us, or at least think of us fondly. I am sure, dear Molly, that you can comfort yourself with this thought. And Harold too: I saw what he was feeling. Do give him my love. In all the excitement I had no chance to speak to him. And my love to you, to all of you. Until we meet again. Dorothea.'

16

In the night a storm broke, waking her from a dream in which she was trying to buy a pair of shoes. The odd thing was that the shoe shop was situated exactly where she remembered it from her youth, just off Putney Bridge Road. She had not been there for fifty years. She shook her head, amused, and got up to make tea. Heavy rain slashed at the windows; she enjoyed the momentary break in the weather, although she knew that in the morning she would find wet yellow leaves plastered to her table and chair on the terrace. With the rain came a release of tension, allaying her memory of recent events.

The dream had given her a desire to visit the old neighbourhood, the old house. Perhaps she harboured a wish to be back in her old bed, the bed in the dark room in which she had always slept so dreamlessly those many years ago. Then she realised that such nostalgia was futile and unrealistic: the house would be unremarkable, one of many such houses in a street from which all the remembered inhabitants were long gone. The remote past was preserved only in memory. Even so it managed to overshadow the life she now accepted as nor-

mal, not least in those moments of reverie, of not quite waking, in which it was so easy to indulge. The journey to the old
neighbourhood had in a sense already been undertaken, in the
dream, and she had been as she once was, young and effort-
less, eager and active. In a sense she had repossessed her youth,
although every increasingly frail bone in her elderly body had
mislaid it.

As for the recent past, it had been diverting, eventful. The
postcard from the children was on her dressing table, and she
glanced at it from time to time. The memory of Steve brought
a smile to her face. The wedding breakfast no longer seemed
grotesque, and even the prospect of Kitty's celebration failed
to bring forth the usual sigh. The great revelation of the night
was that although the past was singular, private, exceptional,
and preserved for ever in neurones to which she had privi-
leged but intermittent access, age—the age she had reached—
could be, must be, an enterprise in which help must be
solicited and offered. There were no precedents for the journey ahead, yet it was felt to be hazardous. Therefore some
form of solidarity was in order. This could no longer be ignored.

In one sense the friends of her youth were still present, and
with them the unthinking acceptance that had characterised
days gone by. By comparison—yet the comparison was unwelcome, faintly ill-mannered—all latter-day attachments
were tenuous. Yet she thought it marvellous that she had some
existence in the consciousness of others. The postcard was
there to prove this fact, as were the many fretful telephone
calls she had received, and discounted, over the years. She was
newly aware of a certain collective fragility. She looked back
incredulously at her recent fantasy of leaving, at her vision of
herself as unkempt, ill-natured. That woman in the sun was

simply the obverse of her real self, a *doppelgänger* struggling for expression. She was valid only as an interesting variation of the truth, whereas the real truth was to be assessed in terms of character, history, even antecedents.

She was not lonely, or perhaps only for ideal company, a fact she hoped she had managed to conceal. What company was presently offered would be accepted, if not actively sought. That she still had access to that company was, she thought, remarkable, given her somewhat remote nature. In the mild morning she felt refreshed, grateful. She thought it marvellous that she could still stand at her window and watch the flight of a bird, could still (occasionally) eat with appetite, could still hear voices other than her own. She was aware of the need to make amends—for joylessness, for fatalism, for caution—in what time was left to her.

When Kitty telephoned, at the end of a day given over largely to reflection, she was not surprised. There was a questing note in Kitty's normally peremptory tone, as if hovering over some as yet unformulated anxiety.

'Kitty?' she replied, unrehearsedly, and undoubtedly with more spontaneity than hitherto. 'Don't worry. I hadn't forgotten. I'll be there. Of course I'll be there. The holiday? Another time perhaps. When we've had a chance to talk things over. After all, we've plenty to talk about, haven't we?'

ABOUT THE AUTHOR

ANITA BROOKNER is the author of seventeen novels, including *Altered States, Incidents in the Rue Laugier, Fraud, Dolly,* and *Providence.* She won the Booker Prize for *Hotel du Lac.* An international authority on eighteenth-century painting, she became the first female Slade Professor at Cambridge University. She lives in London.

ABOUT THE TYPE

This book was set in Bembo, a typeface based on an old-style Roman face that was used for Cardinal Bembo's tract *De Aetna* in 1495. Bembo was cut by Francisco Griffo in the early sixteenth century. The Lanston Monotype Company of Philadelphia brought the well-proportioned letterforms of Bembo to the United States in the 1930s.